My best friend

Juliet Hanson

Contents

1

CHAPTER 1

I felt like, at some point, a girl may get this idea in her head that she wanted to live out some love story that she has read or seen in movies.

The idea of love might sound appealing enough to have her swoon and daydream about her prince charming. And I couldn't blame her.

I'd hate to admit that I was like that girl because that would be silly of me.

There had been parts of life that felt like less of a dream and more of a nightmare, and because of that, it had me questioning just how close I would get to a fairytale if they even existed.

Speaking of a nightmare, I might be living one right now, and the embarrassment I was experiencing would probably haunt me until my ten-year high school reunion. Great.

There was a crowd gathering in the courtyard, and whatever drama was going down, I didn't want to be a part of it. But all the students had their cellphones out filming the whole thing. Teenagers really had nothing better to do than record a personal matter like that.

"Keep your voice down!" I instantly recognized the guy speaking out loud.

"Hell no!" The second voice was even clearer than the first.

It was the last day of my senior year, and when that bell rang, I was ready to start my summer vacation. But leave it to my cheating boyfriend to make a scene and ruin all of it.

James stood in the middle of the crowd with Stephanie opposite him.

She shoved him hard enough to have him stumbling.

James had his back to me, unaware that I was watching this all unfold.

I heard the whispers from the people close by.

"Oh crap, Mia is here."

"Isn't that Mia, James' girlfriend?"

"I don't think they'll be together anymore after this."

"It's a shame. They always looked like the perfect couple." Ha. Funny.

"Mia must be shook, hearing about her boyfriend cheating on her like this?"

"James, don't pretend I didn't get this from you! I always get tested. I start sleeping with you, and BOOM! I get a freakin' S-T-D!" Stephanie shouted.

My jaw hit the ground.

This couldn't be happening.

"For all I know, you could be playing the victim right now when you're the one who gave it to me. But somehow, you're looking for someone to blame," James fired back angrily.

Stephanie's eyes met mine over his shoulder. "Or maybe your little girlfriend gave it to you?"

Nope. Completely out of the question.

James and I never had sex. But I could see that I dodged a bullet right there.

"Leave Mia out of this!" James yelled.

Stephanie laughed bitterly. "No. I want to know. Let's ask her."

All the cellphones and eyes turned towards me as James realized I had been three feet away.

A million stupid questions were running through my mind, but all the answers to them were undeniable.

My boyfriend cheated on me. And by the sound of it, it happened more than once.

Stephanie couldn't have been the only one either.

There was no good way to find out about a cheater. But there were less public ways, and James didn't take that route.

"Mia, I," James began. But I held my hand up, indicating that he didn't have to explain because I didn't want to hear any of it.

I didn't care how regretful and misty his eyes looked or that his face had become sullen. Nothing he could say would make this better.

I cleared my throat and tried to speak up, hoping the emotions hiding inside me wouldn't make an appearance. At least not now. "I remember you wondering if I would regret not making that cliché decision about sleeping with you on prom night."

James swallowed nervously.

"Luckily, I avoided what could have been the biggest mistake of my life. We're done, James." I told him before I stalked off.

"Mia! MIA! MIA!" he called out for me, but I had already pushed my way through the crowd, and I was sprinting at lightning speed towards the parking lot.

I only stopped to catch my breath when I saw my best friend, Grey, leaning against his motorcycle in the already half-empty lot.

Grey had on a sleeveless white tee, exposing those biceps that he was oh so proud of since he spent last summer working out non-stop. He's paired it with dark jeans and his signature black boots. He was rocking the bedhead look today, and he didn't care what anyone thought about it. Except me, of course, but he knew I liked that look on him. I couldn't imagine any look that this guy wouldn't be able to pull off.

Grey was holding his cell phone in one hand, and the other he held up to his chest as he kept making it into a fist, clenching then unclenching.

I wonder if he was watching the video that I'm sure was already circulating in the school.

I let out a sigh.

If this was my junior year, and I knew I would have to come back and face these people next year, I would be horrified. But I was going to college. I wouldn't have to see James again, and I didn't have to worry about those stupid videos. I could start fresh with all of this behind me.

Grey looked up and smiled as if he felt my gaze on him. That was the same warm smile he gave me when I told him my mom had left me. That smile held so many promises behind it. I knew when I saw it that Grey would help me fix my problems and not let me go through anything alone.

Sliding his phone into his pocket, Grey opened his arms wide. Once again, I was running, but this time it was straight into the arms of the person that had never let me down. Not once.

I buried my face into Grey's chest. One, because he smelled heavenly. And two, he loved to comment on how he hated seeing me cry.

I didn't even know why I was crying, but I was.

"I'm sorry. I know you think I have an ugly crying face," I muttered.

Grey chuckled softly. "That was a joke. You're still holding that comment against me after all these years?"

I nodded with my head still firmly placed against his chest.

He gently eased me away from him, and I instantly missed the soothing warmth.

"I don't think you're ugly when you cry. I just know that every time I see you cry, it makes me feel like I wasn't doing my job to protect you. It makes me feel like a shit person. And you know I take my job very seriously. No tears are supposed to fall from these brown eyes with me around. This is literally in my best friend's job description." Grey used his thumbs to wipe away the last few tears that regretfully escaped. "So is beating up the asshole that..."

"Nope!" I pointed my finger at his chest. "It's over. We're over. None of this matters anymore. I have a new life waiting for me at college." I tipped my head up to meet his stormy gaze. "It's fine. I'll be fine. Promise." I gave him a reassuring smile.

Grey brushed back a few strands of my strawberry blonde hair and then used both of his hands to caress my face. His expression went from angry to oddly soft and calm. "Of course, you'll be fine because I'm never letting you date again." He smirked, clearly satisfied with his new mission in life.

I folded my lips into a thin line, trying my best not to be irked or peeved by his words.

I gave him a blank stare for what felt like minutes.

"What?" Grey asked with an innocent expression as if he hadn't tried to put an end to my love life.

I slapped his hands away from my face. "You're never letting me date again? You cannot be serious?" I said, keeping my tone of voice surprisingly even.

He seemed to consider my words for a moment, but it was all an act. "Dead serious," he said, confirming how well I knew his personality. He was too stubborn to change his mind now. "The majority of guys my age are immature jerks anyways." He shrugged his shoulders nonchalantly.

I rolled my eyes. Stating the facts, I was more than aware of didn't make me feel better.

"Greyson, I love you and all, but it's kind of my decision. Don't you think?" I tried to reason with him.

Call me pessimistic, but I knew this wasn't going to work.

Grey bit his bottom lip in contemplation before he nodded. "Ye eaahh... nope."

My eyes turned into slits.

"Come on. Don't be like that." He made a move to place a hand on my shoulder. I stepped back, out of reach.

"You're ridiculous," I gritted the words through my teeth.

"So I've been told. I'd like to think that it's one of my special traits. It makes me totally lovable." Grey winked.

I crossed my arms against my chest. "More like totally annoying," I mumbled under my breath.

"What was that?" Grey asked louder than necessary.

"Oh, nothing. Never mind." I smiled sweetly at him.

He frowned.

"So anyways, James was supposed to take me home today, but..." I trailed off with my mind running back to everything that happened ten minutes ago.

"Forget him. Let's not bring that idiot up again." Grey hopped onto his motorcycle. Cradling his helmet in one arm, he pulled out his phone to send a quick text. He slid it back into his pocket and then put his helmet on. He peeked at me from over his shoulder. "What are you waiting for, Mia? Christmas? Hop on." He twisted his upper body, picked up the other helmet behind him, and handed it to me. I took it.

"I thought you were taking Katrina home today?" Katrina was Grey's girlfriend, the longest one he's had so far. I could say that since they had passed the three-month mark last week.

Grey shook his head. "Nope. I told her to ride with one of her friends instead. My best friend needs me today. I need to cheer her up and then somehow find a way to convince her that she should just swear off dating. For at least a couple of years." Grey added, probably trying to rile me up again to mess with me.

"HA. HA. HA," I said sarcastically. "Not going to happen." I needed to squash that idea pronto. "You have my permission to try and cheer me up, but we have to let go of the last one."

"Why?" Grey asked, lifting the kickstand with his foot.

"What do you mean, why?" I answered his question with one of my own.

"I mean, why bother dating at this age anyway. Nobody that meets as a teenager lasts more than a few years. They're never super serious about each other. So yeah, let me ask again. WHY?"

"I should ask you why when you're dating someone," I countered. "If you think dating at this age is stupid, why do you do it?"

Grey shrugged. He was silent for a second, and I wondered if he would answer me. Or maybe he was thinking of a subject change because he couldn't be bothered to respond. "Let me worry about that." He gestured to the helmet in my arms. "Put that on and let's go," he ordered.

I let the silence grow between us again. I was taking the time to build up the nerve to ask Grey something. "Are you sure there's not another reason that you think I shouldn't be dating?" I was grateful my voice didn't expose the tiny ounce of anxiety bubbling inside me that had made it hard to speak those words in the first place.

The helmet hid most of Grey's facial features except his vibrant Caribbean blue eyes. But that was all I needed to see to know that he was keeping something from me. I think I had an idea of what it was. Or maybe I didn't.

Maybe I wanted it to be something that it wasn't. And that wouldn't be good.

Grey looked away from me and faced forward.

He let out a heavy sigh. "I don't want to see you get hurt. That should be reason enough. Why would I have any other?"

"Right," I muttered so low that he probably didn't hear me.

I slid the helmet onto my head, buckling it in place. Then I held onto his shoulder before swinging my leg over.

Grey turned on the motorcycle, revving it up.

I wrapped my arms around his stomach and leaned into him. "I don't think I want to go home right now," I murmured.

He chuckled. "Good. I wasn't planning on taking you home now anyway."

Then we zoomed off.

2

CHAPTER 2

"Mia Harper," I heard the principal say her name into the microphone as she gracefully strolled across the stage. I jumped to my feet, pulled out my cellphone, and started recording before I began whistling and cheering.

Out of all the graduates, I made a scene like this moment was only about Mia when it was being shared between us. I only cared about her moment.

I heard a blow horn coming from the stands, and I would bet any amount of money that's Mr. Harper cheering for her right along with me.

I watched her face on the jumbo screen as she gave a soft smile to the principal, and he handed her the diploma. A few seconds later, Mia switched her tassel on the cap to the opposite side, signifying that she was now a High school graduate, and she began her descent from the stage.

I cupped one of my hands around my mouth and shouted, "WAY TO GO, MMMIIIAAA!!"

When her gaze landed on mine, she wrinkled her nose at me, and I watched her lips mouth the words. "You're so embarrassing." She rolled her eyes, but I knew she didn't mean it because soon after, her mouth turned up into a dazzling smile, and I could only wink in response.

Like me, Mia graduated with honors. She was the captain of the debate team this year. She had led that team to victory time and time again. There were photos of her and the team up in the champions' hallway at the school's front.

Mia has been immortalized here, and I was so goddamn proud of her.

I watched her walk back to her seat before I quit recording.

The rest of the graduation ceremony went by in a blur, thankfully.

If it hadn't been for the texts from Mia keeping me entertained, I would have probably nodded off due to absolute boredom.

I searched outside the building for Mia amongst the ridiculous number of people when my phone vibrated with a text.

Mia: So, I somehow ended up at the back of the building. Lol.

Me: That's because you have no sense of direction. Stay there. I'm at the front, but I'll come around to find you.

Mia: Okay. Hurry, I want to take pictures!

I smiled, reading the last text. Of course, Mia wanted to take pictures.

Heck, this was one of the few times I felt like taking pictures too.

I slid my cap off my head and tucked it under one of my arms.

I didn't see Katrina a few feet away from me in my haste to find Mia.

"Hey, GREYSON!" She walked up to me, wrapping her arms around my waist as soon as she was close enough.

I wrapped a single arm around her waist. "Hey," I said as my eyes still searched for Mia.

"Were you looking for me?" she asked with excitement.

Crap! I guess I should have been looking for my girlfriend too.

"Of course," I said, giving her my award-winning smile.

"Good because I wanted to talk. I've been thinking about us a lot recently." She backed away from me, leaving about a foot of space between us.

Oh crap. Katrina was about to dump me.

I knew she was upset about how I made her catch a ride with her friends the other day when I had to take Mia home, but this didn't seem like the best reason for a break-up.

Then again, I've broken up with people for more minor things than this. I should get served my karma and accept it.

"I know here's not the best place to say this, but I had to say it here."

My tone of voice dropped an octave. "Is there a better place to do these kinds of things?"

"Yeah, so many better places."

My eyebrows knitted together in confusion. What was going on here? I wasn't even sure I knew at this point.

"I'm just going to come out and say it!" Katrina yelled out. "Where do you see this relationship going? Do you ever see us getting married in the future? Like maybe after college or something?"

There was this huge ass pause between the two of us before I busted out laughing.

She couldn't be serious.

"You're laughing! Why the hell are you laughing?" Katrina asked, shoving one of my shoulders.

If I hadn't seen the expression on her face, I would have never known how damn serious she was about all of this.

I cut the laughter short. "How can you be serious about this?"

"How can I not? We're practically adults."

I interrupted her. "We're 18, and we just graduated from high school less than an hour ago."

Katrina raised her voice. "That's not the point!"

In the few months that I've known her, I've never once heard Katrina yell at me.

"Okay," I said calmly, hoping not to set her off again. "What is the point then?"

She took a deep breath. "They were right," she muttered to herself, shaking her head.

"What are you talking about?"

"I want us to stay together. I don't know if we're a forever thing, but I would like to find out." Katrina shifted her weight to the next foot as she spoke, and her eyes looked down at her feet. "I know we're both going to college, and this whole distance thing might be rough, but I want to make it work. So, I think we should spend as much of the summer together before we both go away to college. This way, we can talk about our future and make some concrete plans that we can both be happy with." She finally looked up from her feet, and her eyes met mine.

"I don't know what to say here," I told her honestly.

"How about you tell me what you want?"

I wasn't sure what I wanted from this relationship.

It took a moment to think about it. Katrina and I had passed the three-month mark, which probably shouldn't be considered an achievement, but it was.

Apparently, I couldn't keep a girlfriend to save my life, which never bothered me. I wasn't looking for my forever but dating someone was nice. Now that I thought about it, I was probably living in the moment.

Katrina huffed, clearly getting annoyed with my delayed response. "Are you having a hard time thinking about us when there's Mia, who is finally single?"

"WHAT?" I said. I must not be hearing her right.

"You heard me, Greyson! You want to throw away our relationship for her, don't you?" Katrina tilted her head back and laughed like a madwoman. "Unbelievable. Actually, No. It's not because every damn thing with you is about freakin' Mia. Mia. MIA! GOD! Do you know there are actually other people on this Earth other than her?"

"Umm." What was going on here? And had aliens abducted my girlfriend because I've never seen her act this way before.

I stood there in disbelief. I felt like the girl standing in front of me was a total stranger. "Where is this coming from?" I asked softly.

Katrina spoke through her teeth. "You want to know, Greyson?"

I nodded.

"How about from having my so-called boyfriend choose his best friend over me all the damn time. Or how about hearing stories about Mia and all her stupid accomplishments and how proud of her you are when you can never congratulate me on a B- that I studied my butt off for. Never mind the fact that I barely see you outside of school. I could go on and on, Greyson. But honestly, it would be exhausting counting the times you've made me feel like crap compared to Mia stupid Harper."

I frowned. I didn't talk about Mia that much. Did I? If so, I was a terrible boyfriend, if you could even call me that.

"I'm sorry, Katrina, truly." I reached out to hug her, but she pushed me away.

Well then.

"If you're sorry, how about you show it by giving us a real chance? Pick me over her right now, and we will take it from there. I need to know you at least want to stay committed to us, whether we're in this for the long haul or not." Katrina made fists at her sides.

I opened my mouth, but no words came out.

Katrina almost spoke again but then...

"GREYSON!" I heard Mia shout my name. I looked behind Katrina and saw her running towards us.

Mia made a dive for me, and I caught her, bringing her into a hug.

When we released each other, Mia turned to Katrina.

Katrina's arms stayed limply at her side as Mia went in for a hug. "Hi, Katrina. Congrats girl! I can't believe we're high school graduates!" she said.

Then Katrina rolled her eyes at Mia.

Since childhood, Mia, my best friend and one of the most prominent people in my life, was the same girl who was sweetly hugging Katrina out of pure joy and all types of kindness.

Mia let her go after a few seconds, and Katrina plastered the fakest grin I've ever seen on her face.

How did I not see this before?

Katrina doesn't like Mia.

Heck, I shouldn't be surprised after everything she had just said to me. I released a harsh sigh, dragging a palm down my face.

If I had found this out a couple of months ago, this relationship wouldn't have lasted as long as it did.

I didn't like anyone that spoke badly about Mia or outright didn't like her. Mia was like family to me; I never wanted to be with anyone who couldn't accept her.

I gently pulled Mia to my side, earning me a glare from Katrina.

Mia, obviously confused, looked up at me and asked, "Why are you being weird?"

I shook my head.

I'd tell her about this later. Maybe not every detail about this conversation, but the most crucial one was that I decided to break up with Katrina after graduation. Which wasn't planned, but she hadn't been making this easy for me.

And I thought having a break up on the last day of school was terrible.

I smiled at Katrina, but anyone who knew me could tell this wasn't exactly my friendliest smile.

"Anyways, we have pictures to take and people to catch up with. I'm sorry about everything, Katrina, but I can't make the choice you're asking me to." Katrina flinched like my words had slapped her in the face, then she got red like she was about to boil over.

Softly gripping Mia's arm, we began to walk away.

Mia leaned into me. "Are you guys fighting?" she whispered low enough that only I could hear her.

I shook my head again.

"I've never seen her so angry." Mia glanced back. "She's always so nice." She frowned, genuinely concerned about the relationship I no longer had. "What did you do to her?"

"ME? Nothing," I said the last word entirely too calmly.

"You-"

I cut her off and pointed to a cherry blossom-looking tree. "Stand over there and let me take your picture." I whipped out my phone.

Mia huffed off in the direction of the tree and stood below it.

Tossing a few locks of hair over her shoulder and readjusting her cap, Mia said, "Greyson, you can't just..."

I changed the subject again. I held up my phone and I said, "Quick! Say 'IloveyouGreysonMcNamara!'"

"Not on your life!" I snapped the picture catching Mia in a mid-eye roll with her arms crossed against her chest.

I grinned, admiring the photo.

If Mia saw this, she'd tell me to delete it. I chuckled to myself.

That was not happening.

3

CHAPTER 3

W e wrapped up the day with a BBQ at the Harper's. That was how Mia wanted to celebrate, and I couldn't complain. I was getting BBQ chicken, burgers, and grilled corn.

Okay, my only complaint was about Mia breathing down my neck, trying to get me to open up about what happened with Katrina earlier.

"Tell me!" Mia whispered harshly while poking my side with her plastic spoon.

"Knock it off." I glared at her in mock anger because let's be honest. Mia wasn't someone who could seriously make me angry. "I'll tell you later," I whispered back.

I would tell her now, but she was doing that adorable pouting thing because she wasn't getting her way. And I was enjoying it too much.

"Is everything okay over there?" my mom called from the patio table.

We both turned to her and nodded. "We're fine," we replied in unison.

I went back to scooping copious amounts of potato salad onto my plate.

Mia put her plate down next to the cornbread. "We talked about James the instant it happened, but you won't talk about Katrina."

I let out a sigh. "There's not much to say." I moved on to the coleslaw. "She wanted a bigger commitment, and I couldn't give her that." This was me trying to tell her the truth while also leaving out a massive part of that conversation.

"Like what?"

I glanced back to make sure our family wasn't trying to eavesdrop before I lowered my voice. "She said that she wanted us to think about the long haul. Whether it be a long-distance relationship or marriage after college," I had muttered the last few words.

"WHAT!" Mia blurted out in shock. "HOW COULD SHE ASK YOU THAT?"

"How can who ask what?" Mom butted into our conversation.

"Yes. We would also like to be a part of the conversation that has had you two pretending to grab seconds for the past five minutes," Mr. Harper said.

"Sorry," Mia whispered guiltily, realizing that her outburst had put the family in the middle of our chat.

Well, now that I had everyone's attention. "Katrina and I broke up." Before they could ask, when I told them. "After the graduation ceremony. It was just, that both of us knew at that moment that it wasn't going to work out for us. So we ended it."

"I'm sorry, honey," Mom frowned.

"It'll be alright, son. With a face like that." Mr. Harper pointed and gestured to my face with his fork. "You'll get a bunch of girls in college."

"Right? He's so handsome," Ava, Mr. Harper's girlfriend, added.

"Exactly," Mom quickly agreed.

"You know, I met Mia's mom in college and," Mr. Harper paused, scratching his head. "Maybe my story isn't the best example since we eventually... you know..."

Mia nodded, then turned to me. "You know what I think you should do?"

"What?"

"You should stop dating for a couple of years." She smiled evilly at me.

I stared at her blankly. She was using my own words against me.

"Okay, okay. I wouldn't go that far now," Mr. Harper saved me.

"Why not? Obviously, he sucks at it. This relationship lasted, what? Three months?"

I snickered. Grabbing my plate, I went back to sit down.

My mom rubbed my shoulders. "It'll be fine, sweetie."

"Can we change the subject now?" I asked, stuffing my mouth full of potato salad.

"Sure," Mia said, taking her seat next to me. "Let's talk about our new apartment." She squealed with excitement, tapping her hands on the table.

Our parents put their money together to lease a two-bedroom apartment close to the university for Mia and me. It was two hours from home, and we were excited just to be independent and do whatever we wanted, like eating leftover pizza for breakfast and ice cream for dinner—just kidding—kind of.

We're supposed to move in August, the week before classes begin.

Since Mia and I had both been saving up from our part-time jobs, she's been spending a crazy amount of money shopping online for house stuff. I've told her to stop because we don't have to buy everything all at once, but then she gave me that puppy dog pout, and I just let her do whatever she wanted.

We both felt incredibly grateful for our parents getting us this place, so when they asked to help us put money towards a few pieces of furniture, we declined. Mia and I wanted to use our own money. I wasn't sure how this would work out, but we'll figure it out together.

I mean, as long as we have food in the fridge and somewhere comfy to sleep, I know we'll be fine.

When I got home, I showered and changed into something more comfortable. I was going over to Mia's for a movie night while her dad left to catch a last-minute flight to Texas for a convention.

"Grey?" Mom knocked on my door as I slipped my black t-shirt over my head. "You have a visitor."

"What? Who?" The only person I could think of visiting me was at home, waiting for me to come over.

"Katrina."

Just as she said her name, I felt my phone vibrate in my back pocket.

I looked at it.

Katrina: Can we talk, please? I know you're home.

I went downstairs and walked out front. I found Katrina leaning against the hood of her bright yellow VW bug.

"Who are you right now?" I said first, breaking the silence first.

She had no clue what I was talking about.

I clarified. "Are you Dr. Jackal or Mr. Hyde? Because I don't think I could handle a repeat of earlier. I'm pretty sure you gave me whiplash." They say you saw someone's true colors after dating them for over three months. They weren't kidding.

"I'm sorry," Katrina started. "I shouldn't have given you an ultimatum. I shouldn't have said those things about you, and I shouldn't have said those things about Mia."

She sighed, shrugging her shoulders. "I was jealous. I always have been from the moment you introduced us. You just don't know how you look at her when she's around you or how you talk about her when she's not."

I opened my mouth to say something.

"No, let me finish, please." Katrina's eyes pleaded with mine.

"Okay," I said.

Katrina told me how excited she was when I asked her to be my girlfriend, how she loved spending time with me but that it didn't always feel like I was present, living in the moment with her. She spent the last few months hoping that things would change eventually, especially after telling me that she thought she was falling in love with me. When she heard that Mia had broken up with James, she felt like she wouldn't get the chance to have the kind of relationship that she wanted with me, so she freaked. She wanted to see if she demanded more of a commitment if I would stay or leave her. She already knew the answer, but she had to try anyway. She admitted that she felt a little broken-hearted over it.

"I'll accept that hug now if you don't mind," she told me afterward.

I leaned in to hug her. "I'm sorry I was such a jerk to you."

"Nah, you weren't a horrible boyfriend." I chuckled with disbelief. "You bought me flowers on my birthday. You took me out on dates and paid for everything. You always opened the doors for me and texted me, 'good morning.' Then you always made sure I got home safely after school. And you always always let me vent about my day to you over the phone for hours upon hours. You never complained and told me I was annoying. I can't tell you how many guys would make the time to listen to me."

Katrina eased out of my arms. "But, even after all of that, you always felt more like a good friend than an actual boyfriend. Why did you ask me out anyway?" she finally asked.

The answer for that was lost on me. I wasn't exactly sure myself. I mean, Katrina seemed cool, she made me laugh sometimes, and she was pretty.

"Is it because I'm the complete opposite of Mia? You hoped that when you were with me that you wouldn't think of her? Or was it because you needed a distraction from the fact that the girl of your dreams was dating someone else?"

What? No.

"No, no. It's nothing like that," I tried to convince her.

Katrina crossed her arms, staring at me with a straight face. "Isn't' though?"

I shook my head. "No. We're just friends."

"But if you could be something more?"

I cut her off. "I wouldn't. I'm not in love with Mia."

Katrina smiled at me. "I never said you were Greyson."

Shoot. "Listen, I do love Mia but not in the way you're thinking."

"It's fine, Greyson, really. But what's not fine is you pretending you can stand by and watch her be with someone else that's not you."

My heart clenched at the thought.

Let's say I did have feelings for Mia. Just hypothetically speaking, I would never tell her because I knew she didn't feel the same. I would make things weird, and I didn't want that. I never wanted that for us.

I bit my bottom lip, contemplating what I should say next.

"You can be honest with me, Greyson. I swear I won't run over and tell Mia everything when you're done."

I dragged the palms of my hands down my face.

"Okay, I see that you may have internally accepted your feelings for her, but you are nowhere close to voicing them aloud. So I'll just tell you this, Mia needs to know that you feel the same way she does."

"What?" I laughed out the word nervously. Then took a sharp inhale, exhaling with a short puff of breath.

"Call it a girl's intuition." Katrina gently punched one of my shoulders. "Anyways, I'm going to head out now. I'm glad we could clear the air between us."

All I could do was nod as I watched her hop in her car.

I saw her wind her window down. "And Greyson?"

"Hmm?"

"I hope everything eventually works out between the two of you. I think you guys would make a great couple, for what it's worth. I don't think I've ever seen two people so in sync with one another. Bye." Katrina winked before reversing out of my driveway and waving goodbye.

4

CHAPTER 4

Grey came hurdling through my bedroom window, gracefully landing in front of my bed with a light thud just as I was slipping a t-shirt over my head.

"Dude!" I scowled at him. I jumped out of the shower when I heard him zooming down the street, and I knew he would pull up to my house soon. I tried to quickly throw on some pajamas, thinking I could beat him to the front door before he knocked, but he decided to take another route.

I'll never understand why Grey would rather sneak in through the window instead of using the front door like a normal human being. It's not like my dad was home, and if he were, he wouldn't care because it was Greyson, and he's known him forever.

"Sorry. It's not like it's nothing I haven't seen before." He shrugged.

I grumbled, sticking my tongue out at him.

Grey ignored me, taking off his boots and then his motorcycle jacket before putting them in my closet.

He took a seat on the edge of my bed and asked, "What's on the movie list tonight?"

I took in his facial expression. It didn't sound like something was up with him, but he looked way too calm right now not to have something going on in that head of his.

I would ask him, but he has been a little weird since my break up with James. And now there was his breakup with Katrina. It's been a rough couple of days for both of us.

I sighed. "I don't know. Maybe we can finish one of the TV shows that we're not caught upon. Or we could re-watch Stranger things." I suggested. That was his favorite show, and we've watched all the seasons twice already.

Grey opened his mouth to reply but got distracted by a text. While he read it, he sucked on his bottom lip, indicating that he was deep in thought about whatever he was reading.

"What is it?"

He glanced up at me and then said, "Nothing."

"Liar, liar." I poked his bicep before sitting next to him.

"It's not a big deal," he added.

I crossed my arms against my chest. "I still want to know."

Grey huffed out a breath, knowing he wouldn't be able to change the subject until he told me. "Fine. That was O'Malley. He wanted to know if I would come in for a race today. I told him I had other plans."

Grey knew I disapproved of this "hobby," if you could call it that, which was why he usually snuck off to race and didn't tell me about it until the next day when he was buying me breakfast with his winnings. He knew how to butter me up before giving me news or asking for forgiveness.

I was surprised he decided to be honest about it, probably because he had no intentions of going in.

"I thought you were done racing?" I've asked him to give it up a few times, knowing darn well that he wouldn't. Grey was too dang stubborn, sometimes.

And eager as I was for him to get over the thrill of illegal racing, I felt like him speeding around on his motorcycle under the stars with only this path lit by floodlights might be precisely what he needed to cheer up a bit.

Grey goes through phases like this a lot of the time. When he was completely caught up in something, he got obsessed with it to the point where it almost seemed like it could become his life. But then he would try something new, and there he went moving from the old hobby.

Grey liked to experience a bit of everything. He was a lot like his father in that aspect.

Grey's eyes met mine. "You think I'm going to be able to afford new furniture on a part-time warehouse associate's salary?" he asked incredulously.

It was about six months ago when Grey started working at this warehouse on the outskirts of town. He hated every single minute, but he got happy when he saw the direct deposit hit his account.

I couldn't blame him, though. I felt the same when working as a receptionist at the Brantley hotel. Don't get me wrong, it was a nice place, and the pay was decent, but that was nowhere close to the dream job that I wanted for myself.

"I think you should go in tonight," I finally told him.

The corner of his mouth tipped up into a smirk. "Wow. You must really want that new 55-inch OLED TV."

I rolled my eyes. When I opened my mouth to deny it, I realized it was kind of true. If he did win a race today, we would be more than able to afford it. But that wasn't the initial reason I had for telling him to go in.

"Yes, but no. I think you should just go in and have some fun. For one last time." I tried to put extra emphasis on the word "last." Hopefully, he caught the hint.

Grey leaned away from me, feigning shock. "You're giving me permission to go in?"

I nodded slowly. "Yes. But under one condition." I held up my pointer finger in front of my face.

"You want me to take you out for breakfast tomorrow?" he guessed.

"No." That would be nice, though.

"You want me to take you to that nice bookstore in the next town over?"

"No." Damn, I said that too quickly! I was dying to make another trip over there.

Grey kept guessing. "You want me to drop the whole no dating rule until you're out of college thing?"

"Yes! No! Well, I never considered that to be in effect, to begin with, so no." I rolled my eyes.

"It's been in effect for days, actually," he grinned. "But that's beside the point. I'm running out of guesses here, Mia."

I hit him with a combo of sweet talk and cutesy smiles. "Grey," I smiled up at him. "Do you know you're like one of my favorite people in the entire world?" I hugged one of his biceps.

Grey was quiet for a few seconds, but he caught on rather quickly. "Nope. Nope." I didn't see him shaking his head, but I felt it. "Absolutely not." He jumped to his feet, sliding his arm out of my grasp. "I cannot take you with me, Mia."

I frowned. "You've never taken me with you!" I argued. It wasn't like I always wanted to go anyway.

"It's not your kind of place," Grey said as if that would change my mind.

"It's just this one time." I reasoned with him. If this were his last race, he wouldn't have to worry about bringing me again.

"No," he said firmly after considering it for a few seconds.

"Please?" I asked nicely, clamping my hands and shaking them.

"No," he repeated.

"Come on!" I shouted with frustration.

Grey's face became stern, and he deepened his voice. "No," he said stubbornly.

I threw my hands up in the air. "So what are you going to do? Leave me here while you go off to wherever to race?"

He nodded. "Yup. Sounds like a plan."

I pouted.

"Don't do that." Grey turned away from me. "I don't want to bring you, Mia." His voice softened. "That's not the best crowd for you to be around. Anything could happen to you when I'm on the track, and I would never be able to forgive myself."

"I'll be careful," I promised. "I won't go wandering off." It sounded like I might be able to win this one.

Grey tilted his head back and massaged his neck with both hands.

"Greyson." If he was adamant about me not going, there must be a good reason, and I didn't want to push it, but...

"Fine," he grumbled. "You can come." He relented, interrupting my thoughts as he turned to face me. "But you have to please listen to everything I say and just follow my lead."

"YES! OF COURSE!" I tried to bite back my grin, but I couldn't hold it in. "I promise." I squealed with excitement before launching myself at him.

At first, he didn't want to hug me back, but I wouldn't let go until he did.

When his arms wrapped around me, no matter what Grey was worried about, I knew he would always protect me.

5

CHAPTER 5

It took us about 50 minutes to make it to O'Malley's.

We were basically in the middle of nowhere on the outskirts of some small town that looked abandoned. If that wasn't creepy enough, Greyson had been on one of the main roads for 5 minutes before he pulled off onto this old, broken-up road, where we spent another 10 minutes riding before we reached an open field with a large abandoned building.

I hopped off first before Grey could even shut off his bike.

I slipped off my helmet, and I took in my surroundings. There was a massive crowd of people, more than I thought would be gathered here.

People were roasting marshmallows and drinking beer around bonfires. That seemed like an odd combo, but okay. I heard music off into the distance, but I couldn't pinpoint the location.

But all in all, this place wasn't half bad.

Grey turned off his bike, took off his helmet, and rested it on the bike seat before taking mine and doing the same.

"So, what do you think?" He gestured to the land.

"I like it," I told him.

"You would. You're like those good girl characters in the movies who go somewhere they've never been that has trouble written all over it, but you're oddly excited about it." Grey sighed, shaking his head.

I narrowed my eyes at him, "Whatever," I responded teasingly. "Where's the track?" I asked since I couldn't immediately spot it.

"Down there." Grey pointed over my shoulder.

I didn't realize we were parked on a hillside until I walked to the edge and looked down.

My mouth opened to form an "O."

"It's a legit track!" I exclaimed.

It was a little run down, much like the bleachers on both sides, but it had authentic stadium lights.

"What you thought I raced on a dirt track with this baby?" Grey patted his bike. "This isn't a dirt bike, Mia."

"I know that. I just don't know. I don't know what I was thinking!"

It was safe to say I didn't know anything about motorcycle racing.

"You figured we'd be racing on dirt since we're in the middle of nowhere?"

"Yeah. I guess so," I mumbled, feeling a little dumb.

Grey chuckled.

"But how do you guys not get caught?"

"Well, I don't know the exact details, but supposedly, the cops around here don't make much, and O'Malley cuts them a profit when he does, so they don't bother us. I even heard that sometimes the off-duty cops come here to gamble, drink, and have a little fun with a side piece or two in one of those tents." Grey pointed to one of the various tents scattered across the hill.

I shook my head in disbelief. "This is unreal."

He released a harsh sigh. "Tell me about it," he muttered.

"What was this place before?"

"No clue. All I know is that the city could care less about it. Anyways, come on, let me introduce you to some people." Grey reached for my hand and led me over to one of the larger tents a few feet away. "O'Malley!" he called out.

A man about my height of five-foot-seven with long shaggy red hair and the equivalent of a Santa Claus beard turned to greet us.

"Hey, champ," he said to Greyson. When his eyes landed on me, he asked, "This your girl?"

"Yes. This is Mia." Grey gestured to me with his free hand.

"Mia, this is O'Malley."

O'Malley sticks his hand out for me to shake. "Nice to meet you, Mia. But you can call me Finn like all the ladies do." He smiled.

Yeah, I wasn't going to do that.

"So when you tell me you're busy...." O'Malley started, but Greyson cut him off.

"I'm busy with her. Or you know, I'm at work since some of us are still employed."

O'Malley chuckled under his breath. "How long will you keep rubbing it in my face that I lost my job?"

"Until the end of time."

"You two worked together? At the warehouse?" I asked curiously. Grey never told me how they had met.

"Yeah. We did, but I got fired a few months back."

"What did you do?"

Greyson exhaled a long breath through his nose, then proceeded to shake his head as if to say, "You don't wanna know."

O'Malley's smile stayed in place. "Nothing too serious. I only seduced the boss's wife in the back stockroom. It wasn't the first time we fooled around like that. Just the first time we did it at the warehouse."

My jaw dropped, but then I quickly composed myself. "Oh. Okay," I replied, not knowing what else to say.

I instantly regret asking.

O'Malley continued. "Listen, in my defense, if she had been getting the attention she needed from her crappy ex-husband, she wouldn't have come to me. Plus, I'm probably the best lay she's had. Anyways, when the boss man caught us, the jig was up, and I was fired on the spot. I swear it was one of the janitors that ratted us out," he mumbled a curse.

"It's not like you guys were quiet or anything." Greyson threw that reminder out there for him.

O'Malley flicked his wrist. "I told her to be, but..."

"I couldn't help myself?" Someone interjected. I watched a woman step out of the tent behind him, pulling down a super skimpy, almost see-through black dress that only fell mid-thigh. She smoothed down the front of her hair and walked over to stand next to him. "Is that what you were going to say?" she asked, slapping his shoulder and making him wince.

I took a good look at her. She had dark curly brown hair that fell to her shoulders and olive skin. She was a tad shorter than me and age-wise, I'd have a hard time believing she was anything over 25.

"Would I be lying if I did?" O'Malley tilted his head in her direction.

"Eh," she replied with a shrug. "You'll have to remind me later so that I can be sure."

"Will do. Will do." O'Malley told her before placing a quick kiss on her lips.

Then she turned her attention to Grey. "Hey, Greyson. What's up? Who's the bombshell blonde next to you?"

I spoke up, "Hi, I'm Mia." I gave a quick wave.

"Nice to meet you, Mia. I'm Caroline. This idiot right here," She bumped her shoulder into O'Malley's. "Is my boyfriend." she smiled.

"So, what brings you out tonight, Greyson?" Caroline said.

"Just squeezing in one last race before it's off college."

"Huh? You think you can give up all of this?" She used her arms to make a wide circle. "After one last race?"

"I'll miss it, but I got bigger and better things to do." Grey's eyes cut to me.

Caroline nodded. "I get it. Anyways, I'm going to get some beer and see if I can convince one of those guys to share their s'mores with me." She walked by us.

O'Malley called out. "I can make you a whole damn tray of s'mores if that's what you want."

"I can make you do just about anything I want, which is why that's too easy and no fun." She blew him a kiss.

"That woman will be the death of me," he said low enough for us to hear still. Grey glanced around the open field. "So, who's racing tonight?"

O'Malley stuffed his hand into his pockets. "Only the best of the best."

Grey rolled his eyes. "I'd like some names."

O'Malley took out a lighter and then a cigarette. "Would it matter?" He brought the cigarette to his lips and lit it. He took a drag and added, "You'll beat them all anyway. You always do. That's why..." he poked Grey's chest, "you're my best racer." He slapped his back.

I glared at the side of his face. "You never told me that!"

Grey bit his bottom lip.

"Yup. Your boyfriend makes me a lot of money when he comes in. He places the largest bets and gives me a more than generous cut."

"He's not my boyfriend," I quickly corrected him, ignoring every other part of what he just said.

O'Malley's eyes looked between the two of us for a few seconds. "If you say so." He smiled.

"How much do you want to put up tonight?"

Greyson looked at the people standing a few feet away from us as they whispered. He pointed to the dimly lit abandoned building beside us. "Let's go inside and talk about it."

"Sure. Step into my office." O'Malley nodded in that direction.

I was about to follow when I heard my phone ringing. I didn't recognize the number, but I've seen it call me before. I think it was earlier, after graduation. I wondered who it could be.

"I got to answer this," I told Grey.

He looked hesitant to leave me standing outside by myself.

"I'll just be right here. I won't move from this spot."

"We have chairs set up inside the tent. You can take a seat in there if you want. We won't be long." O'Malley told me.

I nodded. "Thanks."

I answered the phone as I watched them walk off together. "Hello?" The line was quiet. "Hello?" I said again, a little louder than before in case they hadn't heard me.

I was about to hang up. "MIA! WAIT! Don't hang up. Please." The woman desperately pleaded.

"Who is this?" I couldn't place their voice, but I knew it was familiar somehow.

"It's me. Your mother."

If I could have gripped the phone any harder, it would have crumbled to dust.

Mom?

6

CHAPTER 6

I haven't heard the sound of my mother's voice in over what? A couple of years?

"Mia? Mia? Are you still there?" she asked frantically.

"Yup," I replied in a quiet tone.

"Great. Great. I was hoping, I mean I thought, you would have hung up on me after I told you who I was." She laughed nervously.

"I'm considering it." The words slipped out of my mouth, but that doesn't mean they're not the truth.

Mom went silent for a few seconds. "I'm sure I deserved that."

That reply shouldn't have brought me satisfaction, but it did.

I went inside the tent, wanting some privacy. The interior was not as ordinary as the exterior led you to believe. Not only was this one of the biggest tents I'd ever seen, but the inside also had electric candles and lanterns, a portable speaker, a huge pile of pillows, and blankets that formed sort of made a bed. Then there was a little cooler left open with drinks and right next to it was a box of snacks. This was as good a setup as any. I took a seat on one of the chairs across from the "bed."

"Why are you calling me?" I got straight to the point.

"I, um, was hoping we could talk?" she said.

"Sure. But how about you talk, and I listen because you have a crap ton of explaining to do.." I suggested, angrily nibbling on my bottom lip.

"I know. I know, and I'm sorry." Mom sighed. "Maybe we should meet in person? Are you busy this week?"

I shook my head. "No."

"That's great!" She missed my real meaning.

"No. I mean, I don't think I want to meet with you." My stubbornness, combined with my eight-year grudge, made me unreasonable.

How could I meet with her? My mom pulled one of those, "I'll be back soon, honey, love you!" and then abandoned me. The worst part was that it was right around my birthday. I didn't realize at the time that that would be one of many birthdays. That I would spend without her.

"Mia, everything I have to say would probably be better if I said it in person. I can't just blurt these things out over the phone."

I think I would prefer to hear it over the phone. That way, if she said something I didn't like, I could just hang up. Problem solved. "It's fine. Let's hear it." I leaned back in the chair.

"Okay. Well... um... I don't exactly know where to begin. It's a long story."

I rolled my eyes as if she could see me. "I'll take the cliff notes version. Thanks."

"I'm calling because I want to reconnect with my daughter. I was hoping we could spend the summer together. I've made plans to travel around Asia. I have a few cities I'll be visiting for business. But I loved to take time out to sightsee and explore. I think it would be a good family trip for us and..." She sighed harshly into the phone. "Your sister is dying to meet you."

I gasped. "I-I-I have a sister?" I could barely get the sentence out.

"Yes, Mia. Her name is-"

I interrupted her. "Unbelievable! Of course, you went off and started a new family. Dad said you were unhappy and wanted out. I guess he was right." My heart was broken when I realized she had left for good. Now it was hurting again for a whole other reason.

"No, no, no. It was nothing like that! I may have been unhappy at some point, but that's not why I left. Your sister was sick, and she needed a kidney transplant."

What was she talking about? I didn't have a sister back then? Unless...

"WAIT A MINUTE! How old is she?" The words rushed out of me in one breath.

Her response was slow. "She'll be thirteen next month."

"But how? Does that mean that she's... or did you..." My brain couldn't function from the shock of all this. I leaned forward, placing both of my elbows on my knees, and palmed my forehead.

This was too much.

"There was a time when your father and I separated, and I met someone. It's a long story," she huffed. "After that, I made some very questionable decisions. I'm not proud of them, but I've been forgiven for them. The only person who hasn't forgiven me yet is you, Mia. Your father has finally given me permission to reach out and fix this, so I called as soon as I could."

I frowned. Dad hadn't even given me the heads up that this would happen.

Mom went on. "Please don't be upset with him. I was afraid you would shoot the idea down immediately if he asked you about me potentially reaching out."

"So you thought it would be better to surprise me instead?" I let out a humorless laugh.

"I didn't want to do that either, but I was desperate to hear your voice, Mia. It would have broken my heart to hear you say no." I heard her sniffling. "It's breaking my heart now that you've said you don't want to see me. I will do anything to make up for these last few years if it means that I can see you again. Anything, just name it." The desperation in her voice was evident. I wanted to believe her, but I didn't know her well enough to say that she would keep her promise. This woman was practically a stranger to me. Trust needed to be earned, and she already had a bad rep.

I closed my eyes and took a deep breath. "I need to think about this," I mumbled.

"Okay," Mom sniffled again before I heard her blowing her nose. "It's fine, ba-Mia. Take all the time you need and let me know. Okay?"

"Okay." I know this chat hasn't gone the way she hoped, but it could have gone so much worse.

There had been many things I used to imagine saying to my mom if I saw her again, but I didn't have it in me to say any of them. If it were possible, Mom sounded as broken up about our relationship as I did.

"Okay," Mom repeated. "Great. So um, this is my cellphone number. I'll text you my house and office number in case of anything, really-an emergency or whatever. Or maybe you just want to talk. I want you to be able to reach me no matter what."

All I could think to say was a weak, "Thanks."

"I hope you'll reach out soon," she rushed on to add.

I didn't know how to respond to that.

"And Mia?"

"Yes?" I answered numbly, wondering what else she had to say.

"I love you." And then she hung up.

As I sat there, the minutes ticked by, staring at the ground beneath my feet.

I needed to find Grey. I almost forgot that I was here to watch a street race. This was turning out to be the perfect distraction for us both.

My eyes were glued to the ground, lost in my thoughts, so I was surprised when I stepped one foot outside the tent and collided with someone.

"Hey there, sexy? Is O'Malley in there?" he said, pointing to the tent behind me.

"No."

I watched his eyes quickly scan my body, and he smiled. "Do you have business with him that had you waiting in his love nest? If so, what kind of business is it? Maybe you and me could work out something together instead?" He waggled his eyebrows at me. Gross.

I took one good look at him. Never mind the alcohol stench coating his breath. This guy was far, and I mean far, from my type. Plus, he doesn't know how to talk to a girl properly. That was probably how he got that black eye and a broken nose in the first place. Crazy that none of that had dampened his confidence.

But anyway, if he searched hard enough, maybe a few girls around here wouldn't mind having fun with him.

"No thanks. Not interested," I told him.

I tried to walk around him, but he grabbed my arm and leaned down to whisper in my ear. "I think I can persuade you to change your mind," he said it all cocky as if he had some hidden charm that was bound to work on me.

I was about to give him a piece of my mind when Caroline intervened. "HEY, DOUCHEBAG!" she said, walking towards us with a tray of s'mores in hand. "You might want to ease up off her. That's Grey's girl." His eyes grew wide, and he released my arm with lightning speed. "Luckily for you, he wasn't around to catch that, or you would have gotten a matching black eye but with a busted lip this time, instead of a broken nose." Caroline stopped when she reached us. "Now run along." She swatted the air like he was a bug she wanted to get rid of.

He scampered off like hellhounds were on his tail.

I turned to Caroline. "Grey did that?" He never fought. He was too calm, chill, and unbothered to get caught up in something like that.

"Yup. Word on the street is that they bumped into each other at a gas station a few days ago, and Grey had caught him trying to tamper with his motorcycle. When Grey confronted him, that idiot threw a punch and missed, but Grey didn't."

Holy cow.

Caroline laughed at my reaction. "Your boyfriend has a badass rep out here in these streets."

"Not my boyfriend!" I corrected her. Why does everyone always assume that? "And I can't believe he did that!"

"Can't believe who did what?" Grey said, creeping up behind me.

I whipped around to face him. "You beat up some guy?"

He looked confused. Was he going to stand here and pretend that he didn't know what I was talking about?

"That guy over there!" I pointed to the sleazeball that tried to hit on me.

Grey glanced over his shoulder. "Oh yeah." He put one hand in his pocket. "It was self-defense. He totally had it coming," he said nonchalantly, without a single ounce of remorse.

I rolled my eyes. I really couldn't argue with him there. I just wished he would have told me. "Why didn't you say anything?" I asked him.

He shrugged. "It wasn't that big a deal, and I'm fine. Most importantly, my baby over there is a O-K."

I shook my head. Boys and their toys.

"Anyway," Grey changed the subject. "Ready to watch your first street race?"

This race was becoming a welcomed distraction for both of us.

My face lit up with excitement. "YEAH!"

"Then come on, let's go." Grey took my hand.

7

—·—

CHAPTER 7

Grey rode his motorcycle down to the track. I watched a crowd of people slowly start to gather on the bleachers while some took a seat on the hill, looking down at the track.

I followed Grey as far as the starting line. "Good luck!" I told him.

He gave me a cocky grin. "After everything, they told you about me, do you think I need it?"

I shrugged, smiling. "Nah." I looked around the empty track. "Where are the rest of the guys?"

Grey chuckled under his breath. "They didn't want to race me."

My eyebrows knitted together. "What?"

"Yeah, then there's the fact there's a huge amount of money on the line, and I don't think anybody wants to risk losing that much to me. Except for this one idiot." Grey snickered as he climbed onto his bike.

I heard some girls yelling out his name from the bleachers, waving their arms to get his attention. Grey, being Grey, winked and waved back.

I crossed my arms, rolling my eyes. Of course, Grey had groupies—scantily dressed groupies at that.

One of them ran to the edge of the bleachers and leaned over the railing, "Hey! You should come to my tent after you win the race." She twirled a strand of her matted green hair. She was trying to be flirty and cute. I didn't think she was either of those things.

Grey opened his mouth to answer her, but I beat him to it. "No thanks! He's not interested." I smiled sweetly. She pouted and walked off to take a seat amongst her friends. I watched them whisper and point at us. Great.

"Jealous?" Grey poked my side, causing me to flinch as I slapped his hand away.

"No. Of course not. I just know she's not your type." I was not jealous. I had no reason to be. "Anyways, back to what I was saying. I'm guessing you've raced this guy before?"

Grey nodded. "Twice. And he's a sore loser. He's the last person I would have considered racing tonight, but he agreed to match the money I put up."

I wanted to ask what the offer had been, but I was afraid to. I knew it must be an unseemly high amount.

A thought occurred to me. "But don't you think that's weird? Like he must have something planned if he wants to race you again after losing the other two times. And if he's such a sore loser, why would he put himself in this position to possibly lose again?"

Grey shrugged nonchalantly. "Maybe he's feeling lucky. I don't know, but it doesn't matter. I'm going to beat him like I always do."

I nodded. "Good."

We heard O'Malley speak through a megaphone loudspeaker. He was announcing the racers and saying that the race would begin soon.

"Mia, you can grab a seat over there." Grey pointed to Caroline on the bleachers, who waved at me. He slipped his helmet on and started up his bike. His fangirls started to squeal and scream.

"Okay, I'll see you after the race." I jogged off the track. I was making my way up and around the bleachers when I passed some guy coming downhill with his mustard color motorcycle.

I guess this was the other racer. He had this spikey platinum blonde Mohawk and wore a white biker jacket with stone-washed jeans and a black t-shirt.

Was I the only one that didn't know stone-washed jeans were still a thing?

He had two other guys flanking him as he slowly pushed his bike alongside him. "Are you sure about racing him again?" The guy on his right asked.

He sounded like he thought his friend was making a big mistake.

Since I was biased, I would have to agree.

I slowed my pace to eavesdrop on their conversation.

"Listen, since I've gotten upgrades on this thing, I don't think he'll stand a chance. I mean, his bike looks like some ancient hand-me-down."

Okay, Grey's bike already had a good couple of years. But Grey did inherit from his father. Mr. McNamara could have been a racer in a past life. Grey had a video of him renting out a track to race his buddies. If I remember correctly, he never lost a race either. M

Mr. McNamara's love for the sport was passed down to Grey. So Grey has kept his bike in pristine condition even before he could ride it. His mom had wanted to sell it for years, but Grey always managed to talk her out of it.

I recalled how she used to panic seeing Mr. McNamara ride off on his motorcycle. But with Grey, it was even worse.

She would clench her fists over her chest and shout, "BE SAFE! BE SAFE! PLEASE!" Then she turned her head, tightly shutting her eyes, trying her best not to watch him ride off. It was kind of funny.

Sometimes I forget how much Grey and his dad were exactly alike.

"That's true. His bike is practically crap compared to yours."

The guy on the left spoke after them. "But still, what if he wins? Won't you be embarrassed again? Dude, you barely have any street racing cred like you used to." The guy on the right, his eyes grew wide like he knew his friend shouldn't have said that.

The racer guy paused, then punched his friend in the gut out of nowhere. The poor guy was hunched over on all fours. "Stop talking shit, Jason!" He kicked up some dirt at him. Then they proceeded to walk by him like they could care less about the guy.

I almost felt bad for him.

"What the hell are you staring at, blondie?" He sneered as he got up and dusted off his knees. "You should learn to mind your business," he added, pointing his finger at me.

Agh! Rude. I was going to say something but decided I couldn't be bothered so

I walked away instead.

"That's what I thought!" he shouted to my back.

Real mature.

Never mind. I didn't feel bad for him. I probably would have punched him too.

On the bleachers, I skipped down to Caroline. I was thinking about everything those guys said. It made me want to call Grey and give him a heads up.

I pulled my phone out, and I saw two texts from my mom. I had put my phone on silent after her call. I quickly skimmed the message. It was just her sending the phone numbers, as promised. Then she threw in a "Whenever you're ready to talk, I'll be here for you."

I saved her numbers and then called Grey. I watched him slide off his helmet and then grab his phone from his pocket and answer. At the same time, I watched those three jerks make their way onto the track.

"Mia? You okay?" He twisted around and on his bike, and his eyes instantly found me standing in the middle of the empty bleachers.

I nodded. "Yup. I just," I sighed. "This might sound stupid, but I walked past those guys, coming onto the track, and they said some stuff."

"To you?"

By the sound of his voice, I could tell that he was ready to leap into action if they had said anything he didn't like.

"No. He was bragging about some bike upgrades and how he's finally going to beat you."

I saw him and heard him let out a hearty laugh. "Is that so? Well, I guess I have to see how good those upgrades are when racing."

I bit my lip nervously.

"It drives me crazy when you do that. Stop it." He pointed to me.

I released my lip. "Just be careful. I don't know, but I have a bad feeling about him."

"Noted. I'll be fine. Okay? No worries."

I nodded and hung up.

Grey watched me walk down to Caroline and take a seat before he repositioned himself on his bike, sliding his helmet back on.

"Hey, Mia. I got smores!" Caroline held up a new tray of smores.

Where does she manage to put all of that?

I was still full from the BBQ earlier. Plus, even if I were hungry, my anxiety wouldn't let me eat.

"Gosh! This is so nerve-wracking," I muttered under my breath.

"Don't worry. Your boy got it this." She bumped my shoulder before shoving another s'more in her mouth. "HMM." She groaned into the snack.

I watched Grey and the other racer line up their bikes at the starting line. The guy must have yelled something over to him because Grey gave him the finger.

"So when it's only two racers, Finn lets them do just three laps around the track. Then the winner takes the cash pot. Short and simple," Caroline informed me.

We watched some half-dressed girl walk out onto the track. She reached behind her, then slipped her bra off from under her shirt and held it up.

Oh gosh.

O'Malley spoke, "Okay, get ready..."

The guys revved up their bikes.

"Set... Go!" The girls waved the bra down, and the guys took off.

The crowd screamed while I maintained a death grip on the bleaches. If I had super strength, I would've dented it.

On the first lap, Grey was in the lead. Then the other guy sped up on the second, putting Grey a few feet behind him. For the third lap, I swear my lungs were suffering from the lack of oxygen that I kept forgetting to give them because I couldn't remember to breathe. Grey was in the lead again, but then the other guy sped up, and as he did, I wasn't sure what happened, but they were practically head to head when the other guy looked like he purposely swerved towards

Grey to get him off balance or something. But Greyson must have slightly slowed down, giving the other guy the chance to make it in front and... Oh no.

The crowd cheering for them for the last few minutes got silent as the other guy raced across the finish line.

Grey lost. Ah, shoot.

"OH MY GOD!" Caroline shouted furiously. "NO FLIPPING WAY. HE MUST HAVE CHEATED SOMEHOW!"

I hopped up off the bleachers running to make my way down to Grey.

As I made it to the track, I heard the other guy talking smack, and I watched him poke Greyson in the chest. I stood behind them.

"I knew this day was going to come. How does it feel to lose to me?" he held his arms up, pointing his thumbs down at himself. "Sucks, doesn't it? You walked around here all high and mighty because you thought no one could ever get on your level and kick your ass out on the track. Until today, of course. "

Greys placed his helmet on his bike and crossed his arms against his chest. "Double or nothing? How about a round two, Eddie?"

The crowd gasped as if they didn't expect Greyson to rechallenge him.

"Nah, man. I think I'm good. I need to bask in this glorious victory."

Grey smirked. "I think you're afraid that you got lucky and that it won't happen again, which is true. If you raced me again right now, you'd lose. So I can understand why you would want to save face."

Eddie got up into his face. Grey had about five inches on the guy, and Eddie had to tip his head up to speak. "You're such an effin' sore loser. You look pathetic asking for another chance to race me." Eddie looked at Greyson up and down.

O'Malley came over and handed Eddie the cash pot. He smiled. Digging up the wads of cash, he held it up in Grey's face. "This must kill you," he chuckled. "Three thousand is a lot to lose in one night."

WHAT? I didn't realize I had said that out loud. Not that I cared.

Grey whipped around, finally noticing that I'd been there the whole time.

"Is that your girl?" I heard Eddie say. "Hey sexy, how about..."

"SHUT UP!" I told him, effectively cutting him off from saying some sleazy pick-up line. I already got hit on by one douchebag tonight. I was over it! My eyes went back to Greyson. "I'm going to KILL YOU!" I growled. "THREE THOUSAND DOLLARS? You had three thousand on the line for a stupid race!" I was beyond furious.

Grey didn't respond but instead turned his attention back to Eddie.

OH, I WAS GOING TO... I came up behind him, ready to swing at any body part within my reach. But he caught my hand and pulled me into him, pinning me to his side. I opened my mouth to say something, but he covered it with his other hand.

"Double or nothing. My offer still stands."

Eddie shook his head.

"Did you not pack that much cash on you?" Greyson asked.

Eddie folded his lips into a thin line. I saw his nostrils flare.

One of his guys whispered something in his ear, and Eddie waved him off.

"I'll add another 500 on top to make it worth your while," Grey smirked.

I began to protest. "WHAT ARE YOU DOING?" I yelled, but it was muffled by his hand.

I was practically thrashing around under his huge ass bicep at this point, but he somehow managed to keep me in place.

"Okay, Okay," Eddie said, bobbing his head. "You're on. But," he holds up one finger, "if you lose, I want that bike." He pointed to Grey's bike.

I stilled. He cannot be serious. Grey would never agree to a race with his father's bike on the line.

"Deal," Grey said easily.

Too damn easily if you asked me.

I bit down on Grey's hand, causing him to flinch.

O'Malley wore a grin as he traded looks with Grey, and then he held up the megaphone again. "LOOKS LIKE WE GOT A RE-MATCH!" The crowd cheered. The guys put more cash into the pot.

"Back to your bikes, gentlemen."

Greyson released me but then placed his hands on my shoulders, squeezing them.

"I can't believe you would do that."

Grey kissed my cheek unexpectedly. Then I felt his mouth brush against my ear. "Trust me," He whispered the words so softly.

I hated it when he did that."...Okay..." I whispered back.

O'Malley waved me over to him on the sidelines. "You wouldn't want to signal the start of the race, would you?"

I felt like any other day. I would have said no. But tonight, I was like, screw it, why not.

If I was doing one out-of-character thing already, I might as well make it two.

I knew Grey's eyes were me as I sauntered over to the middle of the track. I held my hands up in the air.

"TAKE SOMETHING OFF!" numerous people shouted at me.

I thought about it.

I also thought about telling O'Malley to tell someone else to do it.

But instead, I pulled off my shirt, leaving me in my Victoria's Secret sports bra. It probably wasn't what all the guys were hoping would be underneath this, but oh well. This wasn't too revealing, and it covered more than your average bra.

With my shirt in my hand, I raised it above my head.

"Okay..." O'Malley began. "Ready...Set...GO!" I flagged my shirt down to the ground as the guys zoomed past me. I ran over to the sidelines, slipping my shirt back on.

"Didn't think you had that in you," O'Malley said with a crooked smile.

I flicked my wrist. "It was a one-time thing. So why not?"

I watched the guys go around the first turn. I've never seen Greyson lean so hard into his turns. His knees looked like they could almost graze the ground. He wasn't racing like this before. The next thing I knew, the guys zoomed past us.

"HOLY SHIT!" O'Malley said, dragging a palm down his face.

"WHAT?" I asked nervously, unsure whether to interpret that as a good or bad sign.

O'Malley shows me this speedometer clock thing, almost like what the cops use to see if you're speeding on the highway.

"That's the fastest Grey has ever gone!" He tapped the screen—100 mph.

"Is that bad or good?" I didn't know anything here.

O'Malley combed through his beard. "It's impressive. It's why he has the lead."

I was flooded with relief. "Okay. That's good. He just has to keep that up for another two laps."

They zoom past on the second lap with Grey still in the lead. I looked at the speedometer again.

105 mph. GASP!

Eddie revved up his bike on the last lap, and I watched him speed ahead of Greyson on the last upcoming turn.

Gone was my relief, and in its place was pure panic. I was clenching my teeth hard enough to break them.

Grey sped up to catch Eddie on the turn, and HOLY CRAP! When Grey leaned in, Eddie tried to do the same but lost control of his bike and slid across the track into a stack of hay. Total Hollywood movie moment, but he doesn't have a stunt double, so that had to have hurt.

That accident put Grey in the lead.

He was going to win this time! I started to jump, rooting for him along with the crowd.

There was no way Eddie could even catch up at this point, but he tried. He picked himself up and got back on his bike, probably going faster than before. But so was Grey. He was a blur when he breezed by, and I checked his speed.

110 mph. JEESH! The crowd roared as Grey crossed the finish line.

My lungs expanded, and I welcomed the deep breaths of air.

Grey circled back around to meet us. He stopped a few feet away from me, shutting off his bike before slipping off his helmet.

"MY MAN! THAT...THAT was insane!" O'Malley used his hands and mimed his head exploding. "Are you sure you don't want to consider professionally racing?"

Grey shook his head, combing through his loose strands of hair. "Nah. This was all for fun and a little cash. I meant what I said. I'm done after tonight."

"That's a damn shame." O'Malley hung his head.

Off in the distance, we heard an engine rev up, and we all turned to watch Eddie speed off the track with his buddies right behind him. I guess he really was a sore loser.

O'Malley gave Grey the cash, and Grey swiped off a couple of the bills on top, handing it to him. "Thanks for everything," he told him.

"No problem. Don't be a stranger, alright. Your handsome mug is the only one that is always allowed to pop in and check up on me anytime. You're good people, Grey." He patted his shoulder before bringing him into one of those manly hugs.

"I could say the same. But I would be lying," Grey replied as a joke.

I knew Grey had a soft spot for this guy, but he wouldn't let that be public knowledge.

"Say whatever you want. I know the truth." O'Malley turned to me next. "Take good care of this one in college." He lightly punched Grey in the shoulder. "I don't think this daredevil is quite done yet."

I laughed on the outside, but I thought he better be done on the inside. "Will do."

I spotted Caroline running over to us.

She threw her arms around me, catching me off guard. "It was so nice to meet you, Mia." I hugged her back, not wanting her to be offended. "You too," I told her, and I meant it.

After all our goodbyes, Grey extended his hand to me, and I took it. "Let's get out of here."

When we hit the main road, Grey finally said, "Go ahead. I know there are all types of questions floating around that pretty little head of yours."

I was quick to deny it. "What? Psh! No!"

I bit my bottom lip. Grey knew me too well. I mean, I have been quiet for the past ten minutes.

"Mia," he said my name in an even tone.

I grumbled. "Fine. Are you done with racing?"

"Yes."

The next one left my lips before I could even think about it. "Aren't you nervous carrying around this much cash on you?"

"Yup. I honestly can't wait to get you back home so I can put our money somewhere safe."

We passed by some more abandoned warehouse buildings. Loosened my grip on his stomach a bit, and I craned my head around to stare at his side profile. "Our money?"

I couldn't think of this as our money. I didn't do anything to help him earn it.

"Yup. I made that for us. We can use it for whatever we want. Or we can save it. It's up to you."

"I think we should," the cacophony of motorcycles cut me off. I looked over my shoulder and saw three bikes gaining on us.

Why did that look like Eddie and his crew?

"Shit," Greyson mumbled under his breath.

AH hell.

"Greyson," His name came out so calmly that I was almost proud of myself for not giving away the fact that I was freaking stressed.

I peeked behind us again, and I saw Eddie rev up his bike going ever faster.

"That's why they left the track in such a hurry. They couldn't wait to get us alone to try something like this," Grey growled. I could feel the anger steaming out of him.

"What are they trying to do? What do they want?" I asked anxiously.

"I don't know, and I don't care, but we gotta lose them," his voice was laced with determination.

Grey let go of one of the handlebars for a split second just to pull one of my arms around him tighter. "Hold on to me. It's going to get a little crazy."

He revved up the engine, and I knew I was about to get a taste of those record-breaking speeds.

8

CHAPTER 8

My heart's had such a workout tonight.

Grey took multiple turns and shortcuts to lose those guys. Ten minutes into chasing us and we lost them. I didn't care what their motives were, but I knew Grey wouldn't let them get anywhere near us.

After experiencing that, I gained a better understanding of how Greyson beat Eddie in the race. Eddie had the faster bike, yes, but he didn't have the control over it like how Greyson had with his. Grey was an expert at any speed.

So when Grey realized that Eddie couldn't handle riding his bike at top speed, he used that to his advantage. He let him win the first race. Then he tried his damn near hardest to convince to agree to a rematch. But with more money on the line, of course. And his father's bike.

I mentally rolled my eyes at that last one. I still wasn't over that.

Anyways, you could say that Grey practically conned him. I would be mad at his methods of making extra cash if I didn't know that Eddie was a complete asshole who probably had that coming.

Grey took us back to his place instead of mine after we took the long way back into town, ensuring we weren't being followed again.

His mom was already asleep, so we snuck. Not that she would mind me coming over to their place at this ungodly hour, but we honestly didn't want to wake her up.

We tiptoed up to his room. Grey flicked on the lights, and I planted myself on his shaggy grey rug in front of his bed.

I watched Grey stash the money in this mini lockbox that he kept hidden inside an old shoebox.

"You want to spend the night?" he asked when he was done.

"Sure," I had responded with a shrug. We had sleepovers all the time-no big deal.

"Okay, cool." He gave me a soft smile. "I'm going to take a shower. You can take one after me if you want and pick out anything of mine that you want to wear."

I smiled back. "I know. Thanks."

He nodded, grabbing the towel hanging from the back of his door, and he left.

I laid down on the rug starfish style, staring at the ceiling.

A lot has happened in the past 24 hours. My brain had failed to process it all.

I pulled my cellphone out of my back pocket, holding it above my face. I reread the text my mom sent me.

She didn't say much, but the shock of hearing from her hadn't worn off. My eyes skimmed the lines a few more times. It was like I needed to commit it to memory, as if it could self-destruct at any moment, being erased forever like it didn't even exist.

This didn't feel real.

But never mind the whole potentially rebuilding a relationship with my mom thing. I had a little sister, and she's been missing from my life for almost 12 years. I could have spent so much time with her. We could have grown up together.

How come no one allowed me to see her? Especially since she was sick.

I wanted to meet her more than anything, but I knew that pretty much came like a package deal. My mom would be included, and I had to think about what I wanted for us first. Do I keep my distance from her for the rest of my life? Or do I somehow try to work on forgiving her for leaving me and slowly build back up a relationship?

I took a deep breath hoping to control all the emotions fluttering underneath the surface.

So much to think about.

"Hey," Grey said, scaring me out of my thoughts and causing me to drop my phone on my face.

"OW!" I whispered harshly, rolling over to my side and holding the bridge of my nose with one of my hands. I glared at my stupid phone lying on the ground a few inches away from me.

Greyson chuckled. I looked up to glare at him too.

That was a quick shower. Or maybe I spent way more time in my head than I realized.

Grey leaned against the doorway, wearing only black joggers, which hung dangerously low on his hips. There wasn't a shirt in sight, so he showed off a slightly impressive six-pack. Okay, it may be more than somewhat impressive, but I would never verbally admit that. His ego was big enough. With the towel draped over one shoulder, he began to dry the droplets of water that were still clinging to his hair.

"Can you spend a week without dropping that phone on your face?" he said teasingly.

I heard the words leave his mouth, but I couldn't answer him for whatever reason. My eyes were focused on the droplets that he missed, which were sliding down his chest, to his abs, and all way down to...

OH MY GOSH! WHAT AM I DOING? WHAT AM I THINKING?!

I quickly averted my eyes, looking anywhere else.

"Mia. Seriously, are you okay?" Grey's voice was soft, but there was some concern in there. I watched his feet walk over to me in my peripheral.

It took no time before he was crouching down in front of me. Grey scooped me up into his arms and placed me in his lap. Wrapping one around my waist, he used the other to remove my hand from my face.

I forgot about the stinging pain at the bridge of my nose because all I could think about was the smell of his body wash taking over my senses.

I swore no guy has ever smelled so good, like fresh laundry mixed with spice and everything nice.

Okay, okay. I was convinced that the tiny vibrations from the cellphone hitting my face must've done something to my brain. That was the only logical explanation I could think of right now. Who was I kidding? That didn't even make sense.

"Your nose is kind of pink." Grey lightly tapped it with his pointer finger. I flinched. "Does it hurt?"

A little. I wrinkled my nose at him, causing him to laugh under his breath.

He kissed the top of my nose and then pulled back.

Our faces were mere inches apart. I watched his blue eyes scan my face before they made contact with my brown ones.

Grey smirked then he snuggled me closer to him. Leaning his forehead against mine, I watched him shut his eyes and sigh. "What's going on in that head of yours tonight, Mia? What are you thinking about?" I felt his breath against my cheek.

You're so close. Too close.

This reminded me of last summer when...

I left that thought incomplete, shoving Grey's hands off me and scrambling out of his lap. My butt landed on the ground with a light thud.

Grey's eyes fluttered open, looking at me, but his face remained neutral, not giving away anything. Sometimes, I wish I could read his mind.

"I um... I'm going to take a quick shower. Yup. Right now!" I got up, bolted for the bathroom, and softly closed the door.

I stood in front of the mirror, staring back at my reflection. I leaned over the sink and said to myself. "What are you doing, Mia? Agh!"

God forbid there would come a day when my reflection talked back.

There was a light knock on the door a few seconds later. I cracked open it and saw Greyson standing there. He held up some clothes. "I realized you didn't bring anything in with you. I thought you might want these."

I opened the door wide enough to take them. "Thanks."

"Um, and if you want to give me your dirty clothes, I could wash them and have them ready by morning."

I nodded. "Just a sec." I closed the door again.

I stripped down to my birthday suit and folded my clothes into a neat pile. I debated whether or not I should give him my underwear and bra. I dangled them up in the air, thinking about it.

Grey's seen my laundry before. Grey has done my laundry before. Once when I was sick and lying in bed. The other times were after a party when some idiot spilled alcohol on me or when the soda can exploded on me downstairs. Not to mention during all the other spontaneous sleepovers we've had. This wasn't the first time I've gotten offered a free laundry service. It worked in my favor when I put them on to leave in the morning, and they're fresh and clean.

So this shouldn't be a big deal. I had no reason to freak out. I shoved my panties and bra between my clothes. Then I grabbed a towel from the linen closet, securing it around me.

Opening the door, I placed my clothes in Grey's hands. "Thanks," I said, avoiding contact like the weirdo I couldn't help but be.

"Sure thing." He winked before walking away.

I shut the door, clenching my fists around the top of the towel. "Pull yourself together," I mumbled. I placed the towel over the shower rod, pulled back the curtain, and got in.

Ten minutes later, I was out of the shower with what I hoped was a clearer head.

I came back to the room to find Greyson sprawled out on his bed, deep in thought. He still had no shirt on, but the sheets draped across his stomach.

In the back of my head, like way wwaayyy way in the deep corners of my brain, a part of me felt a pang of disappointment. Damn.

Grey's eyes flickered to me, hovering by the doorway.

He pulled the sheet up on the empty side of the bed like a silent invitation.

I joined him, resting my head on the opposite end of his king-sized pillow.

"I've been thinking," Grey started.

"That's never a good thing," I interrupted him.

"HA!" He poked my belly, and I slapped his hand away, giggling. "But seriously, I've been thinking."

"Okay." I waited for him to share more.

Grey rolled onto his side, and we were face to face.

"So you know how our lease for the apartment technically starts on the first of July?"

"Hmm."

"Why don't we move in early? Why wait till August? We can move in on the first of July, find a job for the summer that we could potentially do throughout the school year, and settle in before everything gets crazy hectic."

I thought about it. I'd have to break the news to Dad, who hasn't seemed too eager about me leaving him. He's had all year, heck, my entire life to prepare for this moment, but he still wanted to pout and be all glum when I brought it up.

Then there was my job. I wanted to give them a two weeks notice. But a one week's notice will have to do.

Grey was dying to quit his job. I wanted to see what he would do next for cash. That will be interesting. Leave it to Grey to be full of surprises.

"You know, that's not a terrible idea," I told him.

His face broke out into a grin. "Yeah?"

"Yeah. I'm dying to move in. It only makes sense to move in next month. I don't know why we didn't think of it sooner."

"Okay then, it's settled. We'll be at our new place by next Friday." Grey held up his hand for a high five.

I grinned back, slapping his hand. "This is going to be so cool. I have so many ideas on how we should decorate the place!"

"Oh no. Here we go again." Grey dramatically flopped forward onto his stomach, burying his face into the pillow.

I lightly kicked his thigh with the ball of my foot. "HEY! My ideas are good!"

He lifted his head. "If you say so."

"You'll see!" I fired back.

"Whatever you say," Grey chuckled.

I rolled my eyes, resting my head back against the pillow.

Grey already had his eyes closed as he got more comfortable.

"So, are you gonna turn off the lights or what?" he whispered.

"Nope."

"It's going to be so annoying to sleep with them on."

"Oh well. I'm too lazy to get up and do it." I yawned.

Grey sat half up. "Rock, paper, and scissors?" he suggested. "Loser has to turn off the lights."

"Fine." I sat up too. "Best 2 out of 3?"

"Yup."

We played, and I unfortunately lost.

"HA!" Grey said, repositioning himself. "You know I always get what I want. I never lose."

"Yeah, yeah, yeah," I got up and flipped the switch, encasing us in darkness with nothing but hints of the moonlight coming through the blinds.

Luckily, I knew his room well enough to get back into bed without tripping over anything. Not that there's a mess on his floor to trip over anyhow. This guy was an absolute neat freak.

I felt Greyson throw some of the sheets my way, and I slid under them.

It was quiet for a little while, and I knew I would drift off to sleep in no time.

"Good night, Mia," Grey murmured with a yawn.

"Night, Grey," I mumbled with what little energy I had left.

9

CHAPTER 9

I was excited about this new chapter.

But like most of my new beginnings, it was bitter-sweet for me.

I rested my head against the car seat, taking a quick breather before turning off the engine. My mom's mustang seemed loud enough to wake the dead with how eerily quiet it was this morning. Then again, here I was in the middle of one of the town's biggest cemeteries at 7 a.m sunrise.

I didn't see a single soul. Okay, "soul" may not be the best word to use right now, considering cemeteries still creeped me out. Saying "soul" could mean anything like a literal ghost hanging around the place, and maybe there were a few, or maybe there were none. Either way, fingers crossed, I didn't see any because I was not packing any rock salt shotguns in the trunk or weapons made from wrought iron.

Supernatural was taking over my life.

When I was driving in, I didn't see anyone else. Not surprising, though.

I got out of the car, grabbing the bouquet of white and blue hydrangeas from the passenger seat.

I made my way over to my destination. Kneeling on the grass, I placed the flowers into the holder next to the tombstone.

I ran my fingers across the top of the smooth granite, and I smiled. Sometimes when I came here, the last thing I wanted to do was smile, but I knew he wouldn't want to see me sad like that all the time.

"Hey, Dad," my voice sounded hoarse, and my throat felt like sandpaper. I tried again. I took a seat, stretching one leg out and pulling up my other leg so I could rest a hand on my knee. "Hi, dad. I just wanted to stop by before I left. I'm heading off to the apartment with Mia today, we're officially moving in, and she's literally over the moon about all of this. Last night, she complained about how much her cheeks were hurting from smiling so much."

I chuckled at the thoughts before continuing. "We've been moving our things in, little by little, but today, our furniture is coming in, and after we get those settled and carry the very last box in, it'll be official."

I sighed. "I wish you could see the place." And here was where the bittersweetness kicked in. "There are exposed brick walls, and the kitchen is black and white with this checkered floor. Then there's this balcony right off the living room with the best view of the town, but there are also these huge windows that bring in so much natural light, it's insane. It has an excellent layout, too, with a lot of space for Mia and me to still be able to do our things separately. I think you would have liked this place. But I guess I'll have to add that to the long list of things I'll never truly know because you're not here to experience them with me." I closed my eyes, pinching the bridge of my nose right by my tear ducts.

I sat frozen like that until I felt my phone vibrate in my pocket. That was my sign to go.

I stood up, brushing off my jeans. "Just because I'm a few hours away now doesn't mean I won't visit as often anymore. I'll come whenever I can, and when I do, hopefully, I'll have more good things to tell you about."

My memories took me back to elementary school when I came home and found dad in the kitchen, meal prepping for dinner.

"Dad, you want to hear about my day?" I would ask him eagerly. I already knew what we would say, I asked him this every day, and he always gave me the same response.

"Sure, Grey. Tell me something good." He would say with a grin.

And that was our thing.

One of the many things I still couldn't help but miss.

"See you later, Dad." I walked back to the car and drove off.

Back at home, I placed my car keys on the kitchen counter and called out for my mom. "MOM?"

I heard sniffling before I heard a response. "Yeah, I'm up here."

I bounded up the stairs, two steps at a time. I found her leaning against my door frame as she patted her eyes with a single tissue.

"Mom," I said softly, bringing her into my arms.

"Your room looks so empty," she sniffled.

Sure enough, I looked over her head into my room. I still have my furniture here, so I had a place to sleep when I visited. And I left back a few clothes and the TV since Mia, and I bought a new one last week. Other than that, most of the things that made my room look like my room were now in my apartment.

My new home.

If anything, the apartment was just my other home. Or my temporary home for the next few years. And as much as I loved that place already, my childhood home, this home that I've shared with my parents, the one filled with so many memories of my dad and so much unconditional from my mom, will always be my home.

"It doesn't look that empty." I tried to lighten her mood.

"Yes! It does. Your room looks how the house will feel when you're not here."

I watched her bring the tissue to her eyes again.

"Jeez, Mom. You're making me feel like a crap son for leaving you now," I muttered.

She laughed, but it didn't last long. "Sorry. I'm glad you're going out there. I'm proud of you and your academic scholarship and all the goals you have in place for yourself that I know you're going to smash because that's the kind of song I have. A real go-getter, no quitter, type of man."

I smiled. "Well, thank you. I am kind of awesome like that."

Mom pinched my bicep.

"OW!"

"And who do you think you got that from?"

"Dad, of course," I said with a straight face.

Mom slapped my next bicep and wagged her finger at me. "Oh yeah, sure. Your dad was this awesome and super cool indie musician who traveled worldwide. But your mom, she is the coolest of all." She smoothed down her hair. "I would list all the reasons, but it'll sound like bragging, so I won't." she crossed her arms.

I chuckled. "I could tell you one thing for sure. I get my ego from my mom."

Her eyes narrowed, and she folded in her bottom lip. "Hmm..." she shrugged. "I'll take it." Mom smiled before getting serious again. "So, do you have everything? If you don't and you forget something, it's not that long of a drive for you to come back and get it. Or you can call me anytime, and I'll drop it off for you."

I leaned in and kissed her forehead. Best. Mom. Ever.

"What was that for?"

"Because I love you, and I'm going to miss you."

I've never spent this much time away from her. We've been glued at the hip since dad died.

"AWWWEE!!" Mom leaned in to hug me again. "Don't make me cry again. I told myself when I ran out of tissues. I wouldn't cry about this anymore." She held up the crinkled tissue in her hand. "This...this is my last one." She waved the used tissue in the air.

"Good. Now you can dry up all those tears and talk to me without the waterworks."

"HA!" Mom replied. "So, what do you want to talk about?"

I didn't know if this was a good time to bring it up, but I've been holding it for weeks.

"Maybe we should sit down." I led her into my room, and she took a seat on my bed next to me. I didn't know how to start this conversation. "So, um," I nervously rubbed the back of my neck with one hand. "Is there anything you'd like to tell me before I go?" I tried asking.

Mom shook her head. "Nope, can't think of anything." That sounded far from believable.

Okay, let me try this again. "I see you've been having a lot of girls' night outs, which is okay. You deserve it, but I've also passed by your room a few times, and I've heard you talking to someone up until the wee hours of the morning." I slant my head, eyeing her suspiciously.

Mom let out a long exhale but said nothing.

"Mom, are you seeing someone?" I finally asked.

She shook her head rapidly. "No, no. They're just a friend. It's nothing like that."

"You know I wouldn't mind, right? I don't want you to be lonely forever because you lost your husband, my dad. I especially don't want you to be lonely because I'm not here. I want you to be happy. So if there is someone, you can tell me." I wanted her to be honest with me without being afraid to.

There was this long pause where I thought she wouldn't tell me anything, but she started to talk. "I did meet someone a few months ago." At first, the words came out like a whisper before she spoke a little louder. "A doctor that transferred over here from Seattle. He's single. A little younger than me but just by a few years." She rushed on to say, probably hoping that adding that info wouldn't make me want to comment.

But I wouldn't be me if I didn't say something about that. "So my mom is cougar now?" I teased, bumping her shoulder.

"No! No, I'm not!" She rolled her eyes. "He's only five years younger than me. It's not this huge age gap."

"If you say so." I was just pushing her buttons, but she was right. Five years wasn't that bad.

"Anyways, like I was saying, he has two kids. A daughter who just turned 15. And he has a younger son that's about 10. His wife, their mom, passed away two years ago, and he's kept to himself ever since."

It sounds like they have a few things in common already. The biggest one being that they have both lost their spouses.

I never thought about what kind of man I'd like to see Mom with. It was hard trying to envision her with someone that wasn't dad, but I expected this day would come eventually.

Mom let out a long breath, closing her eyes briefly before opening them up again. "I always thought that everyone had one person that the universe put aside from them. They were destined to be with each other and that they would live happily ever after. To me, my one person was your dad. And even though things ended in a way I could have never imagined. I also couldn't have imagined meeting someone after him that makes my heart feel things that it hasn't in a long time."

She turned to face me, and I looked into her same blue eyes as mine. "I really like this guy. And it's kind of scary how much I like him. But what are the odds of me having." She tilted her head from left to right, thinking of the right words. "I don't know two people that feel like my person ?"

I shrugged. "Supposedly, I'm crappy at relationships, so I probably don't know the best thing to say here. But, all I care about is if he makes you happy. If he does, then okay. Who's to say he can't be your person too and vice versa. If anything, I feel like the universe loves to give people like the two of you a second chance at love."

Mom shook her head slowly, and I was confused. Did she disagree with me?

She wrapped an around arm my shoulder. "You know you're kind of wise sometimes when you want to be."

I let out a puff of air. "Oh yeah, and who did I get that from?"

"Me. You get that from me too!" she laughed. "Just kidding, your dad was always the wise one. Oddly enough. He used to give the best pep talks."

I replied without thinking. "Yup."

"Now then, since we're on the topic of this. When are you going to talk to your special person?" Mom squeezed my shoulder, smiling up at me.

I stood up with the quickness. The last thing I wanted was for this conversation to switch and be all about me. "I don't know what you're talking and I think I forgot to pack something." I moved over to the open box on the other side of my room.

"Greyson, I know last summer you and Mia..."

"NOPE! NOPE! NOPE! We are not having this conversation right now." I pretended to search through the box like I was missing something.

"She still doesn't talk about it? She doesn't even drop hints or anything?"

Of course, Mom wasn't going to let this go because I told her to.

I might as well give her answers. "No, she probably doesn't want it to be awkward, and neither do I. It's for the best." No matter how much I've said those four words to myself, I still wasn't sure if they were convincing.

Mom chucked a pillow at my head.

"MOM!" I whined as it hit me from behind.

"Don't be stupid, Grey! You'll be living under the same roof. Seeing a lot of each other. At some point, something is bound to happen!"

AGH.

"Nothing is going to happen."

I couldn't let anything jeopardize my relationship with Mia. Not again.

"Okay fine." Mom threw her arms into the air, finally giving up. "If you say so. But I'll give you guys until thanksgiving to stop cowering away from each other's feelings."

I stared at her unblinking.

She threw another pillow at me, but I was prepared, and I caught it. I gave her a sly grin but with an eye roll. "Don't roll your eyes at me, mister," she said sternly as she stood to leave.

"Jeesh. I feel bad for that new guy. He doesn't know who he's getting mixed up with," I said under my breath with the intention of her hearing it all the same.

When Mom reached the door, she whipped around, sticking her tongue out at me.

I belted out with laughter. And that was Mom, ladies, and gentlemen.

10

CHAPTER 10

"I think I have everything," I said to myself, but I gave my room another once over.

I've been waiting all year for this moment, and still, it felt surreal. I couldn't wait to go, but I also didn't want to leave. A part of me already felt homesick just thinking about it.

The only other place that I've spent this much time at was Grey's house and maybe my grandparents who lived in Canada that we visited twice a year.

"Hey, sweetheart, can I talk to you for a second before you go?" Dad shouted up from downstairs.

"Sure thing!" I walked to my door, one last glance, then closed it behind me.

I skipped down the stairs and walked to the kitchen.

"Have a seat." He nodded towards the breakfast nook. "I made you a caramel cappuccino with blueberry waffles." I was glad dad finally learned to use that expresso maker that his girlfriend bought him for Christmas last year. It's been a godsend and one of our most used kitchen appliances. That's what happened with two caffeine addicts living under the same roof.

"YAY! Thank you!" I told him, kissing his cheek while he finished what looked like the last batch of waffles.

I rushed over to take my favorite seat by the window. I only admired the breakfast spread for about three seconds before digging into my waffles. I took a bite of blueberries with a tiny bit of whip cream and maple syrup. "MHHMM." I crooned. My taste buds were so happy.

Dad slid into the nook, sitting across from me. He only had a cup of coffee in front of him. "I made some for Grey too. I know he probably ate already, but I also know he never says no to a second morning meal," he grinned. "So," Dad began to twirl the coffee mug in his hands, a nervous habit of his. "Remember last week when we said no more secrets?"

After the conversation with Mom, I couldn't wait for Dad to get home so we could talk. I had been dying to do it over the phone, but he insisted that we do it in person.

In proper psychologist form, we sat down in the living room on opposite sides, him on the couch and me on the other.

I had watched him just as closely as he was watching me, probably thinking of how best to proceed.

Eventually, he took a deep breath and said, "First, I'd like to know how you feel about your mom, then we'll talk about what you're thinking about doing?"

I've never lied to Dad.

I knew that sounded unbelievable, but it was true. I've always owned up to my mistakes and have taken full responsibility. Plus, Dad was the easiest person to talk to. I could tell him just about anything, and I knew he wouldn't judge me.

I already had days to gather all my thoughts and feelings about my mom. So when I opened my mouth, everything came out all at once. I told Dad how I felt like she had abandoned us because we didn't make her happy enough. I told him that after hearing about having a younger sister, I wondered if Mom felt like I wasn't the daughter she wanted because she didn't stick around to watch me grow up like she did for her. I said the stuff that I hadn't even completely worked out in my head yet, but I was hoping saying it aloud would clear up any fog surrounding it.

In 30 minutes, I was all talked out.

Dad sat silently for a second, working through his thoughts. I took that as my opportunity to ask him something that had been on my mind. "Dad, how would you feel if I wanted to have a relationship with Mom? I'm not sure if I do right now or ever will. There seems to be so much that I don't know if I can forgive, but she's told me that you had forgiven her, and I want to know if that's true." I nibbled at my bottom lip anxiously.

Dad sleeked back his greyish-copper locks with one of his hands and sighed. I could see a bit of his pent-up emotions being expressed through the way his eyebrows were tightly knitting together and how he tried to focus his eyes on anything but me as he successfully regained his composure. "I don't want this to be about me. But yes, I have forgiven her."

I knew he wanted to move on from that, bringing it back full circle, but I wasn't done.

So I asked another question, much to his dismay. "How could you? She broke your heart. I know you've moved on, and you're happier now. But she left you to raise a daughter on your own. While I know I'm not exactly a troublemaker or anything, and if I'm honest, I can't imagine it being super difficult to raise me, I can imagine there were moments when you must have wished you weren't doing it alone."

"Mia," Dad said sternly but also calmly. His work face was on. Or should I say his "mask" because, in his profession, he needed one.

I knew some people might think.

I didn't need a doctor at that moment.

I needed my dad.

But I knew my dad. This was his way of trying to coolly navigate the situation without putting his feelings in the middle of it. He didn't want how he felt about mom to be the deciding factor for whether or not I chose to have a relationship with her. He didn't want me to live with any regrets if I was only thinking about what he may want instead of what I wanted for myself. And a part of me couldn't help but be curious about his feelings. Also, I felt like if Dad could forgive mom, then maybe I could, too, somehow.

"Dad," I interrupted him. "This affects you too. No matter how unbiased you want to be." I said honestly. Mask or no mask. I saw right through him.

"I have something to tell you. Again." Dad told me that Mom had stopped by when I was at Grey's house a few years ago. He hadn't fully recovered from her leaving, so the minute he saw her face, he told her she shouldn't be here. Dad said he hadn't expected her to listen, but she did and promised she wouldn't show up again. Dad blamed himself for a while and wished he would have handled the situation differently, but he was so hurt that he let his emotions get in the way. He thought that I would have been upset if I knew he was part of why Mom stayed away.

But I couldn't have been mad at him. I was healing slowly, and seeing her face would have set me off. We deserved better, and we didn't get treated that way.

Dad was concerned that I would hold a grudge, but I didn't have it in me. I understood him, and I thought he made the best decision for us. Even if he made it alone, he's more than made up for it.

And he has been the best father a girl could ask for.

"I can't get in the way of this. I swore to myself that I wouldn't. I want the best for you, and if that means forgiving your mother and letting bygones be bygones, you can consider it instantly done." Dad moved from his couch to take a seat next to me. Wrapping one of his arms around my shoulder, he pulled me into him, and I rested my head on his shoulder. "All that being said, sweetheart, I'll support any decision you make." He kissed the top of my head. "Just promise me that you'll think about how you might feel ten years from now before you decide on anything. If you don't like that, though, change the action in the present while you still have the chance."

I nodded and said. "Okay. I'll think about it. But you have to promise me something too." I sat up and held my pinkie finger out to him. "No more secrets?" I said it more like a question instead of a statement.

He chuckled, looking down at my little finger as I wiggled it in front of his face. His huge pinkie dwarfed mine as he wrapped his around it, sealing the deal. "Promise."

Now back to the present.

"Dad, I'm not sure how I feel about surprises and secrets after the last month I've had." I took a sip of my cappuccino.

"I know, and I'm sorry, but this one was kind of sprung on me. And I know I had to tell you."

"Okay, okay. Shoot." How bad could this be anyways?

"Your mom lives in the same town as you and Grey. She moved there six months ago. So she lives 5 minutes away from the university. Which means she lives about 25 minutes away from you." He gave me a tight-lipped smile and sipped his coffee while I sat there in utter shock.

I stuttered, only getting a few words out but not fully forming coherent sentences. "What?...She?...But?... How?... I can't..." I slapped my forehead with my palm. "Wow, this summer is off to a great start, and here I thought I had at least a good enough distance from mom to gather my thoughts. But in reality, she'll only be 25 minutes away from me." I let out one of those humorless laughs. "This is probably the going to be the closest she's been to me in years. Awesome." I angrily cut my waffles this time and chopped down on them.

"Yup." Dad paused, thinking about it. "Nope, I got nothing." He shrugged, giving up. "All I can say is she told me not to tell you. But I warned her you wouldn't like that and informed her that I would tell you as soon as I could, preferably before you moved there, and possibly bumped into her at the grocery store or something. I imagine that would have been awkward." He took another sip.

"You think?" I fired back. "Jeez," I muttered under my breath.

"Yeah." Dad's lip formed a thin line.

We both looked to the front door when we heard a motorcycle outside, followed by what we know is a vintage mustang with a seriously powerful engine.

"Sounds like the McNamaras are here," Dad joked.

All this Mom talk reminded me that I still haven't told Greyson about any of it. This was probably my biggest kept secret at the moment.

Okay, this was one of my biggest kept secrets, but I wouldn't even dare bring up the other one.

I wasn't planning to put out friendship in jeopardy over that because some secrets felt like maybe they should get carried to the grave.

11

CHAPTER 11

"**W**as that the last box?" I asked Grey as he placed it in the living room amongst the others.

"Yup. The very last one, and thank god. It's hot, and I'm beat." He looked around the apartment. "I can't believe we managed to carry all of this in your truck."

I smiled, feeling good about my new ride. My dad passed down his Chevy Silverado to me. It was a few years old with a decent amount of mileage, and it's in my favorite color, gray. Yes, it was a coincidence that my favorite color just so happens to be my nickname for my best friend.

Anyways, Dad had brought this truck brand new, and he promised me that if I wanted to have it for college, I could take it if I got my license by then and proved that I was a safe driver. I've had my license for about three months now, and I've been deemed the "safest of safe drivers." And yes, I was super proud of my title. I mentally patted myself on the back.

"Admit it. My truck is awesome."

Leaning against the wall with his hands crossed, Grey rolled his eyes. "I would never disrespect my bike like that."

"You mean the same bike that you can't drive when it rains?" I pointed out. "Or snows, or when it gets cold or..." I could have gone on and on, but then Grey pushed himself off the wall and strode towards me.

I took a few steps back, and my eyes darted all across the room. I didn't like that look in his eyes. Grey was radiating pure mischief.

This was what I got for teasing him about his baby, which happened to be an impractical mode of transportation, considering it was his only mode of transportation the majority of the time. I mean, it's not like all the stuff I listed wasn't true. They were, but Grey liked to pretend otherwise.

I saw one tip of his mouth twitch as he held back a smirk. Crap. I wanted to make a run for it.

But I really didn't have very far to run from here. Grey would catch me no matter which direction I took off in. One, because he was naturally faster than I am, and two, I was literally in a corner.

So let me say this again... Crap!

"Bet you're thinking about apologizing right now," Grey said, stopping a few feet away from me.

I bit my bottom lip in contemplation. Then I shook my head no.

He raised an eyebrow. "Hmm. So what are you thinking then?"

My eyes cut to the hallway that would take to me to my bedroom.

"You want to make a run for it?" Grey's eyes narrowed. "Okay, I'll give you a head start, but if you lose, I'll definitely be getting that apology out of you." He gave me a smug grin.

I frowned.

"1... 2..." I launched into an all-out sprint. "3..." My hand was so close to the doorknob... "4..."

Was Grey going to let me make it? I thought, but then, I felt my feet lift off the ground as his hands wrapped around my midsection. "10." he whispered in my ear, and I felt his hands skim across my stomach before he began his tickle assault. I squealed loudly.

I hated being ticklish. I hated being ticklish. I hated being ticklish!

"Grey... Grey... Please!" All my words came out breathy. I fought in vain to break free from him. "...I'm sorry... Your bike is awesome! I take it all back!" I practically shouted.

He paused, "What was that?" I could hear how satisfied he was with himself.

So I refused to respond.

"Mia..."

You think I would learn from my mistakes.

He poked my side, and I erupted into giggles again. Damn it.

"I hate you," I said instead, swatting his hands away.

Grey loosened his grip, and I thought he decided to release me, but rather, he picked me up and threw me over his shoulder.

"GREYSON! PUT ME DOWN!" I pinched his back.

"Ow!" he whined.

I watched him walk us back to the living room. We walked past the front door, and then there was a knock.

We both paused.

"Are you expecting someone?" Grey asked me.

I swiped my hair out of my face craning my neck up to peak at the front door as if I could use my imaginary x-ray vision to see who was on the other side. "Nope. You?"

"Nope." He began to walk towards the door. "I wonder who it is then?" "You're seriously going to take me to answer the door like this?" I mumbled. I gave up. I lifted my head placed my chin in the palm of one of my hands. "You're impossible."

I heard him unlock the door.

"Hi! I'm... OH goodness! I'm sorry, am I interrupting something?" A young woman said.

"NO!" I answered before Greyson could. "Put me down!" I growled at him.

He relented, lowering me to my feet.

I turned to greet her. "Hi!" I said, smoothing down strands of my blonde hair that had gotten loose from my messy bun.

"Hello there!" She grinned brightly.

She must be one of our neighbors. I hope she wasn't here to complain about us making a ruckus or something. Then again, she looked too friendly for that. Her smile gave it away.

I wouldn't be surprised if she were a college student too. Mostly college kids were in these apartments. She had a very fair complexion, like just by looking at her. You knew that she was the type to get red if she stayed out in the sun too long instead of tan. She had big grey eyes hidden behind these oversized black frames, and to top it all off, she had an array of auburn curls falling down her back. She wasn't super tall, but she was a few inches taller than me. Outfitted in an oversized Harry Potter t-shirt and leggings with converses, I could already tell that I would like her. I'd like almost anyone who's a Harry Potter fan.

"HI! I'm Freya! I live adjacent to you guys." She pointed to her apartment. "I heard we had new neighbors, and I wanted to

come by and introduce myself." She leaned into the doorway and whispered. "The last person that lived here was a real B. I couldn't wait for her to leave. Phew!" She wiped imaginary sweat from her forehead and pretended to flick it away.

She seemed nice. "Nice to meet you, Freya. I'm Mia, and this is Greyson."

We shook hands. "Nice to meet you both too. I'm a sophomore at the university. I'm majoring in Anthropology. Are the two of you students at the university too?" She asked, looking between the both of us.

"Yup. We're starting our freshmen year this fall," Grey told her.

"And you guys live together?" Freya clasped her hands in front of her heart. "AWEE! You two are so cute! We don't have a lot of couples in this building."

My eyes widened as Grey chuckled under his breath. "Oh no, we're not a couple. Just friends. We've known each other from child-hood," I clarified.

Her expression fell. "Oh. Sorry. When you opened up the door, it looked like..."

I cut her off. "Nope...nope. Just friends," I started again.

Freya nodded slowly, her gaze shifting from mine to Grey's. The skepticism was unmistakable. "Okay, well, stop by if you need any-thing and or if you just want to hang out. I'm hoping we can become friends." She looked really hopeful.

"Sure. Of course," I told her, and I meant it. "Thank you for stop-ping by. We'll talk soon."

Freya started walking backward as I waved goodbye.

As soon as I closed the door, I whipped around to slap Greyson on his arm.

"Hey! What was that for?" he asked, confused, rubbing his bicep.

I raised my chin in the air, and I walked around him without answering.

That was for making our neighbors think that we're an item. Even though I told her we aren't, she still looked like she didn't believe us. I wouldn't blame her, but it's the truth.

Me and Grey, we could never have a relationship like that.

Even if... Agh...Nope... never mind!

A few hours later, we managed to unpack most of the stuff from the boxes. It was a good thing we spent the past week or so slowly dropping stuff off before officially moving in. It saved us the hassle of moving everything all at once and being stressed about how long it would take to unpack everything.

We still had a few deliveries coming in sometime this week.

Like Grey's bedroom set and our dining table. We had everything else like my bedroom set and the living room furniture, etc.

Greyson planted himself on the couch, putting his feet up and resting his head on one of the cushions while I finished placing a few of our new dishes, mugs, and utensils in the dishwasher.

And to think we almost turned down that couch as a gift from my grandparents. We didn't want our families to help us out any more than they were doing now, and we saved enough money for these things, but we couldn't say no to Grandma's gift.

She threatened us and told us we better take the couch "or else." Neither of us wanted to know what that implied, so we thanked her repeatedly and told her how we were grateful for it.

"This mortal form grows weak. I require sustenance." Grey patted his stomach.

I snorted. "Now, I know you're starving when you quote Thor."

"I love how you get me." He opened his eyes to give me a wink.

"Whatever." I walked over to the refrigerator and opened it. "So, our fridge has nothing but water, juice, and milk that we both collectively stole from our parents' fridges. We need to go.

Do you want us to buy food to cook for tonight while we're at it, or do you just want to grab a bite to eat then go shopping?"

Grey thought about it. "The second option gets food in my belly faster than the first one," he said, sitting up.

"Okay, let's try that café we drove past last week. They looked really good."

He nodded. "I hope you're right."

It was a less than ten-minute walk to the café. They looked a little busy, but they had room left for a few people.

When we stepped in, one of the employees grabbed us a few menus and gave us a table inside by the windows. We were close to this stage that they had set up for open mic performances.

"This place is so nice!" I whispered loudly to Greyson. It was dimly lit, but it had a lot of natural light too. It looked city chic, and it came off as a very Instagramable location which would explain why all the people around me had their phones out snapping pics.

"Yeah, it's cool," Grey replied with a shrug as he continued to browse the menu.

"Agh, you men rarely have an appreciation for these things."

I saw him smirk, but he didn't reply.

After skimming the menu, we ordered everything that sounded appetizing. The table between us was filled with multiple dishes when the waiter got back. The both of us tried a little bit from each plate. Nothing was left uneaten.

Our waiter placed the check on the table, telling us we could pay at the register upfront. He also mentioned that if we wanted dessert, we could check out the bakery while we're over there, or he could give us the menu. We thanked him and told him we would check it out for ourselves.

Greyson and I spent about a minute arguing who would pay for the bill until he said he'll just let me pay since I was being stubborn.

When we got up from the table, Greyson walked around me and snatched the bill right out of my hands. "My treat," he said with a smug grin, making sure to hold it up and out of my reach.

I didn't bother to argue that time.

He paid at the register, and I made my way over to the bakery. I stared at the mouthwatering treats wondering how I could decide on just one but also knowing that if I ate two, I'd probably regret the calories at some point. I wasn't skinny by any means. I didn't have a thigh gap, and I had a little roll when I hunched over, which was fine because I loved the curves I had. But I also liked my jeans to continue fitting, which wouldn't happen if I ate my weight in baked goods.

"I'll be with you in a second," a familiar voice called out. I spotted her in my peripheral as she came out of the swinging doors with her back turned to me, carrying a tray of cookies.

"Freya?" I asked, doing a double-take.

She looked over at me. "Mia? HI!" Her face lit up with a smile, and her high cheekbones became more prominent. "What's up? Looking for a sweet tooth fix?"

I nodded. "You work here?"

"Yup. My big brother owns the place."

"Hey, Freya!" Grey said, walking up behind me.

"Hey," Freya acknowledged him with a swift nod. "What can I get for you two?" she asked, slipping the tray onto the counters.

In an effort to help us narrow down our options, Freya described each of the pastries. We decided on two cherry cheese Danishes, two cookies, and one slice of chocolate chip pie.

"Is it always crowded like this?" I asked Freya as we paid, and Grey grabbed the bag of goodies. He'll probably devour more or more of those treats before we make it home. I already saw him peeking in the bag.

"Yes and no. The summer is pretty hectic all day, but the fall season is calm in the mornings than hectic from lunch to dinner. I can't complain though, It's good for business." She shrugged.

I smiled. "So, do you guys need extra help for the summer?" I wouldn't mind working at a place like this.

"Now that you mentioned it, we could use it. My brother has been thinking about hiring an extra person or two, but he hasn't formally advertised it yet. Do you know someone who might be interested in a job here?" She leaned onto the counter, giving me a smirk. "They'll just be a waitress and or help in the bakery, etc. Nothing too challenging, honestly."

I was already sold. She just had to hire me. "Hmmm. I might know of a person who had some experience from working at a hotel."

"You're hired!" she said without hearing any more. "I mean, I have to talk to my brother about it, but he trusts my judgment. And I like you. I think you'll be great!"

I clapped my hands together. "Yay!! Thank you!" I glanced over my shoulder at Grey, who had half a Danish hanging from his lips. He winked, giving me the thumbs up.

"No problem. You can start the day after tomorrow, okay?"

I nodded excitedly. "Sure thing! Thanks again. We'll talk soon." I smiled and waved as we headed out.

Back at home, I prepared myself for bed. I had left my phone on the charger by accident, so I missed a few calls and texts.

My mom had called me then she sent four texts.

Mom: I guess you're busy unpacking. I was just calling to say hi.

Mom: I hope we can meet up soon now that you're living close by.

Mom: But no pressure or anything.

Mom: I'm sorry! I'm going overboard with the texts. Anyways, whatever you decide, just know that I'll always love you, and I always have. Good night, Mia.

Then there was a missed call from James? That was so freakin' odd. We haven't talked since the break-up.

James: Sorry. I'm an idiot. Miss u muchhh. I just caannnt believe we not together. Call me.

What? Did he just drunk text me?

I laughed under my breath. We're not even old enough to drink. Okay, I shouldn't judge him because I've been there. Once. But that was beside the point.

And I wouldn't dream of calling him. I placed my phone back on the nightstand and tried to fall asleep, which came easy considering, I was pretty tired.

Mia! MIA! MIA!! WAKE UP!

I jumped awake, bumping my forehead into Grey's.

OW! I saw his face in the moonlight.

"What the hell are you doing in my bed?"

Grey ignored the question, turning on the lamp closest to him. "What were you dreaming about?"

"Nothing." I tried to forget it as soon as it popped up into my mind.

"You were whimpering and kept saying 'Mom'" I saw concern written all over his face.

I had been dreaming about the day she left and how I begged her to stay. But I didn't want to talk about it.

"You haven't talked about your mom in a while. Why was she suddenly on your brain?" Grey brushed a few stray strands from my face.

I shook my head. "I don't know," I lied.

"You miss her?"

"I don't know." And that was the truth.

Now back to my question. I looked at Grey comfortably lying on the other side of my bed. "Dude! What happened to you sleeping on the couch?"

Grey's bed wasn't coming for another few days, so he said he would crash on the couch until then. I should have known better.

He gave me an innocent smile. "It wasn't all that comfy. Not like your bed, at least." He threw one arm behind his head and shut his eyes.

"Whatever," I huffed. "I'm going back to sleep." I flopped back on the pillow, shutting my eyes.

I thought about how I didn't sleep well for days after my mom left because I wanted to be awake to see her come through the door. Sometimes, I cried myself to sleep on the couch and woke up to Dad carrying me up the stairs to my bed.

Every time I had a bad dream, I remember that mom would be there to run her fingers through my hair and help me feel safe enough to fall back asleep. But when she became the center of all the bad dreams, I didn't know what to do anymore.

I didn't care how old I was. I used to squeeze one of my teddy bears, praying for sleep just to come. Sleep without any dreams of my mother, who never came back. But I didn't have my teddy bear right now.

I looked over at Greyson. "Grey?" I sat up, putting my weight on one elbow as I turned towards him.

"Hmm?" he replied without opening his eyes.

"Umm... Can you just... this might sound weird, but it's platonic, I swear! I mean..." I shook my head in frustration. "Never mind. It's silly." I laid my head back on the pillow, silently cursing myself.

I watched him opened up his eyes in my peripheral as he studied me. "You need a hug?" he asked, opening one of his arms wide for me.

I nodded silently.

"Come here," he said softly.

I cuddled up next to him. Resting my head on his chest, he wrapped one arm around me. This didn't mean anything. I just needed some comfort, and Grey was here. Like he always has been for me. My best friend.

I felt him extend his other arm to switch off the lamp then he kissed the top of my head. "No more bad dreams. Okay?" he whispered.

"Hmm," I said before falling into a deep, restful sleep.

12

CHAPTER 12

After waking up in my arms yesterday, Mia's been acting weird. She got up and went about her day as if nothing had happened. Which was okay with me if she didn't want to talk about it, but I needed to know if she's weird because of us cuddling or if it's because she's been thinking about her mom, and she was silently hoping I wouldn't ask about it again.

"Oh gosh, Grey! I can't find a scrunchie!" Mia said, running out of the bathroom, holding her hair up in a ponytail with one hand. "I'm going to be late on my first day, and I'm going to get fi-AHHH!!" she squealed as she stumbled over my guitar case that I had accidentally left lying on the ground in front of the couch. I took it out of my room, so the guys won't trip over it when my furniture gets delivered later today.

"MIA! Jeez! Are you okay?" I ran over to her aid.

Mia sat up, looking at me through the strands of hair that had fallen in front of her face. She huffed out a breath, blowing a few strands away as she glared at me.

Her finger angrily pointed at my guitar case and said, "Why did you even bring that thing? You barely play it anymore!"

I looked over at it as if I had to remind myself what she was talking about and shrugged. "I figured this summer is as good a time as any to pick it back up again. Maybe, I'll even pay at open mic tonight." I smiled, attempting to lighten her anger a bit.

"No, you won't. You've never played anything in public." She had a point there.

"But I think I could if I want to."

Mia looked unconvinced.

"Do you dare me to?" I asked. If she said yes, then I knew I wouldn't back down. I'd come through on my word.

"I double-dog dare you to get in front of all those people and embarrass yourself since you haven't picked up a guitar in... what? Over two years." She held up two fingers for extra emphasis.

That was pretty close to the last time I played anything on my guitar. I got busy with other hobbies, nothing new there.

I guffawed at her lack of faith in me. "You think I'll look stupid up there and get stage fright or something?"

She smiled sweetly. Too sweetly. "Yes. That's exactly what I think might happen. You don't even like all that attention on you. I don't know how you made it as a street racer with everyone always watching you on the track."

"Never mind that." I flitted my hand in the air. "Musical talent like this just doesn't disappear, Mia," I told her.

Mia snorted.

I ignored it and continued, "That being said, you're on! You know I never back down from a dare." I grinned.

She rolled her eyes as if annoyed by me. "Trust me, you don't have to remind me," she scoffed.

Moving back to the problem at hand. "You okay?" I asked, helping her up.

Mia hopped on one leg, holding onto my arm for support. "I'm pretty sure. My toe is throbbing." She winced.

"Let me take a look at it." I scooped her up in my arms, and to my surprise, she didn't complain this one time.

I rested her on the couch then sat on the ottoman in front of her. Reaching for her foot, I placed it in my lap and examined it. "Your toe is red, but it's not bleeding, which is good. It might swell up later or show some slight bruising. I hope not, though." I rubbed her foot softly. "Do you think you'll be able to stand on it today and walk around?"

She removed her foot from my lap. "Yup. I'll be fine." She launched to her feet, and I saw her bite down on her bottom lip, trying to ignore the slight pain.

"Maybe you should ask if you can start," I began to suggest, but she cut me off.

"Nope. I'm starting today. I got this! I'll be fine."

So stubborn.

I watched Mia hobble over to her handbag and pulled out a scrunchie. Without looking in a mirror, she combed her hands through her hair and made a high ponytail.

"How do I look?" She turned to me. Her hair was neatly pulled back, she was wearing these small gold hoops with no make-up on, and just a hint of what I knew was strawberry gloss. Don't ask me how I knew that.

The café only made the employees wear their black or navy t-shirts with the logo on the front shirt pocket as part of their uniform, and they're allowed to wear whatever they want on the bottom. So Mia was wearing dark jeans with cutouts by the knees.

"You look great like you're ready to work."

"Okay, cool." She smiled, happy with my response.

I observed the way she moved around the living room. She grabbed her handbag and walked to the front door. She was trying not to put too much weight on her injured toe, but she was failing.

I sighed. "Mia." I wanted to try to talk her out of going to work again.

"I don't want to hear it, Greyson," she mumbled, slipping on her sneakers.

"Why are you forcing this?"

"Because I can handle it," she fired back.

Pinching the bridge of my nose and closed my eyes in frustration.

This was more proof that she hasn't been herself. She was hurt, but she refused to listen to me. She spent all day in her room yesterday and only came out when she was hungry, had to shower, and or use the toilet.

I knew she was trying to avoid me. Now, this confirmed it. She desperately wanted this little time away from me. But why?

"What's going on with you?" I blurted out without meaning to.

Her eyes focused on the ground. "Nothing," she said, shaking her head.

"You-"

"Can you just please let it go. I'm going to be late." She gave me that doughy brown-eyed look, and I caved.

"Fine," I said, but I wasn't happy about it. "But let me drive you over."

The café was only a few streets down, but I didn't want her walking on her feet more than she had to.

"Alright. Thank you," Mia said with a breath of relief.

A few minutes later, I pulled up in the parking lot across the street and helped Mia out the passenger side.

I was still five seconds away from saying to hell with all her adamancy and take off with her while I still can.

"You're ridiculous," Mia whisper-yelled.

"I'm obviously more worried about your well-being than you are," I told her.

When I walked her inside, I looked around. It didn't look super busy, so maybe she wouldn't have to push herself today.

"I'm going to clock in," Mia said, eager to leave my side.

"Okay, I'll just head on out then." I hitched a thumb over my shoulder. "Have a great first day." I brought her into a hug. She stood stiffly in my arms before she relaxed and hugged me back.

Whatever is happening with us, I'm going to fix this tonight. I promised myself.

Mia was walking through the "Employees Only" door just as Freya was coming out. They said a quick greeting, and then Freya saw me.

"Hey, Greyson. Can I get you something?" she asked politely.

"Um..." I looked at all the treats in front of me. While I was here, how could I not grab something? "I'll just take a cheese Danish, please."

"Sure thing." I watched her grab it for me and put it in a paper bag before ringing me up.

I leaned over the counter as she gave me the receipt.

"Hey," I whispered, eyeing the employee entrance in case Mia popped out.

"What's up?" She eyed me suspiciously.

"Don't mention this to Mia, but she stubbed her toe earlier. It kind of hurt, but she insisted on coming in anyway, even though she's been hobbling on and off."

Freya's eyes went wide with concern. "Oh no..."

"Like I said, don't mention it. But if you could keep Mia in one place today instead of having her moving around, I think that would help her a lot."

She nodded. "Yes. Of course. We'll just keep her behind the counter. She won't have to wait on any tables or anything. We have enough people coming in to handle that part."

Relieved, I gave her a grateful smile. "Thank you."

"Don't worry about it." Freya smiled back.

I picked up my snack and waved goodbye as I headed out the door.

I would have loved to stick around for a little bit. But the furniture delivery was coming in about an hour. Plus, I'd be back this evening to pick up Mia.

All the furniture was moved in, and now the place was starting to feel homey.

When I checked the time, I realized Mia's shift ended in two hours, and the open mic should have already started by now. I grabbed my guitar case and headed out.

I decided to go to the café at a perfect time because after I and a few others managed to grab a table, a line started to form outside the door.

Some people were just coming in for a drink and or bakery item, while others were here to dine in and watch the upcoming performances-myself being one of them.

Mia hadn't noticed my arrival. She was too busy working the bakery. I watched her politely smile at a few customers and laugh at something funny. I could tell she would like working here, and she seemed to be killing it already.

Then I wondered how her foot was holding up. Mia doesn't appear to be hobbling or anything. Well, not from where I could see her.

"Excuse me." Everyone's attention turned to this young woman on stage. "Oh, great. This is working," she spoke into the mic. "Open mic will begin very soon. We currently have two performers on the list so far, and I want to ask if anyone else would like to sign up. They can write their names on the list upfront with the hostess named Holly. By the way, there's no cut-off time or anything. And in case you didn't know, the open mic doesn't have to be singing or playing music. You can read poetry or do standup comedy if you'd like. Lastly, we will have an open mic right up until closing. Thank you," she said with a firm nod as she scurried off the stage.

I had signed up the minute I walked in. Even though I knew for the past few hours that I was going to do this. What I didn't know was what I was going to sing. I was hoping to maybe go with my feelings, but that's not helping.

"Hi, can I get you something?" I grinned as soon as I heard her voice.

I looked up, and there she was, holding a notepad and pen in her hands, looking all professional and cute.

Mia smiled down at me. "Are you ready to order?" she asked.

Was she planning on treating me like any other customer? Okay, I'll play along.

"Sure. I'll just have an iced Americano for now," I told her.

I figured I'd have a meal after my performance.

"No problem," she said, not bothering to write down my order after all.

I watched her walk off, and I saw it-that moment where her footstep had faltered, and she transferred her weight onto the uninjured foot.

It still hurts. I was going to make her ice it when we got home.

"Mic check, testing 1, 2." A blonde guy said on stage. He looked like he could be in his early 20's if not younger, so did the rest of his bandmates.

The whole group was wearing dark jeans and plain colored t-shirts.

"Hi, some of you may know us formally by another group name but were no longer associated with that group and have decided to pave our own way. So hello, we're 'Save the Knights', and we'll be doing an instrumental cover of Secrets by OneRepublic."

All eyes were on them as the main guy picked up his violin and started. The other guy on the left came in with the keyboard melody and then lastly, the drums.

Somewhere in the middle of the performance, Mia had dropped off my drink and a coffee roll that I didn't ask for but was grateful to get anyways because I never said no to pastries.

Hearing these guys play took me by surprise. They weren't what I expected. If they had a lead singer, they could go off and get a record deal somewhere.

When they finished the last chord, the crowd was going nuts.

I was left to wonder how I would be able to top that but here goes nothing.

I picked up my guitar and made my way over to the stage as the guys were packing up their instruments.

"Good luck, man," the drummer said, patting me on my shoulder.

"Thanks," I said, trying to keep my nerves under control.

Opening my guitar case, I took out my old friend and smiled. This guitar had been one of my dad's. There are four more in the music room back at our house.

My mom and I didn't venture in there much. And we haven't tried to move or touch anything. Stepping into that room felt and looked like a time capsule. Just being in there made me feel like my dad would just come rushing through the doors again.

I was aware of the impossibility, and I knew that sounded crazy, but I couldn't help it. That was the one place that his death hasn't seemed to touch.

With the guitar in my hands, I sat on the barstool. The spotlight was pretty much on me, and it was dead silent. I spotted Mia by the bakery register as she handed a customer their receipt.

I couldn't be sure if she saw me walk up or what. But when I doubled tap the mic and cleared my throat, her head snapped up, and our gazes locked.

I grinned and gave her one of my infamous winks.

"Evening, everyone. My name's Greyson. I'm an amateur guitarist and singer. It's my first time playing in front of a crowd. So please be kind and try not to boo me off the stage." I heard a couple of chuckles. "Hmm... I think I'll do an acoustic cover of "Call you mine" by The Chainsmokers featuring Bebe Rexha." Of course, that song choice was last minute. I wanted to go with the flow.

Mia was obsessed with that song at the moment.

I haven't had much time to practice today, but I should be fine either way. Hopefully, fingers crossed.

I closed my eyes and started strumming the chords as I let the words flow from my lips.

I'd be lying if I said my heart wasn't beating out of my chest. The last thing anyone wanted was to make a fool of themselves in front of a large crowd, but I tried not to think about that.

I didn't miss a beat, and my voice hit all the notes perfectly like this was the most natural and easiest thing for me to do. And I loved every minute of this feeling.

When I finished the song, I opened my eyes, scanning the faces in the crowd. Everyone was silent for a second until they launched to their feet with applause.

My eyes found Mia's, and I watched her mouth the words "Not bad" as she did a slow clap while Freya was jumping and down, clapping excitedly next to her.

"Encore!" someone yelled from the audience.

"Umm." I scratched the back of my neck.

"Sing another song!" Another person yelled.

I sighed. "Okay, sure. Any requests?"

Four songs later, and I had to tell everyone I wanted to call it a night. I'd never sung that much in my life, and all their love humbled me, and I thanked the audience for their warm welcome.

I packed up my guitar and walked through the sea of people. I got compliments from left to right. At this point, the exponential growth rate of my ego will take the roof of this place.

I placed my guitar next to the counter by the bakery. "Do you mind keeping an eye on this for me? I'm just going to use the men's room," I asked Freya. Mia wasn't behind the counter, so she must be in the kitchen.

"Yeah, no problem. Great performance, by the way. I would have never guessed that you could sing like that. You have so much talent that you could do it professionally," Freya told me.

I shook my head. "I don't know about that. This was always a hobby for me."

"And now I'm telling you it should be something to think about and be taken seriously as a potential career choice." Freya pointed to herself. "I have an eye for these things."

"I'll give it some thought."

Freya nodded, "That's all I ask." Then she got back to work.

When I was leaving the men's room, I got flanked by two guys. Then the third popped up in front of me. It was the guys of Save the Knights.

"Hey?" I said to them, my voice laced with both caution and curiosity.

"Sorry, dude. We didn't mean to ambush you like this, but we definitely didn't want anybody else to pick you up before we did. Hi, I'm Dean." The violinist stuck his hand out for me to shake.

"Nice to meet you. I'm Grey." I shook his hand.

"The shrimp next to you is Tatum." I looked down to my right as he stepped away from me to stand next to Dean.

Tatum just gave a solitary wave and said, "Hello." I recognized him as the keyboardist.

The last guy turned to me and held his hand out. "I'm Tobias." He was the drummer. I shook his hand too.

"So, what can I do for you guys?" I asked, my eyes shifting from one to the next.

"Well..." Dean rocked back and forth on his feet. "We were wondering if you'd like to audition for our band. I don't know if you'd noticed but we sort of... kind of ... need a lead singer."

"Okay," I drawled the word.

"So you'll audition?" Tatum spoke up first.

"I don't know. This music stuff is all for fun. I can't see myself taking it seriously."

I couldn't see myself walking in my father's footsteps.

"Could you at least consider it?" Tobias asked kindly.

"Yeah, just come to one practice tomorrow and see how it goes. You don't even have to become a permanent member if you don't want to. You could just do some shows for the summer with us. Our lead singer bailed on us, and we haven't canceled our upcoming summer gigs yet because we promised we would find someone better," Dean added.

I threw a hand over my chest. "And you think that I could be that someone?" I asked incredulously.

"Yup," one said.

"Uh, huh."

"Without a doubt," They all chimed in at once.

"Um..." I didn't want to turn these guys down. I'd feel bad, considering they seemed pretty cool. But if I thought about it, other than moving into the apartment with Mia, I hadn't made any other summer plans. This could keep me busy while Mia was working. Getting to play music all day wouldn't feel like a chore either.

"Just for the summer?" I needed verification.

"Yup. Just for the summer. Unless you decide that you want to stick around a little longer than that," Dean said, with a single hand clap.

I chuckled. "Let's get through the summer first."

We exchanged numbers, and they said they'll text me in the morning with more details.

I couldn't wait to tell Mia about this.

13

CHAPTER 13

"Here, let me help you." I put Mia's foot up onto the ottoman and placed a bag of ice on top of it.

Mia sighed with relief. Her toe was slightly bruised and a little red. It probably wouldn't have gotten to this if she hadn't insisted on walking on it all day.

"Thanks," she said, leaning back onto the couch cushions. "You know, I didn't do a ton of walking today. I was mostly working the bakery alongside Freya. She's pretty cool and super funny." She giggled.

"I bet." I smiled. "Now, back to the topic of my performance." I took a seat next to her.

"Hmmm... Performance?" Mia tapped her pointer finger on her chin. "There was only one band on stage tonight. I don't think anybody memorable came on after them," she teased.

My eyes narrowed into slits. "Hahaha. Not only was the second act so utterly fantastic that the audience asked for multiple encores. But he was so memorable that he had that same instrumental band ask him to join them."

Mia's jaw dropped. "What! OHMYGOSH! THEY DID NOT !" she slapped her hands onto her cheeks.

I chuckled at her reaction. "They did. Their singer-less, and they need a temporary fill-in. So I'm joining the band for the summer, and we'll see where it goes from there."

"Wow. You picked up your guitar again for the first time in forever, performed in front of a large crowd, and got yourself into a band? You're seriously overachieving this week, don't you think?" She bumped her shoulder into mine.

I smirked, shaking my head. "Not even close."

"I'm surprised, though." Mia carefully angled her body towards mine, making sure not to move her injured foot around too much. "I didn't think you wanted to live that kind of life. Even if it's only for a little while."

She wasn't wrong.

Being in a band and performing was my dad's thing. I never thought I would be able to follow in his footsteps.

I shrugged, placing both arms behind my head.

"Let me guess. It's one of the many things Greyson McNamara has to try just for the sake of trying because he lives for the thrill of jumping from one hobby to the next." Mia said, accurately describing what could be my worst but yet most fun personality trait.

She might be the only person who can list all the hobbies and activities that I've gotten into over the years.

I think even I might have forgotten all of them.

Mia continued, "I swear that's like your special skill. Now you've gone from street racing to singing. At least this hobby is legal," she jested, aiming straight for my heart.

I poked her ribs, causing her to flinch. "You're just full of jokes this week, aren't you?"

"Maybe," she replied playfully, drawing out the syllables.

I hung my head. What am I going to do with her?

"Anyways, I'm going to hop in the shower first." I stood up from my comfy position. I pointed to her foot. "Don't keep that ice pack on for more than 15 minutes. Okay?"

She gave me the universal "OK" sign with her hand.

I took about a ten-minute shower. I didn't bring any extra clothes in the bathroom but a fresh pair of boxers, which wasn't a big deal since Mia has seen me like this before plenty of times. I wrapped my towel around my neck and walked out.

I was going to ask Mia if she wanted to have a movie night, but when I approached her, she didn't even hear me walk up behind her. She was too busy, furiously texting someone.

I'd be lying if I said I didn't occasionally become curious about stuff that didn't concern me. And I may or may not be tempted to spy. Like I was right now.

I peeked over Mia's shoulder at her texts.

Mia: Listen, the way things ended, they sucked. But I don't believe that it's my fault. It's yours.

She couldn't be talking to who I thought she was.

I looked up at the name on top of the screen. JAMES.

What the actual hell?

He texted her back a few seconds later.

James: Can we talk about it? I feel like crap, and I haven't stopped thinking about you. I want to apologize in person. Can we meet up? Please.

Mia started down at the screen. Everything she started to type, she erased. I had no idea what she was thinking, but I've been nosy long enough.

"HEY!" I shouted, stepping into her line of vision.

Mia jumped, clutching her phone to her chest and giving me a deadly glare.

She opened her mouth to yell at me or something, probably, but I beat her to the punch.

"What are you doing texting that cheating asshole?" I gritted through my teeth. The mere thought of him had my blood boiling.

She frowned. "Why were you spying on me?"

I ignored her question. "How long have you been talking to him?"

Mia stayed silent.

"Mia?" I practically growled her name.

She averted her eyes from mine. "He reached out a few days ago," she said quietly.

"Why didn't you say anything before? Is this why you've been acting so weird?" I asked, trying to get to the bottom of this.

Her eyes went wide, and she shook her head rapidly. "No, no, no." She started to make an "X" gesture with her arms, wildly waving them in the air.

I crossed my arms against my chest. "Either way, I hope you're not considering meeting up with him. He's not good enough for you, and he never was." I hoped my words stuck. I wanted to talk her out of making another mistake.

"He doesn't deserve your forgiveness, and you don't need to meet up with him so his conscience can be cleared. He was wrong. Let him live with that. He'll be fine," I added.

I expected Mia to agree with me. I didn't know what to make of her silence when she didn't reply. "You can't seriously be thinking about this Mia." My voice rose higher than I intended.

"So what if I was Grey? It's my decision," she shot back.

The hell it was!

I walked around the couch and stood in front of her.

I saw she still had the ice pack on her foot after telling her when to take it off. I picked it up and put it aside.

"See, it's responses like that make me hyperaware of your inability to find a decent guy in this world. I mean, come on, Mia. You're not stupid or blind," I said sharply.

She let out a humorless laugh. "That's rich coming from a guy that's had how many girlfriends in High school? If I have an inability to spot good guys, then what's the thing that you have called?"

Commitment issues, possibly. Or maybe I wasn't sure what I want. But we didn't have to talk about that.

"OH! Don't turn this around me!"

"Why the hell not, Grey? You always think you know everything..."

I laughed obnoxiously at that statement. "I think we can both agree that that's a common trait we share."

"Fine, sure, or whatever." Mia flicked her wrist dismissively through the air.

I sat across from her on the ottoman. I needed to try a different approach.

I sighed. Biting each other's heads off like this for something so silly wasn't worth it. I lowered my voice and tried to calm myself. "Promise me you won't go see him, Mia. Promise me you won't waste any more time on guys that are just not right for you?" I said softly.

My eyes pleaded with hers, hoping that she would listen.

Something about her potentially being in his presence again was rubbing me the wrong way. I didn't like him from the very beginning. Then again, I was not too fond of a lot of the guys that approached Mia.

None of them seemed right for her.

Mia leaned forward with her face just a foot away from mine. "And what kind of guys are right for me? Who should I date?" she whispered the last bit, staring intensely into my eyes.

I looked away. My palms felt sweaty suddenly, and I tried to wipe them in the towel covertly.

How could she ask me that?

I licked my lips nervously and thought about what she said. A million different responses flooded my head. But what came out of my mouth was the most cliché line ever. "You should date the guy that sees you as his entire world."

There! I said, what I said!

And I was leaving no room for regrets.

Mia's eyes were glued to me, but she didn't utter a word in response. I could only imagine what she could be thinking and... Crap!

Never mind. Never mind.

I'd take it all back. I started to send a prayer out to the universe.

Dear whoever was listening, please grant me the power to turn back time to five minutes ago.

"Do you know any guys like that?" Mia finally spoke, breaking the silence between us.

No.

And if I did, I sure as hell wouldn't tell her about them. I was tired of pretending to be okay with every guy being exactly where I wanted to be.

I paused. Did I really just think that?

Eliminating most of the distance between us, I rested my elbows on my knees. I gazed into Mia's warm irises so profoundly that I could see my reflection.

Where did I want to be with Mia? I had to ask myself.

I've spent almost a year trying not to dwell on last summer. I've tried not to think about the "what ifs" and the "maybes." But that was hard when I didn't know the truth.

What if the moment that had the potential to change our lives was just a mistake? What if Mia hadn't seen it the way I had? The way I still did?

Because it wasn't a mistake for me. It was a decision, and I used the excuse of being slightly intoxicated as the logical reason behind my actions, but that's not true.

I didn't know if it'll break me to hear the truth, but I also knew there's no one to me like Mia. I couldn't admit that before, but now, things had changed.

I got nothing to lose, right? I meant, it wasn't like Mia's going to turn around and hate my guts.

I gulped. My throat felt dry, and my heart was galloping out of my chest.

"Me," I whispered it so quietly. Who knew if Mia heard it. I tried to speak louder the second time, feigning cool and confidence with my words, but instead, what I said next came out a little deep and breathy. "You should date me."

14

CHAPTER 14

Did he just?...

I held Grey's gaze waiting for him to tell me that he was joking.

He had to be.

There was no way Greyson McNamara wants to date me?

"Mia?" he spoke my name softly.

I felt like I was on the brink of having heart failure. Why did it feel like all the oxygen had suddenly been sucked out of the room?

Oh gosh! The tiny people in the control room located in my brain must be receiving a lot of "warning" and "error" messages.

"Y-y-you..." Damn it! Where were my words? I tightly closed my eyes and tried to take a few deep breaths.

I felt Grey's hands cradle my face, and my eyes slowly flickered open.

There was this unmistakable electricity zinging from his finger-tips.

"Yes, Mia. I want to be with you." The words flew out of his mouth like it was the easiest thing for him to say.

I inhaled sharply.

I was not freaking out.

I would not freak out.

Who was freaking out?

NOT ME! NO! NO! NO!

"Do you like me too?" Grey rushed to add. "I mean..." He took a deep breath as if he was trying to muster the courage to continue. I almost found it hard to believe that Greyson was all nervous. That was totally not like him. "Do you like me as more than just your best friend?" His Caribbean blue eyes searched mine for the answer that I was having trouble giving him.

There were a crap ton of words dancing around in my head, but my brain was malfunctioning to the point that I couldn't seem to put any of them together to form sentences.

I wanted to ask if he was for real. Never mind the fact that he straight up confessed. I still couldn't believe it.

"No. No, you don't!" I blurted out, and I wanted to slap myself for it.

Grey's eyebrows knitted together, creating that cute little wrinkle in the middle of his forehead. I was confusing him.

I had confused my damn myself.

I felt one of his thumbs gently brush across my cheek, giving me goosebumps up and down my spine.

"You don't believe me?" Grey caught on quickly.

I shook my head. "All of this is quite unbelievable," I murmured. Maybe even too good to be true.

"No, it's not. And you didn't answer my question, Mia." He gave me a hint of a smile. Small enough to express that he was trying to be patient and understanding.

How did he make confessing look so effortless?

"I don't know how to say this...?" I started. Instantly, I knew that was the wrong way to begin when a frown formed on Grey's lips, and he tore his eyes away from mine.

His hands slipped from my face, and he began to pull away.

"Are you saying you don't have feelings for me?" he mumbled under his breath. His shoulder's dropped with defeat.

God, I was an idiot.

"Grey..." I tried again.

"It's fine," he replied in a clipped tone before he got up. "Never mind. I'm going to my room." He began to walk off.

I launched myself off the couch. "How can you think that I don't have feelings for you?" I hurried to say as if my life depended on it.

Grey paused mid-stride, then he slowly turned to look at me over his shoulder. "What?" he asked cautiously.

I told my rapidly beating heart to calm the heck down so I could say this without butchering my words or causing any more miscommunication. "How can you think I don't have feelings for you when there's no one else in my heart that occupies the space that you do."

He turned, fully facing me. Frozen in that exact spot, he made no moves towards me. So I took that as my cue. I stepped forward until I was standing mere inches away from him. I craned my neck up to meet his gaze, and I watched his eyes dance all over the features of my face.

From the looks of it, his brain was working a lot like how mine was a few minutes ago.

I smiled at the thought. I placed my hands on his shoulders and stood on my tippy toes to place a kiss on his cheek.

When I pulled back, a handsome grin lit up his face. The pure radiance from it brought a calming warmth that confirmed everything I already knew.

This really wasn't one side.

Everything I felt, Grey felt it too.

But there was a reason I never said anything until now, and what if...

"Nope. Nope. Nope. Whatever you're thinking in that pretty little head of yours don't."

"We need to talk," I said sternly.

Grey shook his head adamantly. "Not if you're going to give me all the reasons that you think we shouldn't be together."

"I wasn't going to do," I trailed off, sucking in my bottom lip.

He raised a brow and pinned me with a look that I instantly knew meant, "Really, Mia?"

"Could you blame, though?" I fired back. "All my reasons are probably the same reasons you didn't tell me how you feel."

Grey opened his mouth, then closed it, then repeated the action once more.

"HA!" I poked his chest. "I'm right, aren't I?" I said, awfully pleased with myself right now.

He rolled his eyes while crossing his hands against his chest. "That's beside the point!"

"That IS the WHOLE point!" I threw my hands in the air from pure frustration.

"So what are we supposed to do then?" he asked exasperatedly. "You want us to go back to pretending we don't feel anything for each other because doing that for the past year has sucked."

I sighed harshly, fidgeting from one foot to the other. "I don't know," I replied truthfully, not hiding the distress in my tone of voice.

That answer appeared to calm Grey. He seemed like he needed a minute to recollect his thoughts before he said anything else. He rubbed his chin and ran his fingers through the wet strands of his hair.

"How about we make a deal?" he proposed.

I narrowed my eyes. "What kind of deal?" I asked hesitantly.

I knew my reaction to his question had him amused when the corner of his lips tipped up into a smile. That same smile was usually followed by trouble.

Oh no.

"Let's spend the summer acting on all those feelings. We don't hold anything back. And see where that takes us and how we feel when it's all over. If it's all over." He gave me a smug grin.

I had to play the devil's advocate. "And what if it ends?"

"Then we go back to being friends like nothing happened," Grey said, adding a casual shoulder shrug for good measure.

Being friends was one thing. We've been doing that for years. Being something more meant we'll practically be playing a whole other ball game, on a completely different field, getting ready to bat curveballs out of the park, or simply striking out of the game.

No pressure or stress there.

"So what you're saying is..." I needed clarification as I processed this whole idea. "You want us to date for the summer? And if it works out then, it works out, but if it doesn't, we'll magically go back to being friends, somehow avoiding the awkwardness of just having broken up with each other from over the summer. And we'll continue to live our lives with the knowledge of this, but it won't change anything?"

Greyson began with a slow nod like he had to make sure the words I had spoken lined up with the terms of the deal. "Yup. Pretty much."

I stood staring at him like deer in headlights.

There was no way this would work.

The words were easy to say, but if it got to the point where we had to put them into action, would I be able to hit the rewind button and go back to the way we were?

"Come on. It's a win-win." Grey tried to convince me. "We were afraid of our friendship ending if we were ever to get into a relationship, and now, we don't have to," he said it like it was the most genius solution.

"Because we'll always be friends no matter what?" I repeated the words he used to tell me when we were kids, and I would ask him if he would grow up and start hanging out with more guys instead of me.

"Yup. We got noth-"

"Don't say it!" I held up on hand. "Are we really bringing that phrase back?"

Greyson smirked. "Of course, it's my catchphrase!" He winked.

"Yeah, when we were like ten, and I'm way over it now." I rolled my eyes.

"Every awesome person has one."

"I don't have one," I countered.

He chuckled under his breath. "Who said you were awesome?" he teased.

I folded my lips into a thin line and sighed. "Wow. Way to charm the girl you're asking to date you for the summer," I said dryly.

Grey grinned, closing the distance between us. He wrapped one arm around my lower back, drawing me close up against his broad chest. If I wasn't acutely aware of his half-nakedness before, I was now. I tried not to be a creeper as I low-key sniffed the scent of the shower gel that lingered on his skin.

Irish Spring? I guessed.

I sniffed again. Yup, totally Irish spring. The scent of the heavens and gods themselves.

Grey's free hand tipped my chin up to meet his gaze. "Go out with me, Mia?" There was no hesitation. Now, that was the confident Grey I knew.

I cast my gaze off to the side. "Eh... I have to think about it." I decided to mess with him a bit.

He pouted adorably.

I tried to cover up my laughter as I cleared my throat.

"You just want to make me grovel, huh?"

I gave him an evil grin. "Maybe."

Grey exhaled a long breath. "Okay, fine. Then you leave me with no choice."

I looked back to him, just in time to see the flicker of mischief glowing in his eyes. I knew that look, and much to my dismay, I wasn't quick enough to avoid what came right after seeing it.

Grey's fingers slid over my stomach, and I erupted in giggles.

Damn it!

"Greyson! Greyson!" I pleaded, but he kept a firm yet gentle grip around me.

"What's your answer, Mia!" he asked over my squealing.

"This... This..." I said in between breaths. "THIS IS SO WRONG!" I told him as my legs began to give out beneath me.

"And I'm okay with that," he whispered in my ear.

After a few more seconds of torture, I gave up. "OKAY! OKAY!" I yelled.

Grey stopped his tickle assault.

I brushed a few loose strands out of my face and stood up straight. My eyes drifted up to Grey's again, taking in his ridiculously smug grin.

"Okay. Yes." That was all that I said.

"Yes, what?"

My eyes flickered to the ceiling as I feigned annoyance. "Yes, we have a deal." I held out my hand for him to shake.

He looked at my extended hand and said, "I think we should add in another clause."

"What?" I asked in horror. What more could he possibly want?

"From now on, I think we should seal every deal with a kiss."

Before I could comprehend what he had meant, I was pulled into his embrace. I peered up at him, and without hesitation or any stalling, Grey's lips crashed into mine.

There was nothing soft or slow about how he completely consumed me. When he traced my bottom lip with his tongue, I let him in. I felt molten lava as I melted into him, finally unafraid of holding back and giving him everything.

Grey pulled back only a few inches as the two of us tried to catch our breaths.

"Deal," he whispered before taking my lips once more.

15

CHAPTER 15

I felt myself being swept off my feet and swung around our living room.

"GREYSON!" I squealed in between my laughter as he continued to spin us.

I was getting dizzy but catching those glimpses of pure joy etched across his face. How could I tell him to stop? And why would I ever want to?

Grey was spinning me fast enough that I almost felt like I was flying. And that weightless feeling, like gravity, couldn't hold me down. My heart was soaring.

While I hadn't given Grey the exact heartfelt confession that I've kept buried deep within in my soul, I gave him a sneak peek. And that felt like enough for now, but it wouldn't be all that he'll hear from me.

Grey spun us until it looked like he was getting deliriously dizzy himself, then he flopped on the couch, cradling me in arms close to his chest. He placed a kiss on my forehead, and gosh, I was a sucker for those forehead kisses. I was a sucker for everything Greyson-related.

Wow. My life just became a Jonas Brothers song. But we didn't have to talk about it.

My body relaxed against Grey's as I placed my head to rest on his shoulder.

Grey ran his fingers up and down my arms, and it gave me the best kind of goosebumps.

"Can I ask you something?" Grey said out of the blue.

"Hmm?"

"Why have you been so weird the last few days?"

My shoulders instantly tensed.

"Is it because we slept together? Cuddled up? Or has something else been bugging you? And if so, what is it?" I could tell by his tone of voice that he had been worrying about this. "You always like to distance yourself when something's bothering you, and I know that's what helps you think. But that's also what drives me crazy. I try to give you time to work it out alone and let you come to me when you're ready. Other times, I admit that I get impatient, and I find some way to persuade you into telling me."

That dang finger poked my rib and let out a giggle. Sometimes I wished his methods weren't so effective.

"Hmm." I agreed, thinking of all the times he persistently nagged the heck out of me to talk to him. "You could be so annoying some-times." I scrunched my nose at him.

"Shush," Grey said with a soft chuckle. "Don't change the subject." He continued, "We've always been in this together, so talk to me."

I haven't mentioned my mom to Grey in years. I kept my thoughts of her locked away, and he knew that. But lately, it hasn't been that easy. I did want to talk to him, but it wasn't the right time.

Then there's the cuddling thing. I had woken up in Grey's arms feeling safe and cared for. Grey had one hand cradling the back of my neck as my head was snuggled into his chest, and the other rested on my lower back while our legs were tangled together. I could've stayed like that until he woke up. I could have enjoyed the moment that may have never happened again, but instead, I chose to tell myself to be realistic. My best friend would never want to be with me like that.

I got up from the bed and tried to create the space that I felt necessary to keep my heart safe. Trust me. I hated knowing that Grey was under the same roof as me 24/7, and we weren't spending time together.

"It was the cuddling thing," I muttered, it was the half-truth, but I prayed he couldn't pick up on that little fact.

"I figured as much," Grey said confidently. "What bothered you about it?"

Since our feelings were out in the open, as might as well say it. "I thought it was nice. So nice that I wanted it to be real. I wanted it to mean something more than you just comforting a friend."

Grey sighed, then maneuvered me in a way that I was now sitting next to him but with my legs draped across his lap. He angled his body towards me, so we were face to face. "It meant something to me. Everything I do for you means something more than friendship to me. Yes, I wanted to comfort you, but I also selfishly wanted to hold you."

Grey ran the back of his pointer finger down my cheek. I shivered, and he smiled at my reaction. "As if it wasn't obvious, I'm glad we are where we are right now. This was all I've ever wanted and more."

I leaned in and kissed him. It was a quick peck, nothing like how we were kissing earlier. But it was enough to let him know that I appreciated everything he said.

I took one of his hands in mine. "You think anyone will be surprised about us."

Grey barked out a laugh. "Psh! Nope. My mom gave us until Thanksgiving to get together."

My jaw went slack with surprise. "What do you mean?" My voice went high-pitched.

Grey grinned, clearly amused by the outburst. "She knows how I feel about you. She thought after months of living with you that I was bound to crack and tell you everything. She was right. Like always." He rolled his eyes, but I knew he was honestly happy about it all.

"What do you think my dad will say?" I blurted out as soon as the thought popped into my head. For the first time, I was eager to tell my dad about who I was dating.

But Grey didn't share my excitement. His face turned to stone, and I busted out laughing.

"I don't want to think about what your dad might say," Grey said dryly as he pinched the bridge of his nose, looking slightly distressed.

"Come on!" I slightly slapped his bicep. "Dad has always loved you."

"Yeah, I'm sure he did. But that's because we were childhood friends. Now that I'm dating his daughter, I'll probably become public enemy number one." Grey held up one finger. "Every dad likes that one guy friend that only seems to be a friend until they start dating their daughter." Agh, he dramatically threw his hands upon the air before slapping them on his face and slowly dragging them down. He kept his gaze straight ahead as if he was watching a video of a dark, dank future that only he could see. "I'm a goner." He shook his head slowly. "A dead man walking," he said sorrowfully, slumping back into the couch cushions.

He was being silly.

"I think your logic might be flawed." Then again, there have been some cases like that, but I wasn't going to confirm it for him.

"Nope. I'm speaking facts," Grey said stubbornly like he has already accepted that he wouldn't live to see our college graduation.

"Okay, how much do you want to bet?"

Grey rubbed his smooth chin. "Hmmm." He was acting as if he had to think about it deeply.

"Listen, my dad has known you for pretty much 80% of your life. He's watched us grow up together. He's been just as proud of your achievements as he's been proud of mine. He was never afraid to scold you when we both did something stupidly fun. And when you lost your dad, he tried his best to be the man you could talk to about anything if you needed to talk." I added a pause for dramatic effect. I'm also hoping these two microseconds would give him enough time to process the first half of my mini-speech that I had going on.

"You're right." Grey agreed faster than expected. "He's been the best male figure in my life, and I'm grateful to him for that."

I watched him stare off into the distance.

Yup, the speech was loading. I rolled with. "It was important for him to be there for you because you have always been important to him. Trust me. He loves you. He'll be glad it's you with me instead of me with a total stranger that he has to spend hours psychoanalyzing and giving them the third degree." I huffed, thinking of all the embarrassing and overprotective stuff my dad had in his arsenal to scare guys away from me.

"He didn't do that with James," Greyson replied gruffly.

James was the last person I wanted to insert into this conversation but okay.

"Um, well." I looked briefly looked away from Grey. "So I never told you this because I knew you would laugh, but he never liked James." I sped through that sentence.

Greyson gave me a blank look before the tips of his mouth broke out into a grin, then he tried to reign it back in, folding his lips together.

I couldn't even be mad. I almost told him to laugh it out and get it over with it.

"What didn't he like about him?" Grey asked calmly, but I heard the humor laced throughout his voice.

"I don't know," I shrugged my shoulders. I told him that when James came to pick me up for our first day, dad had opened the door before I could get there. James introduced himself, stuck out his hand for him to shake. My dad took one good look at him, slammed the door shut, then turned to me and said, 'I don't like that boy.'"

Greyson tried to covertly cover his mouth with hands as his shoulder shook with silent laughter.

"Go on," I waved my hand forward. "Let it out." I encouraged him, much to my dismay.

Greyson broke out in a laughing fit.

I decided to let him have his moment.

After what felt like a good minute, Grey wiped an imaginary tear from the corner of his eye. "Please, Mia. Continue."

I went on to tell him that Dad said he disapproved of James. He also said that if I liked him that he'll let this one slide. But that the next guy he didn't like, he would leave them outside. So dad let him in and decided to be civil for my sake.

Grey's face became neutral. "After the break-up, he must have wished he wouldn't have let him take you out that night."

There was a bitter howl of laughter. "Oh yeah, he definitely wanted to go back in time and put his foot down, but it's whatever now. He's happy that I'm not depressed or crying my heart out over it. Now," I leaned forward, drawing his attention to me. "Back to what I was saying, dad's not gonna freak out."

Grey still looked torn about it. "He just might. Especially since I didn't ask for his permission."

I gasped, placing a single hand over my heart and leaning away from him. "Who are you?" I asked. "You know if the real Greyson got kidnapped by aliens and you're like a clone or a shapeshifter or something, this would explain a lot." I pointed out.

My fingers went to the back of his neck. "Where is the zipper for this human meat suit? Show me what you really look like, alien."

Grey captured my hands, putting them together. "I'm not an alien clone, whatever." He kissed my knuckles. "Listen, the loser buys dinner and pastries from the café when your dad freaks."

"If my dad freaks," I corrected him.

We were getting so addicted to those pastries. Soon I'd need to start hitting up the gym if I kept this up. Then again, it couldn't hurt to work out just for the sake of being healthy and not worrying about whether or not I had to stay a specific size.

My phone vibrated with another text from James. I forgot about him. He was practically the reason Grey and I were having this talk.

I opened the message and ignored whatever he wrote me. Instead, I typed back what I should have said from the beginning.

Me: I'm sorry, but I don't want to see you. I don't think there's anything left to talk about.

Me: Please, don't try to text me anymore. I've moved on, and I think you should too. Anyways, I hope you have a wonderful life, James.

I included that last bit to be nice.

Greyson kissed my cheek right after I clicked send.

"Would I sound like a terrible person if I said I'm happy he screwed up?" Grey asked with a lopsided grin.

I shook my head. "You're ridiculous. And since we're on the topic of break-ups, what happened with you and Katrina, for real. I know there's something else you're not telling me."

Grey paused, then launched off the couch. I almost toppled sideways, but I caught myself and glared at him. "Don't you want to hop in the shower? It's getting late, and you have an early morning."

I checked the clock on the wall. He was right, but regardless, I hated how fast he had changed the subject. "Fine," I grumbled, placing my feet on the floor.

"Great. Um..." Grey's eyes traveled down to the ground. "I'll finish getting dressed then." He walked backward in the direction of his bedroom.

I pouted. Did he have to? It took maximum effort to keep my eyes on everything from the shoulders up. But I failed miserably.

Looking away, I said, "Yup. You do that." I awkwardly gave him a thumbs up.

I watched him grab his towel and walk off. I waited until I heard his bedroom door shut before I got to my feet and dragged myself into the bathroom.

About 20 minutes later, I completed my nighttime routine, moisturized my freshly washed hair, put on my PJs, and I was more than eager to hop into my bed.

I pulled the sheets back and climbed in.

Should I text Grey goodnight? The thought crept into my mind.

He might be sleeping already. He hasn't made a peep.

I reached for my phone on the nightstand, and suddenly, a text came in from Grey. I smirked, opening it.

Grey: Sleepover?

Me: On the couch?

The couch was comfy, but it had nothing on my mattress.

Me: How about we just sleep on my bed? I suggested.

Grey: OR we can sleep on mine. ;)

What? Oh, wait! I forgot his bedroom set came in. I hadn't even checked it out yet.

I scrambled out of bed and flung the door.

Grey was standing on the other side with his fist raised. "You want to see my room?" he asked excitedly. "It feels like I've officially moved in." He reached for my hand, and we take a stroll across the hall. He opened his room door and stood off to the side, allowing me to enter first.

My eyes went wide as saucers. "DUDE!!" Grey had a king-size mahogany bed like the one back at home, in the middle of his room, and it was taking up the majority of the space. The bed was spread with gray and white cotton sheets, about four king-sized pillows, and one white fluffy-looking throw blanket was folded in half and draped across the edge of the bed.

"Wow!" Grey had a chest of drawers and a single nightstand with a lamp to the right of the bed. Other than that, the décor in here was pretty simple. Grey had three photos in silver frames, one of us, one with him and his parents, and one picture with the two of us and our parents. There were two other frames on the wall. Both of which had some of his favorite quotes. He probably couldn't fit anything more in here if he wanted to, but Grey doesn't like much furniture in his space, to begin with.

"You like it?" he asked, still standing behind me.

I ran over to the bed and dived on top of it. "OH MY GOD!" I laid across the mattress in a starfish position. "This bed feels like a cloud," I told him.

He chuckled under his breath. "Ready for bed?" he yawned.

I didn't answer him. I just lifted one end of the sheet and crawled under. Then I patted the space next to me.

Grey took the hint and got in. He didn't turn off the lamp. For a few minutes, we laid peacefully in silence.

I turned my head to him while he was lying on his back with one arm behind his head. I could tell by the pattern of his breathing that he hadn't fallen asleep yet.

I still couldn't believe this was real.

I thought last summer was a fluke. I had believed that that would be as close to Grey as I would have ever gotten, and I had to live with knowing he didn't want me beyond that. So after that night, I acted blasé about it. He didn't seem to mind, and that was all the proof I needed to never bring it up again.

"What are you thinking about?" Grey asked softly, interrupting my thoughts. He opened his eyes and turned on his side towards me.

"A lot of things." I wouldn't even know where to begin.

"Like?" he urged me to continue.

"Last summer," I whispered it like I was in fear of someone possibly overhearing me.

"Hmmm." Grey reached over, tucking a loose strand of hair behind my ear." I thought you didn't want to talk about that." he quirked a brow.

"I think now is as good as any. Especially since we're supposedly dating," I bit my bottom lip.

"We are dating. For the summer. Maybe longer. If you're lucky," he winked.

"Why are you making this relationship sounds like a summer fling or a trial testing thing." I sat up, bringing my knees to my chest, and wrapped my arms around them.

"Let's just take it one day at a time and not worry about that."

"Sure." I nodded. "So about last summer..."

Greyson exhaled a heavy breath. "There was alcohol involved. But I know that I don't regret anything. Do you?"

I didn't have to think about my response. I just knew. I knew it then, and I still felt the same.

Out of complete boredom last summer, Grey and I snuck a bottle of wine from his mom's cabinet. His mother had picked up a night shift, and my dad had been away at another one of those doctor conferences.

Now mind you, Grey's mom is not a big drinker, and she hardly kept alcohol in the house, but she hosted a bachelorette party one weekend when Grey was spending the night at my place. She had more than a little booze leftover from that night.

So Grey and I decided to play one of those drinking games.

Long story short, we ended up making out. I swear we weren't shit-faced drunk, only a tiny bit buzzed. And since we had already been on the floor in his room, naturally, we made our way over to the bed.

There was a moment when Grey's lips left mine, and I remembered whispering something about wanting my first time to be with someone I trusted, and someone I knew wouldn't hurt me. But it was more than that; I had wanted Grey for years. I thought he would have turned me down, but to my surprise, he didn't.

Grey said he wanted this with me too, and in that moment, I didn't care if it was the alcohol talking or what, but we lost our virginities to each other that night. I knew people at this age often complained about their first time being shit and how they regretted it. But what I had with Grey that night was... At the risk of sound cliché... it was so dang magical.

When I woke up the next morning with a slight headache, but luckily, I didn't have one of those hangovers where I was running for the toilet to throw up the contents from the night before. Grey seemed pretty okay, too, from the looks of it. He had been sleeping soundly when I got up, got dressed, and snuck out of his place at about 6 a.m.

I hadn't planned to leave things like that. I needed to think about my next move. But all my brain wanted to focus on was the fact that I had slept with my best friend, and that could have drastic consequences. I panicked and did the dumbest thing I could think of. I bypassed the whole topic and acted as nothing had changed.

When I noticed it worked, I was beyond relieved. I didn't have to lose Grey.

All my feelings for him went nicely back into a bottle until now, when I shattered it.

"It was the best decision I ever made because it was with you. I wouldn't change any of it," I told him honestly.

"Confession?" Grey said.

"Hmm?"

"I haven't stopped thinking about it since then," he smiled sweetly.

I lost count of the number of times I found myself grinning like an idiot tonight.

There was something silly I've meant to ask while we're on the topic. "So as far as 'first' times go..." I trailed off, hoping he would catch on to what I was asking instead of forcing me to finish the question.

"What do you mean?" He looked at me, so curious and lost.

Oh crap. "I mean... Do you think that I was... that you... Did you feel like...?" My brain failed to put the words together, and I felt the heat, my cheeks threatening to turn crimson. I flopped on the bed and buried my face into the pillow. "Never mind. Forget it."

The horror. The embarrassment.

"You wanted to know how I felt about our first time." Grey easily worded my silent question.

So he did know what I was trying to say. Jerk.

He poked my side, and I flinched, blindly slapping his hand away with one arm.

"Stop it!" I shouted before he could take it any further, but the pillow muffled my words.

I lifted my head.

"Answer me," Greyson demanded softly. "Is that what you wanted to know?"

I couldn't meet his eyes. "Possibly," I mumbled.

He leaned over and brushed his lips against mine. Once then twice. God, these kisses were going to fry all my brain cells. "It was the best," Grey whispered. Then he placed a kiss on my forehead. "You were perfect. You are perfect, Mia."

"Thank you." I didn't know what else to say, and I felt kind of stupid after speaking it. But I loved hearing that. My heart was starting to swell.

"Okay," Grey yawned again, stretching out one of his free arms. "It's officially sleepy time." He extended his arm, and I curled up into him, getting cozy.

I'd get to do this all summer long. That thought made me absolutely ecstatic.

Maybe we'd last beyond the summer after all.

Maybe all those irrational fears of losing him as a friend and or something more would all fade away because I wanted to make this work.

And I knew Grey did too.

16

CHAPTER 16

Kisses were being peppered all over my neck and cheeks.

I felt myself smile despite my sleepy haze.

"Good morning, Mia," Grey whispered in my ear.

"Morning," I mumbled, refusing to pull my face away from the warmth of his chest.

"We gotta get up, sweetheart."

"Sweetheart?" I repeated, only opening one eye to peek up at him.

Grey was smiling down at me. "Yeah, sweetheart." He kissed the tip of my nose. "I think I'll be testing out nicknames for the rest of the summer."

My lips curled up into a smile. "I have absolutely no problems with this."

He chuckled. "Good. Now come on, or we're both going to be late."

Grey and I shared the bathroom as we brushed our teeth, did our skincare routine, then we decided to take turns showering even though he offered to shower with me.

Real jokester that one.

I didn't respond. I couldn't because I'd be lying if I had said it was a terrible idea. So instead, I gave him a tight-lipped smile and slammed the door in his face.

Five seconds later, a teeny tiny part of my brain was reconsidering his offer, and it rolled with it. My thoughts automatically went to the dirtiest place imaginable. Grey, naked, wet, droplets of water trickling all the way down his broad chest then down his rock-hard abs to... JESUS CHRIST! STOP THIS, MIA! I squeezed my eyes shut and palmed my forehead multiple times.

I was going to go crazy if I let my thoughts stay there.

I heard a soft double tap at the door, causing me to jump. "Hey, Mia. Don't finish all the hot water."

"Okay," I mumbled, just barely loud enough for him to hear.

"Then again, now that I think about it. I just might need a cold shower if I keep thinking the thoughts I am right now." Judging by his tone of voice, I knew he wasn't the least bit ashamed to admit that. As a matter of fact, he wanted me to know that he was thinking about me too.

I slapped my hands onto my cheeks that were probably burning red. "GREYSON! FOR GOD'S SAKE!" I muttered a curse under my breath.

I could hear his light chuckle from the other side. "Never mind. Take all the time you need."

I rolled my eyes. Was he going to be this unbearable for the rest of the summer?

I took a quick ten-minute shower, then wrapped my towel around me as I peeked out the bathroom door looking for any signs of Grey. Nowhere in sight, I hurried down the hall into my room and softly closed the door before letting out a light sigh.

"AHEM!"

I jumped. That was twice this morning, in case you weren't counting.

I whipped around to find Grey laying down on my bed with a knowing grin. "Avoiding me already?" he placed a hand over his chest. "That hurts."

"I can't even...." I didn't bother finishing that sentence.

I firmly grasped the towel with both hands at the top, holding it in place. "Can I help you?" I asked with some extra sass in my voice.

Grey pretended to think about it. "Nah... just came to borrow your charger." He held up his phone and waved it, showing me that he was indeed charging his phone. "Mine's been acting up. I need to buy a new one."

"Right. Anyways, here's an idea. How about you take the charger, leave and let me get dressed."

He smirked, typing something into his phone. "Or..."

"I don't want to hear it!" I moved to cover my ears with both hands when I realized the towel was slipping. I gasped and grabbed for it.

Grey busted out laughing at my mistake.

Kill me now.

I was not going to survive the summer like this. Let alone the next two years that we're supposed to be sharing this place.

"Grey..." I whined, hoping he would get the hint.

"Okay, okay. I'll leave," Grey said, still laughing in between.

He got up as if he was walking towards me. I shuffled aside to move out of his way while trying my best to avoid his gaze.

I figured he would walk around me, but he surprised me by grabbing my shoulders planting a quick kiss on my forehead. "I'm going to shower. Then I'll make us some breakfast."

He waited for me to respond, but all I could do was nod like an idiot.

Grey didn't go all out for breakfast this morning. I thought I would have French toast, scrambled eggs, and the works, but I remembered we are both crunched on time today. So he made egg, cheese, and bacon croissantwiches. My taste buds were far from disappointed. I almost made coffee but opted to wait for when I get into work to beg Freya to make me one. That girl made the most magical caffeinated drinks.

"I'll do dishes since you have to go like right now," I told him when he rested his plate in the sink. Grey was already dressed and ready to head off to his first practice session with the band. "Where's their practice anyways?"

He checked his phone. "It's a 20-minute walk from here."

"You're walking? Why don't you just borrow my truck? Then you can put the guitar in the back."

I could tell that he was about to decline the offer, so I talked him into it.

"It takes me less than five minutes to walk to work. I wasn't going to drive and waste the gas if I don't have to." I picked up the keys from the counter, took his hand, and placed them in his palm.

Grey smiled gratefully. "Thanks."

I walked him to the front door, where he slipped on his boots and grabbed his guitar case. I was too busy in my own head this morning to realize what Grey had put on.

It was a simple crew neck color-blocked t-shirt that seemed like a nice fit, hugging him in all the right places. Much like the dark jeans, he was wearing.

"Are you checking me out?" he asked with a smug grin.

I diverted my eyes. "What? NO!" My tone of voice made it very obvious that I was and that I had been caught.

Why is he like this? Inwardly groaned.

"It's fine. I like it." He winked.

Of course, he does.

"Anyways." I stepped forward to hug him.

A hug? Should I hug him goodbye? I lowered my arms hesitantly.

Maybe I should just kiss his cheek and tell him, "I'll see you later." Or do I give him one of those quick pecks on the lips and then say goodbye?

I contemplated all of these options.

Why was I complicating things?

I never worried about how I should say bye to him before. But this was different. We're dating now, and I felt like I was trying and failing to navigate through it all.

I looked to Greyson, who I was guessing had spent the past few minutes or so silently watching me work through my thoughts.

"So um..." I began without knowing where I was going with all of this. "I'll see you later." I gave him one of those single rainbow wave goodbye.

Grey's eyebrows furrowed, and he shook his head. "You're acting weird again," he said, slowly sauntering over to me.

I quickly denied it, but I knew he wasn't convinced.

I hurried to explain. "This whole thing is weird. The more I think about it, the more I worry about how to act now." I sighed, knowing I was silly. "I was here overthinking about how I should say goodbye to you."

"What do you mean?" he inquired.

I was dreading bringing this up now. I just knew he was going to laugh.

"I mean..." I was wracking my brain to think of the best explanation. "So when we're saying goodbye..." I started. "Would a hug be sufficient? Or would it be cool if I was in the kitchen and I stuck my head from around the corner and waved goodbye? Or do we always say goodbye with a kiss? Or..." I wanted to ramble on, but he kissed me, effectively shutting me up.

"Mia." Grey said my name sternly but then added a soft smile. "What did I tell you last night?"

I couldn't pinpoint exactly what he was referring to. So much was said. I shrugged in defeat.

"I said, we'll take it one day at a time," he repeated softly, tucking a loose strand of hair behind my ear.

I blew out a breath of relief.

"Don't stress it too much," Grey added. "Hug, no hug. Kiss, no kiss. Single wave, no wave. It's cool. I just want it to be natural. Whatever you feel in the moment, go for it."

I nodded. "Got it. No more overthinking." I gave him two thumbs-up.

Grey laughed. "Alright." He kissed the top of my head.

Well, that was kind of perfect.

"I'll see you." Grey walked to the front door and opened it. "I'll pick you up after work, okay?" he said, looking over his shoulder, waiting for confirmation.

"Okay." I grinned, watching him leave.

Back in the kitchen, I glanced at the clock above the stove, noticed I had precisely 35 minutes to get to work. I wanted to wash the dishes and wipe down the counter before leaving.

When I noticed two keys lying next to the fruit basket, I realized that Grey had forgotten his house keys.

I took out my phone to text him and let him know, but a knock on the door stopped me in my tracks.

Grey must have discovered he didn't have them and came back.

I started to speak to the person on the other side before actually answering it. "I was just about to tell you that you forgot your-" I swung the door open.

It took a second to register the stranger standing in front of me. I haven't looked at pictures of them. I haven't bothered to watch old homemade videos to keep the memory of who they were to me and what they meant to me. I had closed my heart and pushed away from the idea of them possibly making their way back to me.

That being said, she was the last person I expected to show up at my door.

She was nervously shifting from left to right as she tightened her grip on the handle of her handbag that she held in front of her like a shield.

She looked the same. She was wearing a yellow sundress that complimented everything about her. Her mink brown hair was cut short, falling just above her collar bone. I remember she used to keep it a lot longer, and it used to make me think that she was a brunette Rapunzel. She wasn't as tall as I remembered since I've grown a few inches taller than her. Her brown eyes, though, are an exact match to my own. But where I once saw warmth and familiarity, maybe even unconditional love, I now saw confusion and regret.

"Mother," I said coldly. It hadn't been my intention to sound like that, but I couldn't help it. It was as if the years of hurt had seeped its way into my voice. There was only, but so much I could hold in at this point. I never thought I would have the opportunity to see her again, and I didn't know if I would want it. I still don't.

"Hi," Mom rushed on to say, ignoring my harsh tone of voice. "I know, I should have called, but I was afraid if I asked to stop by, you would have said..."

"No?" I finished the sentence for her. "You knew that would've been my answer but chose to come anyway?" I asked in disbelief.

What would have happened if she had been here five minutes earlier before Grey left?

Crap. I would've had a lot of explaining to do.

Mom was silent for a few seconds, "I was just dying to see you." She stepped closer, tilting her head up ever so slightly to get a better look at me. "You're so beautiful," she whispered.

I wondered if she was saying that because I was her clone but with blonde hair.

I tore my eyes from hers. "Thanks," I mumbled.

"Can I come in?" She took a peek over my shoulder. "I'd love to see the place."

I didn't answer, but I stepped aside, silently giving her the go-ahead.

What in god's name persuaded me to do that? I didn't know.

Mom slipped out of her sandals by the welcome mat and walked forward into the living room. Dragging my feet, I followed at a short distance behind her.

"Is Greyson here?" Mom looked back at me.

I shook my head.

"Oh, maybe I'll catch him next time then," she said like she was so sure she would be here again.

There was only a handful of times I remember mom seeing Greyson. Those few years were the start of our long-lasting friendship, and she hadn't been around much for that.

Mom stopped in the living room and admired the entertainment stand. The few pictures we had managed to hang up on the walls and the view from the balcony.

Then she walked over to the kitchen. "This is a great size for the two of you. Do you cook much?"

I shrugged one shoulder and scratched my forearm nervously. "Occasionally. Greyson's the better cook, to be honest. But I can bake just about any cake or pastry. It's amazing. I don't look like a balloon with all the pastries I like to consume."

Mom cracked a smile. "I see some things haven't changed about you." I was tempted to ask her what she meant by that. But I wasn't in the mood to bring up the past.

"Yup." I popped the "p" at the end.

"I had my doubt about letting you share this place with a boy, but your father trusts him and thinks of him as a family so that I couldn't argue with him on that. Your father says, you two are just friends?" She turned to me, awaiting an answer.

"Yup," I repeated my previous response. It's not like I would tell her I'm dating my best friend before telling dad that I was dating him. "So, do you want to see the rooms?" I changed the subject. Talking about almost anything other than my current love life would be preferable.

"Of course!" Mom nodded gingerly.

I quickly showed her my room, then the bathroom, followed by Grey's room.

"Isn't it going to be awkward for you when Greyson invites other girls over?" she asked.

Other girls? My heart painfully clenched at the thought. I didn't want that to happen. Then again, if we knew things weren't working out between us and we ended it at the last week of the summer as we planned, I'd have to deal with that at some point.

Well, this sucked. Why didn't I think about this before?

"I mean, and vice versa," she added, not making the situation any better.

No longer wanting to think about her question, I clapped my hands together. "Well, that's everything there is to see here." I gently nudged her forward in the direction of the living room once again.

A part of me hoped she would be pleased and leave now, but then she took a seat on the couch.

Smiling over at me, she said, "Let's talk."

Oh no.

"I have to get to work." I was grateful I had a legit excuse to avoid this. "I let Grey burrow my car today, so I'm walking."

Mom nodded, but she had disappointment written all over her face. "Your father mentioned you have a job at the café a few minutes away." She stood up, smoothing out the front of her dress. "Let me drive you."

I flicked my wrist, dismissing the offer. "It's fine. I can walk." I gave her my best reassuring smile.

Mom shook her head. She wasn't having it. "Nonsense. I'm going that way anyway. It won't be a bother."

I opened my mouth to refuse again, but then she said. "I think you can survive just a few more minutes with me. You've been doing great the last fifteen."

That may be true, but still. I sighed. "Sure. Fine, thanks." I muttered unenthusiastically.

"Great. Finish up getting ready, and I'll bring the car around front. Okay?" She sounded a bit too happy about this if you asked me.

I gave her two thumbs up and headed for my room to throw on my work shirt.

I texted Grey about the house keys before I forgot again, and I grabbed my bag, locking the door.

When I walked out front, the only car I spotted was a sleek silver Maserati SUV with tinted windows. Mom whined the down and waved me in after I spent more than a few seconds just gawking at the vehicle.

Opening the door, I hopped in and buckled my seatbelt. I did a glance around the car. Well, this looks fancy.

"You like it?" Mom asked, pulling away from the curb.

I pretended like it wasn't a big deal that she was driving an outrageously expensive car. "Yeah. It's nice." I turned my head to the window, counting down the seconds.

"I just bought it. I'm not sure how much your dad told you, but I work with my..." she paused. I could see in my peripheral that she was debating whether or not to share this info with me yet. "My husband, Michael." She gave me a nervous side glance.

"That's great, Mom," I muttered, uninterested.

You've moved on from dad and me. Good for you.

"He's your sister's father." She included that info as if that was supposed to make it better.

I stayed silent. Not knowing exactly what to say.

Mom continued to ramble on. She was trying to squeeze whatever she could into this thankfully short ride. I was basically scrambling to get out of the car when she pulled up in front of the café. "Thanks," I mumbled, opening the passenger door.

"Wait!" She called out before my feet could hit the ground.

I paused.

"Have you thought about everything I asked? The summer trip? Me? Your sister?"

I looked over my shoulder and spoke the one thing that I was sure of. "I don't know about everything else, but I'd like to meet my sister someday."

Mom released a sigh of relief. "I can do that. No problem. Just say when."

I nodded. "Okay, thanks."

"I'll be in touch!" Mom said before I closed the door.

I politely waved goodbye, not bothering to watch her drive off after turning my back.

17

CHAPTER 17

I turned the GPS off when I pulled up at the corner of this bar called "Lila's."

Putting the car in park and pulling the key out of the ignition, I finally read the text I got from Mia.

Mia: You forgot your keys.

My hand fell to my empty pocket to double-check. Dang.

I quickly typed back.

Me: Crap. Bring them both with you. If anything, I'll stop by the café after practice to grab them. :)

Mia: No prob. See you later!

I slipped the phone back into my pocket and got out of the truck.

The text I'd gotten from Dean told me to walk around back and knock on the side door.

I followed his instructions. Spotting a dark wooden door, I knocked twice.

"Coming!" I heard a girl's voice shout from the other side before opening it three seconds later.

A petite girl, emphasis on the word "petite," her head didn't even reach my chest. She has a head of curly jet black hair and caramel skin. She had to crane her head up to look at me from the doorway.

If I had to take a guess, I would say she was around my age or a little older, but that's only because she was rocking a sleeve of arm tattoos. Smiling politely, she said, "Hi, you must be Grey?"

I nodded with a smile and held my hand out for her to shake. "Yup, that's me."

She shook it firmly. "It's nice to meet you. The guys have been bragging about their new lead singer all morning. I'm pretty sure they're excited to have you on the team. Come on in." She waved me inside. We went into the hallway, then through another door, and down a flight of stairs. "I'm Mari, by the way," she told me over her shoulder, halfway down.

I smiled. "Mari? Is that short for something," I asked out of curiosity.

She cast her gaze downward. "Unfortunately, it's short for Mariposa. My mom thought it was cute." She shook her head. "Don't ask me why," she muttered.

I chuckled. "It's nice. I like it." I reassured her.

Mari shrugged her shoulders. "If you say so, dude." I saw her hide a little smirk.

We made it to the bottom, which I was guessing was the basement, but it looked like it could pass as a studio apartment. It was very modern and sleek. The floors had a grey wood laminate, and the walls were a crisp white that almost looked blinding with the recessed lights on. In the middle of the room was an oversized black leather sectional couch and in front of it was a glass entertainment stand with a TV and what looked like PlayStation underneath it and a record player. To the far left was where all the music equipment and instruments were set up. There was a glass dining table on the right with some books stacked on both ends like it was used more for studying and homework than eating.

"Guys! Grey's here!" Mari announced to the empty room.

The three guys came scrambling out of one of the doors under the staircase.

"Hey, Grey!" Dean waved with a burrito in one hand. He used the other to smooth over his disheveled hair that fell past his eyebrows.

"Yo man, what's up?" Tobias said next, leaning one shoulder against the door frame with his arms crossed against his chest.

"Hi!" Tatum said last, pushing himself out from between the two larger guys.

Mari pointed an accusing finger at the group. "Did you guys already devour the breakfast burritos I bought down?" she yelled.

They all put on a mask of innocence while Dean hid his half-eaten burrito behind his back.

Then they all blurted out at once.

"No!" Dean replied, rapidly shaking his head. He denied everything, never mind the fact that he had been caught with the evidence. And that he had a string of melted cheese hanging from the side of his mouth.

"What?" Tobias looked at her in feigned shock. He appeared to be offended by the accusation.

"Of course not!" Tatum said like it was the most ridiculous thing he had ever heard.

Mari marched towards them and went into what I can now tell was the kitchen. "You guys are unbelievable!" Her yelling continued from behind them.

"Sorry!" They mumbled in unison, but not one of them looked guilty enough to mean it.

"When mom finishes baking the peanut butter cookies, I'll tell her not to send a tray down here for you jerks," Mari threatened, taking her time to glare at every single one of them. "Minus Grey, he can have some to go."

I grinned.

"Awe, Mari, don't be like that," Dean opened his arms to hug her, and she slapped them away. He pouted looked like a wounded puppy.

"Now that wouldn't be nice," Tatum muttered under his breath, fidgeting with his fingers.

"How dare you try to rob us of all that deliciousness!" Tobias complained. "I demand justice! Who's with me?" He raised his fist in the air.

Well, this was getting entertaining.

I leaned against the armrest of the couch and stuffed my hands in my pocket. If only I had some nachos to eat.

"I second this motion," Tatum spoke up, raising his pointer finger in the air while still managing to avoid eye contact with Mari, who no doubt was waiting to unleash her wrath onto them.

"Me three. I demand peanut butter cookies! We demand peanut butter cookies," Dean took a quick bite of his burrito that he brought out from hiding and then raised it in the air.

All three of them looked to Mari for a reaction, and she simply quirked a brow. She looked more amused than anything but also a tad bit annoyed with them.

Mari closed her eyes and huffed out a heavy breath before opening them again. She mumbled something inaudible. Putting both hands on her hip, she said, "You think you guys are in a position to make demands of me right now?" she asked in a dangerously low tone.

Dean took a step back, shielding himself behind Tobias, and Tatum shuffled to the other side of the kitchen, out of the line of fire. "You greedy bastards left me nothing to eat!" She threw up her hands.

I watched Tatum move behind her and open the microwave, reaching for something inside. I smiled when I realized what he had grabbed.

"How could you guys be so self-" Mari gasped.

Tatum interrupted her rant, holding up a plate of untouched burritos in front of her face.

Mari's eyes went wide, and the biggest grin spread across her face with dimples and all. "OMG, I LOVE YOU!" she squealed. She threw her arms around his neck. "You're so sweet." She stood on her tiptoes and kissed his cheek.

The poor guy was beet red, but Mari didn't seem to notice. Not like the other guys did.

They made little kissy faces behind her back, teasing Tatum. He mouthed something that looked like "F off."

"See, we saved you some." Tobias jumped in, studying his hands into his pockets.

Tatum looked at him with a stony expression. "No, I saved you some. He..." He gestured to Tobias. "Wasn't going to leave you crumb."

Tobias jokingly gave him the finger, and Dean stepped in between them, playing peacemaker.

"Guys, guys guys!" He held up both hands like he was surrendering even though he didn't start this war. With the way he was acting, I thought he would bust out with some quotes about peace, love, and friendships. But instead, he said, "You're making us look bad in front of the new guy," he whispered, nodding his head in my direction. "Behave," he added in a stern tone.

I laughed out loud, bringing everyone's attention to me.

These guys are a trip! We're going to get along just fine.

The actual practice went on for about an hour and a half. All of us had quickly fallen into the rhythm of playing together. We practiced a few songs that they had sang at some earlier gigs, and luckily for me, I knew the words to all of them. The guys didn't have a certain genre that they stuck to, and they liked making a song into their own.

I understood that. Last night I was singing an acoustic version of a pop song. Putting my own flare on music was kind of my thing too.

We practiced a few slower songs with Dean on the violin, and then he switched it for a bass guitar. We worked on getting the exact sound we wanted, fiddling with certain chords and asking each other their thoughts on it. I went back and forth between simply singing and then singing while playing the guitar.

Rarely off beat, these guys were no joke. I was impressed last night, but I was even more so now.

I almost doubted the little talent I had. I didn't spend years honing my skill like them. I played by ear, but I also learned a lot from dad. Music was just an outlet for me growing up. One that I gave up to chase other things.

I wondered if they would soon realize I might not be as awesome as they initially thought. But nothing I've done so far has made them question my talent. Either that or they're just being all-around nice guys.

After a four jam session, we decided to call it a day.

Mari had been in and out, taking trips upstairs and then coming back down to work on some summer class assignments. She mentioned that she was helping her mom bake for a family friend's baby shower tomorrow. So she had her hands full, juggling between the two tasks.

I figured she must be used to listening to the guys practicing because she didn't get easily distracted by them, but she did pause a few times to listen to a specific song she liked.

And I couldn't help but notice how her eyes always seemed to find their way to Tatum every time.

I thought something might be going on with these two. And I have to say, I could see them as a couple. There was chemistry there that I imagined made them perfect for each other.

Not that I was a relationship expert or anything.

Oh dang. Was this how everybody felt about Mia and me? I mentally sighed.

During one of our little snack breaks which thankfully, included peanut butter cookies and milk, I learned that Mari's parents owned the building. The bar upstairs was her mom's, and she ran it with the help of her dad, who was also the co-owner of one of the biggest law firms in town. The top two floors were divided into three apartments. Mari lived in the biggest one that the guys described as the "penthouse," with her parents. They rented out the other two units to none other than... you guessed it, these guys.

Dean and Tobias share one and Tatum, shared the studio apartment by himself.

"Okay, guys, I have to head out," Mari said, piling up all her books onto one side of the table. If I'm not mistaken, they appear to be law books. I didn't get the chance to ask what she was majoring in.

"Where are you going?" No surprise that Tatum spoke up first.

Mari gave him a slight shrug as she continued to pack away her books. "Some guy I met at the mall asked me out for a late lunch today. He seems nice so, I said I would go." She peeked up at them from under her eyelashes while nervously waiting for the guys to respond.

"YOU'RE GOING ON A DATE?" Tatum said, jumping off his keyboard bench and knocking it over in the process.

Mari's eyes went wide. "Um...Umm..." she began to stutter. I didn't think she expected that exact reaction from him. She might be regretting bringing it up at all.

All the guys were now sporting straight faces.

Slamming a book onto the table, Mari pointed at them. "See! This is why I should never tell you guys anything!" she grumbled.

Dean stepped forward, slipping the guitar strap from over his head. "I just want to know who he is and what's his name?" he said calmly like he wasn't asking for too much.

"If he does anything you don't like, you better call me. Put my number on speed dial," Tobias said firmly.

Tatum stayed silent this time with his eyes on his keyboard, deep in thought.

Mari looked to me next. "I'm not sure if I'm supposed to say something here or what. But I can understand where these guys are coming from." I thought back to how overprotective I always was with Mia. It was worse when I thought about her dating other guys. Guys could be real jerks sometimes to the sweetest girls.

"Of course you do!" she shouted, slapping her hand on her forehead.

I smiled apologetically.

"Anyways, I don't want to be late. So you guys are free to continue to be all..." She flitted her hands in the air. "Whatever you all are right now. Bye!" She wiggled her fingers.

There was a mixture of "See you later, bye and yeah, whatever." From the guys. Minus Tatum, who didn't utter a thing.

Dean turned to him, "You alright, man?" His eyebrows furrowed with concern.

Tobias frowned, glancing over at him too.

"I'm super," Tatum said with his face remaining emotionless as he walked off to the kitchen for a drink.

I knew the last thing Tatum must want right now was to talk about how bummed he was feeling.

I placed my guitar back in the case, packing it up.

"So, what are your plans for the rest of the day, Grey?" Dean asked, plopping onto the couch while Tobias played with his phone.

"I don't have anything planned." Not until I needed to pick up Mia.

"Okay, so Pizza on us, and we can watch a movie or something. Let's get to know each other better." Dean cringed after speaking the words.

Tobias snorted upon hearing them, while Tatum just shook his head at his choice of words.

"Lines like that are the reason why you're still single," Tobias remarked.

Dean shot a glare at him. "Anyways, What do you say, Grey?"

"Sure," I replied.

A few hours, two empty pizza boxes, and multiple cans of fruit punch later, I think we had covered the basics as well as the most random things about each other's lives.

So here was the cliff notes version of it all.

Dean Walker and Tobias Graham are both 20 years old, born and raised in Portland, Oregon, and they've been best friends since they were ten. They met at this music summer camp and then realized they went to the same school but never met. They grew up together, playing music and a few sports like lacrosse and basketball. They moved 4 hours away to this town for college two years ago, which is how they met Tatum.

Tatum Reed was born and raised here. He's 18, just like me, but he started college at 17. He has been living on his own since he was 16. He didn't specify why but judging by the looks on everyone's faces when they were treading around the topic, he had a rough upbringing. He taught himself how to play the keyboard when he was 13. One of his neighbors tossed his keyboard out on the curb, and he picked it up, cleaned it off, bought a book on how to play keyboards, and boom! He became the most talented keyboardist I've met to date.

The guys had another member too up until a couple of months ago, but he got signed to a label who only wanted him, not the band, so he up and left them hanging. What an A-hole. I hoped he grew to regret that move in the future.

This group had more potential than I think they knew. They haven't decided where exactly they wanted to take this band, but they're just having fun playing music for now. And I think that one was of the things I liked about them the most. They tended to live in the moment.

The three of them haven't known each other for long, but they've been through a lot together.

"So Grey, did you ever take music lessons?" Tobias asked, chugging down the last of his drink.

I shook my head, leaning back on the couch. "My dad taught me everything I know. Growing up, I thought he was some musical god because there wasn't an instrument he couldn't master. He played the harmonica, the piano, guitar, and drums. I used to love watching him perform backstage when he used to switch out the instruments in between songs." I said, thinking back to the memories of my dad, rocking in out on stage with his band.

"Your dad was in a band?" Dean asked incredulously. "Was he like famous or anything?"

I shrugged a shoulder then began to massage the back of my neck with one of my hands. "Uh, it was an indie band, so you probably never heard of them," I told them the name, and all three of their jaws were left hanging.

"No flipping way!" Tatum exclaimed with his eyes going as wide as saucers. "Your dad was Roman McNamara? He was an indie rock legend!"

"I have all his CDs!" Dean yelled out with that look of shock still itched on his face. He looked at me like really looked at me. "I don't know why I didn't see it before. You're like his carbon copy. We're in the presence of indie rock royalty," he added a gasp, making the moment more dramatic than it needed to be.

Tobias interjected, "I would have done anything to see him in concert growing up. I missed so many opportunities. It's literally like a lifelong regret." His voice held a tinge of sadness. His eyes met mine, and I recognized the expression on his face instantly. I've seen it half my life. Sympathy. "I hope I don't kill your mood by bringing this up, especially since this was a long time ago, and I'm sure you've heard it a million times, but I'm sorry for your loss."

Dean quickly added, "We all are." The guys nodded in agreement.

I felt a ghost of a smile on my lips. "Thank you. I appreciate that." And I meant it.

There was this almost awkward silence as if no one knew what to change the subject to from there.

Tobias spoke first, "I hope you know that we don't think of your dad as a legend because of his music alone. It was his outlook on life that moved us and his selflessness when it came to helping others. The way he passed was a tragedy, and he deserved better than an ending like that. All in all, nobody can't say your dad wasn't a hero in his own right."

"Agreed," Dean chimed in.

"No doubt about it," Tobias said after him.

My gaze traveled around the room. A part of me almost got choked up. Minus Mia, who was like one of my dad's favorite people in the world and vice versa, I've never met anyone close to my age that were fans of my dad who thought so highly of him. The mark you leave on the world will continue to touch people long after you're gone. "That means a lot to me," I said with a calmness that gave away none of the emotions that I had stirring up on the inside.

They all nodded. "You're welcome," they replied in unison.

My phone vibrated with a text. I smiled upon seeing Mia's number.

Mia: I think I forgot to tell you what time to pick me up. My shift will be over in an hour.

I checked the time.

I replied. No prob. I'll be there

"You have to leave?" Tatum asked.

"Not this very second," I replied to him as I was replying to Mia.

"Was that your girlfriend?" Dean asked, nudging me with his elbow and waggling his eyebrows.

A huge grin took over my face. "Yes."

"Is it that blonde-haired girl you were talking to at the café? She's hot!" Tobias said with a smirk.

"Yup, that's her. My Mia."

The next thing I know, we were gossiping about my relationship. I told them how we'd been friends forever and all the dating drama from high school, leading up to us moving in together, etc.

"AWE! You guys are cute!" Dean pouted with hands over his chest.

"Dude." I mumbled under my breath, shaking my head.

Tobias rolled his eyes. "Ignore him. His life is lonely and sad."

Dean scowled at him. "Your heartless that's why you're single. In case you didn't know," he fired back.

Tatum chuckled under his breath. "He isn't wrong," he mumbled.

Tobias took offense, and his face turned expressionless. "I'm single by choice. I don't do relationships. Who can take anybody seriously at this age anyway?"

All their eyes shifted back to me as if to say, exhibit A was sitting right over there.

Tobias pointed to me, "He's a special case. He met his dream girl when he was in elementary school. They're practically soulmates. How often does that happen?" Tobias crossed his arms against his chest. "Let me answer that, hardly ever," he huffed out a breath.

"Can I ask you something?" Tatum said out of the blue five seconds later.

"Sure thing."

He leaned forward, resting his forearms on his thighs, and he started twiddling his thumbs nervously. "How did you get out of the friend zone?" he mumbled, keeping his eyes cast downward.

The room grew silent.

I wasn't sure how to answer that. Maybe because I didn't know for sure if I was entirely out of it, it was uncertain what would happen by the time summer was over. Mia might not want this like I did or she might get scared and want things to go back to the way they were before. I knew she had feelings for me, but what if her fear of us falling apart became bigger than the possibility of us staying together?

My mind flashed back to this morning, how she seemed to over-think the small stuff. It was so easy for me to slip into boyfriend mode because it felt natural. Those little sleepovers, sharing a bathroom, forehead kisses, I did all those stuff when she was my best friend. Mia was so much more.

I felt my heart start to race. Mia always had this effect on me.

"I was honest," I told Tatum. "I saw an opportunity to speak up, tell her how I feel, and I took it. Luckily, she felt the same. A part of me felt like we were on the same page, but I was never sure until recently." I smiled at the thought.

Tatum nodded with understanding. Finally meeting my gaze, he said, "Thanks."

"No problem."

My phone buzzed in my pocket, and I checked it.

Mia= Um, no rush or anything, but you're kind of late. Did you forget about me? LOL

I launched to my feet after rechecking the time. "Gotta go, guys."

I snatched up the guitar case. "Same time to tomorrow?" I asked, heading for the staircase.

"Yup," Dean replied. "See you later." He gave me the two-finger salute.

"Peace out, bro." Tobias lifted up the peace sign.

Tatum offered a smile and did a short wave, "Sayonara." He would be the one to say something like that.

I laughed, "Later!" I shouted over my shoulder.

I bounded up the stairs two at a time. I couldn't wait to see my girlfriend.

18

CHAPTER 18

"Dad, she can't just pop up whenever she wants!" I told dad angrily over the phone. My shift was almost over, and the café was kind of slow.

I gave him all the details of this morning, and he listened intently, throwing in his few cents here and there.

"Mia," Dad's voice was calm and even. The complete opposite of mine that was tangled up with distress and confusion. "In her defense, you haven't been responding to her texts. She was worried and figured it would be best to talk to you in person. She wants to tell you her full story before you decide on anything."

I huffed out a breath and furiously began to clean the already immaculate kitchen counters with a paper towel while everyone else worked around me. I needed to do something to get out my pent-up frustration. "I don't believe I owe it to her to sit down and listen to what she has to say," I said bitterly, trying my best to keep my voice low.

How could someone who spent years without making time for you suddenly ask for you to make time for them?

I didn't expect dad to agree with me. "You're right," he said. My hands froze on the counter. Did I hear him correctly?

As if he could sense my disbelief from all those miles away, he repeated himself. "You have every right to feel that way. But you also have the right to the truth, so you should take it. Then see how you feel afterward."

Why did he have to play Mr. Logic all the time?

"I'll consider it," I replied noncommittedly.

I checked the clock above the kitchen door. Grey should be here in 30 minutes. "Anyways, I have other things to focus on right now," I said, thinking about the deal I made with Grey.

"What do you mean?" Dad sounded suspicious, which was why he had asked cautiously.

I shrugged, "Nothing." It was probably best not to share this over the phone.

"No, no. Something else is going on with you. What is it?" Dad rushed on to ask.

I laughed nervously into the phone. "Just girl stuff. Don't worry about it." Typically, when dad's heard anything surrounding the words "girl stuff," he left it alone.

But instead, Dad snickered. "If I found out this has something to do with some new boy in town..." he began to warn me.

I rolled my eyes. "Oh please, dad. He's not some new guy." I quickly covered my mouth, silently cursing myself for letting that little admission slip.

"WHAT?" Dad's voice boomed on the other end. I had to pull the phone away from my ear. I knew he wasn't mad or anything, just in a tiny bit of shock and mostly likely drowning with curiosity. "Mia..." he began.

"Dr. Harper. Your next patient is here," I heard his assistant say, interrupting him.

Boy, did she have good timing?

"I have to go," Dad hurried on to say. "But we'll pick this up later, okay." There was no mistaking it. That was not a question but a statement.

"Sure thing, Dad," I mumbled, already developing a slight hint of anxiety over that future phone call.

"Alright. I love you."

"Love you too. Bye."

"Bye." He hung up first.

I let out a deep sigh.

I tossed the paper towel that I had been using in the trash bin and washed my hands.

One of the bakers asked me to bring out the fresh batch of Danishes and cookies.

"Sure, no problem." I slipped on the oven mitts. Grabbing the trays, I pushed open the kitchen door with my hip.

I placed the trays on the counter behind Freya as she removed the empty trays from the display cases.

"Everything okay with your dad?" Freya asked, piling one empty tray on top of the other.

I gave her a slow nod. "It's complicated."

Freya frowned.

Smiling softly, I quickly added, "But it's nothing that we can't handle."

I watched her expression become light and easy-going once more. Freya was one of the nicest people I've ever met, but I couldn't imagine burdening her with my problems.

"All right. But I'm here if you ever want to talk," she began to reassure me. "I know there are things happening in the real world, to real people," she sighed. "Regardless of the fact that I prefer to keep myself buried in my fantasy books."

I agreed. "I wouldn't mind living in a fantasy world," I told her. "I can't tell you how long I waited for my letter from Hogwarts to come in the mail." Just like every kid at 11 years old did at some point.

Freya giggled. "Every day, I ask myself why can't Hogwarts be real?" She whipped around to face me. "Out of curiosity, from one Potter head to head to the next, what classes would you be signing up for a Hogwarts."

I bit on my bottom lip in contemplation. "Hmm... Alchemy and Apparition."

Her mouth formed an O. "That would be so cool! Learning to teleport. And Alchemy is just a great mix of Human chemistry or muggle chemistry as they would call it, and potions but lastly, transfiguration." She clapped her hands together, getting carried away with the thought of it all.

"What about you?" I asked, leaning against the counter with both hands supporting me.

"That's easy. Divination and potions. Mostly, I want to concoct a love potion."

I paused, thinking I didn't hear her right. "A love potion?" I repeated in disbelief.

Freya's gaze shifted from me and fell to her feet. If I didn't know any better, I would say she was embarrassed.

"Well..." I thought about it some more. "It's not a terrible idea. If I didn't have Grey and my only real experience dating anyone was with my cheating ex, then maybe I'd be considering the same thing. I can't blame you." She seemed to pep up again. I didn't want her to think that she was the only one who felt like that.

I was sure lots of women had been there too.

With an all-knowing smirk on her face, she asked, "I thought you and Greyson were just friends?"

I paused, remembering how the first time we met, that's what we had told her. In my defense, it had been true in that moment.

"You see..." I started hesitantly. "What had happened was..." I bit down on my bottom lip.

Folding her arms across her chest, Freya urged me to continue. "Hmm..."

"It kind of just happened." I shrugged innocently.

Freya quirked a brow.

"I mean, like last night, happened," I confessed.

Her eyes grew wide, "OH MY GOSH!" She started doing a double hop in place. "I don't even know what to say!" She clasped her hands in front of her chest. "You guys are the cutest!"

"Thanks," I said, not knowing how to feel about that compliment, considering I was still letting it all sink in.

Freya continued, "And I know Grey cares about you. Not just by how he plays around with you but how he takes the time out to make sure you're going to be okay."

I scrunched my brows together, trying to think back to what she could be referring to.

She sighed, indicating that whatever she was about to say, she hadn't been planning on mentioning this. "Yesterday, when you went around back, Grey told me that you had hurt your toe and asked if I could keep you from walking on it too much."

I gasped. It was such a Grey thing for him to do. But the lengths he goes to sometimes occasionally baffled me.

Freya watched my reaction to the news before telling me more. "I told him it wouldn't be a problem. So I kept you in the bakery."

"I...he..." And here I was, failing to make coherent sentences. If I knew Grey was going to do this beforehand, I would have been kind of upset. I didn't want it to seem like I couldn't do my job well on my first day. Without complaints, I would have pulled through like the champ that I liked to think that I am. I wouldn't have asked for special treatment.

Leave it to Grey to take care of my smallest problems.

"Don't sweat it," Freya told me. "The minute I saw you limping, I would have done the same thing." She winked.

I smiled gratefully at her. "Thank you."

Freya nodded. "So anyway, back to potion-making. I've had the worst luck in the love department. I need some help. Magical help because I don't see it happening any other way." She slumped against the counter disappointedly.

"Maybe you're just looking in all the wrong places." I pointed out. It was a cliché line, but sometimes it rang true.

"I just want a decent guy. I don't even care anymore if he's super handsome or not." Freya said it like she was trying to convince herself as well as me.

I arched a brow.

It didn't take long for her to take it back. "Okay, okay. I would prefer that he was easy on the eyes..." She paused for a nano sec. "I want cute babies, alright!" she blurted out the last bit, throwing her hands in the air.

I busted out with laughter, catching her off guard.

"Hey, Mia," Freya's big brother Robbie aka my boss, greeted me.

"Hi, Robbie. Do you need me?" I asked politely, trying to recover from my laughing fit. I slipped off my oven mitts and rested them on the counter.

"No, I actually need to grab Freya for little." His eyes flickered to his sister's.

"Sure thing," she replied.

You know, as far as bosses go, Robbie might be my favorite. He was kind, smart, and generous. He treated all of his employees with respect and genuinely told them how much he appreciated their hard work. I couldn't think of one person that didn't like him.

"I know it's almost time for you to leave, but can you cover the bakery for a few extra minutes? You can take a pastry on the house." Robbie bribed me.

"It's fine. I don't mind." I gave him a thumbs up.

"Thanks," Freya and Robbie said in unison, then they walked off to his office.

I stood in front of the register and looked around the café.

There were few people seated, but this was our slow hour before the evening customers arrived.

When my eyes reached the furthest corner, I noticed the small table meant for two was being occupied by a young girl. She looked like she had a cup of tea or maybe hot chocolate on the table with a half-eaten cherry cheese Danish next to her.

I wonder why she was here alone.

This wasn't exactly a hangout spot for kids her age.

I decided to walk over to check if she needed anything and ask if she was doing okay.

She seemed to be hardcore focused on the work she had laid out in front of her.

Her small head of jet black hair didn't lift once. She wasn't easily distracted by the slight noise around her. She was in her own little world.

The closer I got, I realized that she had a math textbook open in front of her, but she wasn't working on it. She was focused on a sketch of a dragon instead.

I smiled. "That's really good!" I said, now hoovering over her, admiring her work.

She whipped her head up, and her cinnamon-brown eyes went wide. "Y-y-you..." she began to stammer.

I offered her an apologetic smile. I must have startled her.

"I didn't mean to scare or distract you from your drawing. I just came over to ask if you were okay and if I could get you something else."

She just sat staring at me with the pencil still glued to the paper. "I...I... I'm..." she began but then shook her head, clearly frustrated with herself.

"I'm sorry," she mumbled, putting her pencil down and sliding her hands into her lap. She kept her head down. Her dark hair parted in the middle, almost reaching down to her elbows, curtained her features. I couldn't tell what expression she wanted to hide from me.

"It's fine. It's my fault. If you don't need anything, I'll leave you to it." I motioned to her drawing. I almost felt guilty for bothering.

She slowly rose her head, meeting my gaze. She looked a little tense. There was something brewing in her brain, and her eyes looked like she was uncertain or maybe nervous about communicating something. She could only keep eye contact for a few seconds before tearing her gaze from mine, only to bring it back again. Then she shifted in her seat.

"I'm okay," she muttered.

I looked down at her empty cup. "Would you like for me to get you a refill?" I offered.

She shook her head then remained quiet as she pretended to be fascinated with something happening outside.

I had to look behind me just to make sure I wasn't missing anything out there.

I peeked over my shoulder. Nope. Nothing.

I spotted a skateboard under the table by her feet, and I saw a helmet resting in the empty chair opposite her. I would have never pegged this girl as a skateboarder.

"Do you like to skateboard?" I asked her randomly. I didn't know why I felt like I wanted to keep her talking to me.

She nodded, still not looking at me.

Focusing my attention on the math textbook, I turned it around to me.

"Are you in summer school?" I asked.

She pouted, shaking her head. "I didn't do so great in math this year, so my parent's hired a math tutor for me for the summer. This." She pointed to the textbook. "Is the homework that I'm supposed to be doing, but it's so boring." She tilted her head back and let out an exaggerated sigh. "AGH!!"

I laughed. "Let me guess. You'd rather spend your time drawing mythical creatures and skateboarding?"

Her eyes lit up, and she grinned, flashing me the cutest smile. Her blue braces were exposed, and the two dots of dimples in her cheeks became more pronounced.

My eyes scanned her features. She has the most adorable button nose that compliments her face. Her cheeks have a sprinkle of freckles, and she has these rosy pink lips, like think of sleeping beauty's lips. Then those teddy bears eyes, as Grey liked to call them, the color almost resembled mine but maybe not. My eyes tended to change colors. I wondered if hers did the same.

All in all, she was possibly one of the cutest kids I've ever seen.

"Plus," she continued. "I don't get all of it. Even though she, my tutor Ms. Gracie, explained it a million times." She pouted, taking a deep breath and dropping her shoulders. "If I'm honest. After about the fourth time of her explaining it, I think I saw her getting annoyed and impatient. So I pretended I understood buuuttt I don't."

I didn't like teachers like that.

She shouldn't have felt like a bother when she didn't understand the material. Sometimes the teaching methods need to be tweaked for the student to understand a little better. Who's to say a little extra patience wouldn't have been the key.

I skimmed a few pages of the textbook to see what lesson she was on. These problems look easy enough. Then again, as much as I hated math, I was oddly good at it. My dad used to say it was a natural talent, one that he felt I got from him. He was probably right.

Mom math wasn't mom forte. She had a passion for the Arts, Literature, design, and all of that stuff. She used to be a museum curator back in the day, and I thought it was one of the coolest jobs.

I took another look around the café, making sure I wasn't needed back at the register or anything. I was in the clear.

Then I smiled down at the girl. "I could help you if you'd like. I'm pretty good at math."

She raised her brows in shock. "Are you sure? According to my parents, I have a pretty thick skull. My brain only processes foreign languages, K-pop dance choreographies, History, and Art everything. Don't ask me about anything that involves numbers. Agh." She rolled her eyes, closing her drawing book leaving only the pencil inside to hold her spot.

I smiled warmly. "Yes, I have a little free time. I think I can help you get a better understanding of all of this. It's real simple. I promise. I'll break it down as best as I can." I assured her.

She nodded excitedly, eager to get started. She handed me a spare sheet of paper with one of her pencils.

Ten minutes later...

"Seriously, that's it?" she asked, completing the first equation with very little assistance, I might add. I was exceptionally proud of my teaching skills at the moment.

"That's so easy!" she exclaimed, holding up the paper in front of her face with a huge triumphant grin.

I giggled at her reaction to finally making sense of it all. "I told you! Pre-algebra is a piece of cake."

She shook her head. "No. I think I just have a good teacher." She peered up at me. "You wouldn't want to take my tutor's spot, would you?" She asked in all seriousness.

I barked out a laughed. "Oh no. I'd hate the idea of putting someone out of a job."

"Eh." She waved off my response. "I don't think she would mind."

I smiled. "I doubt that."

I looked over my shoulder at the register and see that Freya has come back. She gave me a thumbs-up, indicating that she had it all under control from here.

"Do you want to sit down?" the girl asked me suddenly.

"Sure." I looked down at her helmet on the seat.

"Oh. I'm sorry," she said, leaning over the table to remove the helmet. "There." she placed the helmet off to the side.

I sat down and watched her begin to breeze through the problems. She understood it so well it almost makes me wonder if she was faking it earlier. I laughed in my head at the thought.

"So," I began. "What are you doing here all alone? Do you live close by, and do your parents know where you are?" I rested my arms on the table and leaned forward.

She didn't look at me, but I noticed the second her mood and face fell.

"I live about 20 minutes from here by car. On my skateboard, maybe 30 minutes. As for the reason I'm here..." She lowered her voice. "I came to meet someone," she said softly. Her eyes flickered to mine briefly.

"Oh yeah? And what happened? Did they not come to see you?" Who wouldn't want to meet her?

I wanted to ask who she was meeting and why. But was it any of my business? I mean, it could be a schoolmate, a long-lost relative, or... What if it was some child manipulator she met online or something crazy like that? Kids of all different ages were online, and they could get caught up in just about anything if they didn't have the proper supervision. Yet, as sweet as she looked, she didn't strike me as a girl that would take crap from a school bully, let alone fall for any online traps.

As if she could read my mind, she said. "Don't worry. They're not someone who would ever hurt me. Not physically anyway."

I nodded slowly. I wanted to know what she meant by that.

"Are they like a crush or something?"

She slammed her book shut, causing me to jump. Then she stood and started to pack her things into a backpack. "I have to go," she mumbled hurriedly.

I watched her slip on her helmet then pick up her skateboard.

"Wait..." I reached out and touched her shoulder.

She turned her head slightly. "Thanks for all your help," she spoke over her shoulder but kept her eyes downcast.

My hand slowly fell back to my side. "No problem," I said. "Maybe you can stop by some other time?" I couldn't explain it, but it didn't feel right watching her run off like this.

"Sure," she said, but I wasn't convinced that she meant it.

A part of me hoped she would keep her word anyways.

19

CHAPTER 19

I sent Greyson a quick text when it looked like he was running a few minutes late.

Grey: Sorry, Mia. I lost track of time. I'm on my way.

I decided to keep myself busy until then. I helped one of the guys clean off the tables and pick up the dirty dishes, etc. About twenty minutes later, I heard a tap on the glass as I was putting fresh flowers into a vase at one of the tables.

I looked up and saw Grey with his pointer finger on the glass and a huge grin spreading across his face.

He was so freaking cute.

I mirrored his smile and waved.

Grey stood back from the glass, and I watched him mouth the words, "I missed you."

My heart started galloping in my chest.

I never blushed so fast in my life. "Stop!" I said out loud in between my light laughter. I knew he couldn't hear me, but he could read my lips.

Looking smug, he shook his head. I hadn't expected any other response from him.

I held up one finger and mouthed, "One second." He gave me a single nod. I watched him walk to the passenger door of the truck and leaned up against it with his hands in his pockets.

I ran to clock out then told everyone goodbye.

When I stepped outside, I saw Grey open his arms wide for me, and I ran right into them, letting the familiar warmth comfort every inch of me.

"You hungry?" Grey asked, nuzzling my neck.

"Hmm." I nodded against his chest, inhaling his scent like the total weirdo I was.

"Okay, let me take you out," he replied smoothly.

I pulled away slightly to peer up at him. "Is this a date?" I asked in feigned shock, whispering the words like it's supposed to be a secret between the two of us.

Grey's face broke out into a handsome grin. "Just dinner, sweetheart. I want our first official date to be more special than this," he teased.

I quirked a brow. "So what you're saying is you already have something planned?"

With a chuckle, Grey leaned in to place a tender kiss on my forehead. "Yeah, I do," he confirmed.

"What is it?" I tugged on his arm excitedly.

With one arm against my lower back, he drew me into him. I felt his lips gently brush my cheek, and goosebumps exploded all over my body, sending shivers up and down my spine as he brought his mouth to my ear. "I'm so not telling you anything," he whispered before pulling away.

I pouted. "Tease," I mumbled.

Grey barked out a laugh then took a step back to open the car door for me. "It's called a surprise for a reason." He gestured for me to go inside.

"I hate surprises," I grumbled, letting the lie roll off my tongue while I climbed in.

Grey stood next to me, resting his hand on top of the roof. "You love my surprises," he countered with a wink.

I folded my lips into a thin line, successfully restraining myself from smiling.

I couldn't deny it.

I lived for his surprises.

Greyson took me to this seafood place on the outskirts of town. One of those restaurants he looked up before we moved here said he wanted us to check out.

When I had picked up the menu, Grey said, "Order whatever you want." Four of my favorite words.

This place wasn't overly pricey, so Grey told me to order both when I had trouble deciding between the fish and chips or the fried shrimp with fries. I regretted nothing, and I ate almost everything. Grey had ordered shrimp scampi with a side of broccoli. I tried a bite, and I felt like my taste buds had been sent to heaven.

During dinner, Grey told me about his bandmates and the practice. I could tell he really liked them about how animatedly he described them. It was pretty adorable. There might be a bromance in the making yet.

Grey also mentioned that they have a gig at that same bar in a few days, and he wanted me to come to support them and meet the guys. Plus, there was this girl named Mari, a friend of theirs, that he thought was cool and that we would get along.

When Grey asked about my day, I kept it simple. I briefly mentioned catching up with my dad but conveniently left out the parts
about my mom. Then I told him about work and that little girl I met.
She kept popping up in my mind, on and off. It was the strangest
thing. He had asked if I had gotten her name, and I was upset when
I realized I didn't think to ask. We skipped introductions, launched
into a conversation, then a quick tutor session. Then in the blink of
an eye, she was racing out of there.

"Maybe next time," Grey said. Always the optimist, that one.

Back at home, I kicked my shoes off at the door and braced one
hand against the wall as I massaged my foot.

"Does it still hurt?" Grey asked with concern before swooping in
behind me to lift me. We sat on the couch with me in his lap.

I watched him slip my socks off one by one before stuffing them
into each other and putting them off to the side.

Softly, Grey picked up my semi-injured foot from yesterday, examining it.

"I'm fine," I said, finally answering his question. "My feet were just
pulsating earlier because I did more walking today than yesterday."

He nodded with understanding. He pulled me up against him,
cradling me in his arms, and instinctively, my head landed on his
shoulder as he rested his head on mine.

There was a comfortable silence between us for a little while until
I opened my mouth.

"Greyson?" I asked softly.

"Hmmm?"

"Thanks."

Grey laughed briefly, lifting his head. I angled mine up to look up at him. "For what exactly?" he asked, slightly amused but more confused than anything.

There was a list of things I could have said, but I went with, "For being you." I thought that covered all the bases.

He smirked, and I earned myself a forehead kiss.

"But if you had to be specific..." Greyson urged me to elaborate

I giggled. "How about the fact that you told Freya to take it easy on me yesterday."

"Oh..." Grey smiled a little, hanging his head bashfully.

I couldn't help but smile too. "That was very sweet of you."

"I guess. But if someone hadn't been stubborn in the first place because she was trying to avoid me and her feelings for me, then I wouldn't have felt the need to step in." Grey tilted his head to the side. I could only imagine the following few words that would be coming out of his mouth.

Grey made a scene out of dramatically clearing his throat, "Now that we're dating, I think you can come clean about all of those times you failed to avoid me because you didn't want to own up to your feelings. Chicken." His Caribbean blue eyes twinkled with humor.

"Greyson." I caressed his face with one hand, and he leaned into my touch. "I have no idea what you're talking about," I told him, keeping my face as neutral as possible.

The twinkle in his eyes faded. His face became kind of like that emoji with the two straight lines for eyes and the single straight line for the mouth.

I bit my bottom lip, effectively holding back the laughter bubbling up inside me. Grey snickered. As an apology for messing with him, I leaned in to kiss his cheek, but he dodged it.

Rude.

But that didn't dissuade me. I decided he was going to get one anyway. I brought my other hand to his face and pulled his forehead down to my lips, and Grey just let me.

A few seconds later, I admitted that he was right and that I was being stubborn.

Grey was all too happy to hear it. His smirk made a comeback.

"Yeah yeah, whatever. Moving on," I rolled my eyes.

His grin grew wider. He was relishing the moment.

"AGH!" I'm leaving." I hopped out of his lap, and he didn't make a move to stop me.

"I'm going in the shower," I told him over my shoulder.

"Okay," Grey replied. I didn't need to turn back to know that he was still smiling. I could hear it in his voice.

20

CHAPTER 20

"Hey, can you send this over to the little lady by the window?" One of the baristas asked me and pointed.

I followed their finger and spotted the same little girl from the day before, sitting at that same table by the window.

I hadn't seen her walk-in, or I would have stopped by and said hello.

"Yes. No problem." I told him, carrying the tray with a cup of green tea and a glazed donut on the side.

She didn't have her homework laid out in front of her today, and she appeared to be skateboard less too. She did have her sketchpad, though.

"Hey there!" I chirped. "It's good to see you again."

She lifted her head, giving me a toothy grin, showcasing those dimples. If she had siblings, they must be as adorable as she is.

"Hi Mia!" she said excitedly.

I placed the tray on the table as she moved her sketch pad over to make room. I slid the green tea in front of her along with the donut.

My eyebrows furrowed. "I don't remember telling you my name," I said to her.

Her eyes widened for a fraction of a second, but then she looked at my shirt and silently pointed to it with her pencil.

My eyes followed her gaze. Name tag. I palmed my forehead.

"I'm so stupid, of course. My name is right there." I thumbed my name tag. "But still, let me formally introduce myself." I stuck my hand out to her. "Hi, I'm Mia, and you are?"

She shook my hand. "I'm Ella." She squinted her eyes at me, searching for something in mine.

"Umm..." I began, but then her eyes softened as she slumped down into her chair. If I didn't know any better, I'd say she was disappointed, but I didn't know why. "So, what are you working on today?" I asked, bypassing that slightly odd exchange we just shared.

She slid her sketchbook over to me before taking a cautious sip of her tea.

This place looked familiar. But it wasn't somewhere I'd been physically, but maybe I've glimpsed it on TV or in pictures. It was a field of Tulips. Everything was in black and white at the moment, but her attention to detail brought it all to life without colors. She had drawn it so well that it would be solid competition against an actual black and white photo. This kid has some serious talent.

"Wow," I said under my breath in amazement.

Ella cleared her throat. "Thanks. I think I'm almost done with it." She tilted her head to look at it from my angle. "Yup. Just a few more additions."

I shook my head in astonishment. "I think I would rather suck at math if it meant that I could have a talent like this." I doubled-tapped her sketchpad with my pointer finger.

Ella giggled. "I don't know. Math is pretty handy. Maybe even handier than drawing." She sighed, biting her bottom lip.

"But drawings, art in general, makes you feel something. It teleports you to different places and moments in time. Trust me, I'd take those experiences overmastering calculus any day," I told her. I didn't want her to believe that her talent had no value. Her talent was a gift.

Her lips curved up into a beautiful smile, then they slowly parted to show those pearly whites. "Thank you," she paused. "Hey, your shift is almost over, right?"

I nodded.

"Do you think we could chat for a little?" Her cinnamon eyes sparkled. "I mean, you don't have to..." She shook her head rapidly, forcing her dark locks to follow the movement. "But I thought it would be nice to have some company until my dad comes to pick me up." Her eyes flickered back and forth from me to her green tea. Then she began to twirl the mug in her hands nervously.

"Of course. I would love to," I said without hesitation. Who knew what she wanted to talk about, but I didn't care. I just knew for a fact that I wouldn't mind spending some time with her.

Ella looked like she wanted to jump out of her chair and hug me, but instead, she clapped her hands together. "YAY!"

Adorable.

"When I clock out, I'll grab a snack and join you. Okay?"

Ella took a quick bite of her donut and nodded eagerly.

"Cool." I winked, walking off.

Thirty minutes later, I was officially off the clock and sent a quick text to Grey asking him if he could pick me up in an hour instead of right now. When he said, "no problem," I grabbed a cherry cheese

Danish and made myself a small cup of coffee. I would have paid for them, but he told me it was on the house when Robbie saw me at the register. Boss. Ever.

I thanked him multiple times, and he just smiled before heading back to his office.

When I made it back to Ella, she was laser-focused on her sketch-pad again. She hadn't noticed me until I began to pull out the empty chair across from her.

"Oh hi," she mumbled in surprise.

Ella hesitantly put her sketchpad off to the side, stuffing her pencil within the pages to hold her spot.

I shook my head, sliding onto the chair. "You don't have to stop on my account. You can draw, and we can still talk at the same time."

"Really?" She sighed with relief and picked up her sketchpad again. "It drives my parents crazy when I'm drawing, and they're trying to talk to me. They think I'm not fully listening, and they always ask for my undivided attention." She pouted.

"It's fine. Continue." I encouraged her, picking up my Danish. "I'll watch."

The corner of her mouth tipped up. "Okay."

Within the time it took me to stuff my face and gulp down my coffee, her masterpiece had been completed.

"Finished," Ella announced confidently. She held it up for me to see.

Speechless, I couldn't use any words to describe how beautiful her drawing was. "I love it," I told her.

Ella beamed with pride. "Thank you." She put the sketchpad down, closing it. "I haven't been drawing landscapes or anything like this for long. I just started. I figure I needed to branch out a bit and see how well I could do. So far, I think I've been killing it. And judging by the reaction you gave me, I'm right."

I admired her confidence.

I laughed softly. "Definitely," I said with a firm nod. "So Ella," She lifted a brow, and I took that as a sign that she was listening. "What else do you do when you're not drawing, skateboarding, and or procrastinating on your homework?

A small smile graced her lips. "Well, I got this terrible habit from my dad where I always feel the need to keep myself busy, so my list of hobbies and interests are all over the place. I wouldn't know where to begin." She shrugged a shoulder.

I rested my elbows on the table. "It's fine. We have time."

Ella immediately launched into a conversation about her favorite TV shows, which were the inspirations behind some of her favorite things to draw. All her American favorites were mine, too, like the Flash, Marvel Agent's of shield, and Once upon a time. But she surprised me when she mentioned that she had a few Asian favorites as well.

"So Legend of the Blue sea is about this gorgeous mermaid with super cool powers played by Jun Ji-Hyun, who was honestly one of my favorite actresses, next to Park Bo-young. OHMYGOSH! Don't even get me started on Park Bo-young. But anyway." She flitted her hands in the air. "It's about a mermaid who falls for this con artist and turns out they're like reincarnated soul mates. They had a tragic ending in the past, so they never got a happily ever after. So this is like their re-do. Then there's all this family drama from his side and killer on the loose. It's a great show."

Ella held up her pointer finger as soon as she remembered that she forgot to add something. "Also, the male lead, Lee Min Ho, looked so handsome in this show," she sighed, looking off into the distance.

I quirked a brow, waiting for her to come back down from the clouds.

"Okay, okay, so he might be one of my celebrity crushes, but if you saw him, you would understand why."

I smirked. "One of your celebrity crushes?"

"Yes. A girl needs to have her options." She dramatically flipped her hair. "Plus, there's a lot of eye candy out there. How can I just stick to crushing on one guy? I mean, it's not like I'm hurting anyone."

I shook my head, laughing under my breath.

"Who's your celebrity crush?" she asked.

I thought about it, only to realize that I was in the same predicament as her.

"Well." I bit my bottom lip then released it. "So there might be more than one."

It was her turn to quirk a brow. She was looking awfully amused right now too. With her hand, Ella gestured for me to continue.

"Alright, so there's Sam and Dean Winchester, Oliver Queen, and Barry Allen. But if I had to pick one out of the four to spend the rest of my life with..." I spent a few seconds giving it some serious thought. "It would probably be Barry Allen. I would give you an explanation, but it'll take me all night."

Ella chuckled. "The flash is pretty cute," she agreed. "Then again, I'm biased because he's my favorite superhero."

I agreed. "Mine too."

"Now, back to the K-dramas. Do you think you'd be interested in trying one of them? I mean, I know a lot of people get annoyed with reading subs all the time. It's easy for me to watch them because I'm fluent in Korean, but..."

I gasped. "Wait, what?" I blurted out. "You speak Korean?"

"And Japanese," she added casually as if knowing one foreign language wasn't impressive enough.

My jaw dropped.

"The thing is..." She went on to tell me that she used to live in South Korea with her father and her grandparents, who are actually her dad's godparents. They adopted him when his birth parents died in a car accident as a child.

"If you don't mind me asking, what happened to your mom?" I figured since we were on the topic of family that I'd ask. She hadn't mentioned her yet. She mostly talked about her dad and grandparents.

Ella bit her lip, something I often did when I wasn't sure of what to say, or I don't want to say anything. But she spoke up anyway. "She and my dad split up before I was born. Then they got back together a few years ago. She's been a part of my life ever since."

I nodded. "Do you have any siblings? I can't imagine your parents not wanting to make more of you." My eyes started to gaze upon all her unique features. "You're so beautiful."

Ella looked away from me, focusing on her hands resting in her lap. "Th-thank you," she said ever so softly. "And um... as for siblings. I-I-I..." She took a deep breath. "I have a sister. She's a few years older than I am, but we don't talk much. We're not super close or anything." She frowned.

I felt my heartache for her. "Her loss," I told her honestly.

She gave me a sad smile with a slight nod.

Okay, next topic. "I feel like I've gotten to know a lot about you, but I haven't told you much about myself." I leaned back in the chair. "To be honest, I'm kind of boring. So you probably don't want to hear my life story." I shrugged.

"Nope! Uh-huh. Tell me everything."

I started with the basics, age, birthday, hometown, etc. I told Ella about my dad and how my parents divorced a while back. I told her about the few hobbies I had, including watching TV, reading, playing video games with my dad. I used to do ballet too up until my mom left. This means about six years of dance classes went down the drain. Then there was this brief time that I was into soccer, but I stopped playing a sophomore year of High school to focus on the debate team and making sure I got good enough grades to get into whatever college I wanted. And, of course, Grey was mentioned now and then.

"Do you have a boyfriend?" Ella asked out of the blue.

I felt my cheeks heating up from the simple question, maybe because Grey's smiling face popped into my head and those blue eyes.

"So I'm taking that as a yes?" Ella guessed. "You literally dazed out as soon as I mentioned him. Wow. You must be in love." She waggled her eyebrows and shimmied her shoulders.

This was one of those moments where if I were drinking coffee, I would have spat it out and ended up in a coughing fit.

I shook my head. "No, no. I don't... I mean... I've known him my whole life..." And I do love him but am I in love with him?

Ella crossed her arms. The look on her face was daring me to deny it.

"Listen, we just started dating," I began.

She interrupted me. "What's his name?"

"Um... well... you see... SO he's actuallymybestfriendGreyson," I blurted out in one breath.

Ella gasped loudly. Placing a hand over her heart, she leaned away from me. "You two have known each other practically your whole lives."

"Doesn't matter! It's too soon to throw the L-word out there!" I whined.

"There's no time limit for these things. If you feel it, say it. He'd be crazy not to feel the same," she huffed.

I was experiencing that feeling you get when you realize a 12-year-old was far wiser than you. She may be correct, but still.

My thoughts trailed off, but it didn't last long because the minute I heard what sounded like a motorcycle out front, my head instantly whipped around to look outside the window.

Speak of the devil, I was right. Greyson had just pulled up.

He turned off the bike, slipping off his helmet. In my mind, it was like someone had clicked the slow-motion button, and I swear I was watching his biceps and back muscles flex as he took off the helmet and then run his fingers through his hair. Oh boy.

Grey pulled out his phone, and my pocket vibrated a second later.

"OHMYGOSH! IS THAT HIM!" Ella shouted and pointed.

"Yup, that's Grey." My lips curved up into a grin.

"EEPPP!" She squealed. "He's so cute, and he rides a motorcycle!" She shook her head. "Does he always pick you up from work? Awe!! That's so sweet." She gave me the puppy dog eyes.

"Sometimes, I drive myself or walk, but Grey also liked to pick me and or drop me off. We don't live far from here."

Ella focused shifted from Greyson and then back to me. She stared at me blankly, blinking a few times. "Did you just say 'we'?" she asked carefully.

I smirked. She doesn't miss a thing. "Yes, I did. We live together. That's another part of my story. I'll have to tell you about some other time." I winked, making a move to get up.

Ella's eyebrows scrunched together, "You really want to talk to me again?" she asked skeptically.

"Of course. I liked spending time with you, and I'd love to do it again." Her eyebrows knitted together, making little crinkles in the middle of her forehead. "Is that alright?"

Her face softened. She opened her mouth, but no words came out, so she just nodded instead.

"Awesome!" I replied with a grin.

"Mia." Ella stood abruptly. Opening her sketchbook, she ripped out a page and rolled it up before handing it to me. "Here, since you like it so much. You can have it." She smiled up at me.

My grin grew even wider. "I don't like it. I love it. Thank you." I covered my heart with one hand so she could understand how much this meant to me.

I extended an arm to hug her. She visibly stiffened, her eyes filled with uncertainty. Maybe this was too much. What if she was not a hugger?

I was about to put my arm down when she dashed towards me, knocking me back a step as she wrapped her arms around me in a firm hold.

Instinctively, I did the same.

I didn't know what this kid had going on at home that made her want to run here almost every day and try talking to me, but I wanted to learn more about her if she'd let me.

Slowly, she pulled away from me, not meeting my eyes. "Is everything okay?" I asked her. I feel like her vibes had changed entirely.

Ella nodded, putting on a halfhearted smile. "It's fine. I'm totally fine."

"Do you want me to wait with you until your dad comes?" I offered, I don't want to leave her alone if she's not okay with it.

She shook her head no. "It's fine." She repeated the exact words that I didn't believe.

"You sure because I can wait. Greyson, won't mind at all." I tried to reassure.

Ella tilted her head up to meet my gaze. "I don't want to keep you."

"Okay," I smiled, but it was forced.

Tucking a strand of her behind her ears, I told her. "I'm off for the next few days. But I'll be back working the same shift after that. So you can swing by then if you want to."

That sparkle was slowly coming back into her eyes once more. "Okay."

"Okay," I repeated. "I'll see you then. Bye." I waved, watching her get comfy in her chair to draw something else on a blank sheet waiting to be blessed by her artistic talent.

I saw Freya walk in after saying hello to Greyson. "Hey, Freya."

"Mia, I thought your shift was over an hour ago," she asked, confused.

"Yeah, it was. I stuck around for a friend." I glanced over at Ella one last time. "Can you make sure she's okay after I leave? Her dad is supposed to pick her up, she said."

"Yeah, of course. No problem," Freya replied.

"Great. Thank you. I'll see you later!" I waved, heading out the glass doors and running straight for Grey.

He caught me as I leaped into his arms, wrapping my legs around him and planting a quick kiss on his lips.

Grey rested his forehead against mine. "Miss me?" he asked smugly.

I pulled back and scrunched up my nose. "Eh..."

Those Caribbean blue eyes turned into slits. "Liar," he whispered accusingly.

I playfully rolled my eyes.

"You made a new friend?" Grey asked. He tips up his head in the direction of Ella, who he can see through the glass.

"Yup," I grinned. "You might have a competitor fighting for your best friend slot." I teased.

He shrugged like it was no big deal.

"You're okay with that?" I asked incredulously.

"Yup," Grey replied with absolute certainty. "For one, she looks absolutely adorable. I wouldn't dream of competing against her. And two, I'm not only your best friend anymore. I'm also your boyfriend." He leaned into me, lowering his voice to a husky whisper that had goosebumps traveling up my arms. "I don't mind sharing you because only I get to have you in a way no one else can."

I licked my lips and folded them into a thin line, and took a long deep breath through my nose. "Why are you always like this?" I grumbled.

"Because it's fun. And I love it when you blush because of me." Grey used the back of his hand to brush across my cheeks that are now burning scarlet.

"You are so annoying sometimes," I mumbled.

"You like it," Grey replied without missing a beat. He planted a kiss on my forehead. "Come on, let's go home."

21

— ◦ —

CHAPTER 21

At Dean's request, band practice was short. He wanted us to save our energy for the gig at Lila's tonight. All the guys seemed pretty hyped up except for Tatum, who looked like he had a lot weighing on his mind.

I had asked him about it, but he brushed it off, saying it was just nerves. Of course, I didn't believe him.

Either way, I let him know he could call me anytime if he wanted to talk, especially about Mari.

I wasn't saying that I am a relationship expert or anything now, but I knew what he was going through.

When it came close to the end of Mia's shift, I decided to walk and meet her at the café. It was a nice enough day to ditch the truck and the bike for some good ole fresh air.

I had been crossing the street to the other side when my phone started ringing. "Clocks" by Coldplay began playing through my jeans pocket, my mom's favorite song, and her ringtone.

"Hey, Mom!" I said excitedly. I haven't heard her voice in days.

"Oh wow!" she said sarcastically. "You remember me, do you? I wasn't sure if my only child, who carried in my belly for over nine months, went through an excruciating 17-hour natural labor just to have him never call me..." She took a swift intake of breath before continuing. "...Would recognize the sound of my heartbroken and distressed voice," she began to fake weeping.

"Mother, you do realize I've called you the past two days in a row. If anyone should be heartbroken, it should be me. My mother obviously has no time to talk to me. I even left you texts. "

"What! When?"

"The last two nights in a row," I replied.

"You lie!" Mom whispered harshly. "I didn't see any texts!"

I sighed. I knew Mom must have overlooked them.

"Look, I am telling you," she began to sing terribly. "There's no way, n-n-n-n-no way!!"

"MOM!" I said before she began singing the entire chorus.

"Oh! Hey, I found them," Mom said softly. I heard a few tapping motions from her end.

"Hmm..."

"In my defense, you see what had happened was," she paused.

"I'm waiting."

"I dropped my phone. The screen cracked on the side where my messaging app is. So, yeah. It's unbelievably bad. I'm surprised it still works. "

"How do you explain the missed phone calls?"

"Did I mention I love you?" She answered my question with one of her own.

"Mom."

"Okay, I must have looked at them. Then I made a mental note to call back, but then I got distracted every time. I forgot." I could feel her guilt through the phone.

"I believe you owe your only child, the one who taught himself how to make chicken noodle soup when you were sick, the same one who stayed up late to make sure you always made it home safely from work, an apology."

"I'm so sorry, my loving son. Will you ever forgive me?" she said, only half sarcastic.

I cracked a smile. "Ahh... I'll have to think about."

"I'll bake you banana bread with extra walnuts."

"You are forgiven," I said instantly.

We laughed. "So what's new?

"A lot of things," I said vaguely.

"Wow. That sounds so exciting. Thanks for telling me all about your new life," Mom replied blandly.

I crossed the next street. I could see the café now.

"Mom, I think... UMPH!"

I heard a tiny squeal as a little human crashed into me. I tried and failed to catch her before she got hurt.

"Ow ow ow ow owww!!" She whined with one arm, bracing herself and one knee to the ground.

Initially, I had reached out to grab her, hoping to hold her up, but she might have managed to scrape her knee a bit.

I stared down at the girl in the metallic silver helmet, kneeling next to her skateboard.

"Mom, I'll call you back later," I said hurriedly.

"Sure thing. Love you."

"You too." I hung up.

My attention went back to the girl who collided with me. "Hey, are you okay," I asked her.

She began to tilt her head up slowly.

Her maple syrup eyes scanned my face as I helped her up. She hopped on one leg for a few seconds before she stood firmly on both feet.

I think I've seen this girl from somewhere. I took in her long dark wavy hair, freckles, high cheekbones, and button nose. If I hadn't seen her somewhere before, I probably think she looked familiar because she reminded me of someone. I couldn't figure out who, though.

An adorable smile took over her face as she continued to peer up at me.

"You're Mia's boyfriend! Greyson, right?" she asked, looking like she already knew the answer to that.

I tilted my head. "Yeah. But who...how..." As soon as I had a light bulb moment, I snapped my fingers and pointed. "You must be Ella." I remembered seeing her face from the window a few days ago.

She nodded excitedly.

"Mia talks a lot about you," I told her, causing her smile to grow to a megawatt grin giving me a full view of her blue braces. I knew when those came off that her smile was going to be even more gorgeous.

I squatted down to her eye level. "Are you on your way to see her?"

"Yes. I know her shift is almost over."

"That's right," I confirmed.

Ella tore her gaze from mine as a frown replaced her smile. "I'm sorry, I crashed into you. I wasn't paying attention. I got a text." She held up her phone and waved it in the air. "And I wanted to take a quick peek at it. By the time I looked up, I had tried to swerve to avoid you, but it was too late. Sorry." She bit her bottom lip guiltily.

I rested my hands on her shoulders and gave them a light squeeze, "Don't worry about it. I'm all good." I smiled, hoping to reassure her.

I watched her eyes examine me for herself like she didn't believe me.

I did the same and stopping at the bloody scrape over her bare knee. Ella was wearing a helmet, elbow pads but only one knee pad. Maybe it wouldn't have been so bad if she was wearing jeans or something, but she had jean shorts that fell just above her knee, offering little to no protection.

"That doesn't look good." I pointed to her injured knee.

Ella tightly closed her eyes. "I'm trying really hard not to think about it because every time my mind regains awareness of it, I think it starts to hurt more." She let out a long sigh. "Of course the day, I think I'll be okay with one less knee pad is the day I get hurt." She opened them, gestured to her leg, and rolled her eyes. "Ridiculous."

I chucked under my breath. "I'm sorry." I grabbed her skateboard. "Can you walk?"

Ella hobbled towards me, twisting up her face. "I think I'm good," she mumbled in obvious pain. "As long as I don't think about it. That's proving to be a lot harder than expected."

I turned and squatted down in front of her. "Hop on," I demanded. I patted my back.

"No, no, no. I'm fine. That's not necessary." Ella stalled.

"I'd feel better if you let me take you to the café to get that bandaged. It's just at the end of the street anyhow."

"You have a point there."

"Yup. Come on," I insisted. "Don't be stubborn."

"I am not stubborn," Ella grumbled, hopping onto my back.

Not even a minute later, I opened the café door when Mia saw us; her eyes widened with panic and concern as she came running over.

"OHMYGOSH, ELLA! What happened? Are you okay?" Mia asked in a rush.

"Yeah, it's just a scrape," Ella replied nonchalantly.

Mia's eyes traveled down to her knee. "That looks like more than a scrape! You could have skinned your whole knee. Why aren't you wearing your knee pads?"

Ella wiggled her opposite leg. "I could only find the one."

"Then, at the very least, you should have worn pants," Mia told her.

That was true.

Ella sighed. "I know, I know."

"If you're done scolding her mom," Ella giggled while Mia narrowed her eyes at me. "I think we should take care of her scrape. You guys have a first aid kit, right?"

Mia took a deep breath, calming herself. "Yes. We have one in the back. Let me go grab it." She hurried down the hall through the employees' only door.

I looked over my shoulder at Ella, who had just gone quiet. "You want me to put you down now?"

I saw her shake her head in my peripheral. "Nah, I kinda like it up here. The view's great." We both cackled.

When Mia returned, we went to an empty table, and I gently placed Ella on top.

Opening the first aid kit, Mia bent down to examine her knee. She drew a sharp breath through her teeth. "So what happened?"

Elle's eyebrows pinched together as she looked at me. I knew she must have been feeling guilty again, but she had no reason to. It was an accident.

"We kind of bumped into each other. It was an accident," I told Mia, and Ella corroborated the story.

"Alright." Mia took out an alcohol swab. Ella cringed, automatically recognizing what it was. "This might sting just a bit." Mia held up her thumb and pointer finger an inch apart.

"Want me to hold your hand?" I said jokingly, but when she gave me a quick nod, I put her hand in mine and gave it a light squeeze. "It'll be quick. Promise." I winked.

Ella still looked uneasy as she removed some of her gear and put them next to her.

"Yup. What he said." Mia slipped on some gloves, cleaned her wound with the pad while Ella hissed, biting her bottom. Mia put the garbage into a paper bag then whipped out an antibiotic ointment and a cotton swab. She glanced at Ella apologetically before gently applying it. Ella looked away, tightly shutting her eyes. When Mia was done, she blew on the wound. "Luckily for you, we had a band-Aid big enough to cover your scrape."

Ella opened one eye, taking a peek at Mia. Mia smiled kindly. "The worst is over," she told her. She ripped open the band-aid and smoothed it on over her knee. "All done."

Ella admired Mia's handy work. "Thank you," she whispered with a sigh of relief.

Mia slipped her gloves off, tossing them into the garbage bag too. "No problem, beautiful." Mia stood up. "We should probably call your parents to come to pick you up. I don't want you to skateboard back home if your knee hurts."

"NO, NO, NO, NO!" Ella shouted in response, making an X with her arms repeatedly. "It's fine. Don't worry about me," she said more calmly.

Mia frowned. "It's definitely not fine."

"I don't want to call them!" Ella blurted out.

Mia looked torn. "Then how about we take you home?" she suggested instead.

We had a little time before I needed to be at Lila's for my gig, so I wouldn't mind dropping her off. I just wanted to make sure she got home safe.

Ella kept trading looks back and forth between the two of us. "Nope. Not necessary," she said.

"There's that stubbornness I was talking about earlier," I mentioned to Ella teasingly.

She pouted. "Listen, guys, I appreciate the offer, but," She was preparing to hop down to her feet. But I stood in her way.

I had an idea. "Okay. I'll make a deal with you freckles."

Her eyebrows furrowed. "Freckles?" she repeated with confusion.

"Yes, freckles." I lightly tapped the tip of her nose, causing her to erupt into giggles. "How about I buy you something to eat, anything you want, and then you'll let us drive you home."

"OH!" Mia said in surprise. "That's a good deal! You better take it quick. I would!"

"I mean..." Ella's eyes softened. "How can I say no to free food?"

Mia busted out with laughter.

"Sounds a lot like somebody I know." I looked to Mia with a smirk.

Mia, without a doubt, would never say no to free food.

✳ ✳ ✳

We spent an extra hour at the café, chatting it up with Ella. This girl was something. Her personality meshed with ours perfectly. Our interests were pretty much the same, minus her love for art. I couldn't draw to save my life, but we both had a creative side and could appreciate how different people liked to express themselves. I never thought I'd have something in common with a 12-year-old, but here I was.

I saw why Ella and Mia got along so well. At one point, I was just listening and watching them converse. They had a connection. I couldn't explain it, but they were probably sisters or something in another life.

I chuckled in my mind at the thought. Only I would think up something like that.

When it was time to go, all three of us walked to the apartment together. I had left the keys for the truck at home. I came back down and found Mia and Ella laughing about something in the lobby. Their laughter died down a bit when they saw me, but they smiled in my direction, and I felt my steps falter.

All I could think about was two sets of practically matching brown eyes staring back at me. My eyes shifted between one and then the other. My teddy bear brown eyes that warmed my heart to the maple syrup ones that held so much light. I got this weird feeling in the pit of my stomach. It wasn't a bad feeling, but I couldn't quite explain it either.

"What's wrong?" They both asked, then exchanged looks with each other as if to say, "Stop reading my mind."

I shook my head. "Nothing. I just had a strange feeling of sorts."

They both looked confused, and a bit worried.

I shook it off and gave them a warm smile. "I'm just weird," I said with a shrug.

"Nothing new there," Mia quipped, making Ella laugh under her breath.

I rolled my eyes. "Anyways." I walked towards them. "Let's get you home, freckles."

Ella lived about 25 minutes away from us. Her neighborhood was nice. It had an old-timey feel considering it was smack dab in one of the historic districts. The houses here were massive, with a decent amount of space between neighbors. Each house had its unique design. Some you could tell had been renovated to look more modern while others have been kept well enough to maintain their old-fashioned charm.

"My house is coming up on your left. The all brick one with the navy blue door," Ella informed me.

I pulled up in front of it, and both mine and Mia's jaw dropped. Now, this was the kind of house I'd buy for Mia and me.

"Ohmygosh! I love your house. If I didn't love my dad, I would ask you to ask your parents to adopt me," Mia jested.

Ella laughed in the back seat, unbuckling herself. "Yeah, we haven't been living here long, but it's been great so far." She opened the door and hopped down to the sidewalk, turning back to grab her gear and board. "Thanks again for the ride, you guys!"

"No problem!" Mia and I both said.

"And good luck tonight, Grey," she told me, picking up the nickname Mia always called me. No complaints here, though. I liked it.

"Thanks. See, I'll see you around."

"Bye!" Ella waved, slamming the door shut. She jogged up the walkway to the front door. We watched her slip a key out of her pocket and unlock it. Opening the door, she turned and gave us a final wave goodbye. We returned it before she went inside.

"She's pretty dang adorable, isn't she?" I said to Mia before driving off.

"I know, right? Those cinnamon eyes can get to anyone."

"Maple syrup," I corrected her.

"What?" Mia asked, laughing.

I got more specific. "Her eyes are the color of maple syrup. Not cinnamon."

"I think they change colors like mine," she said, thinking about it. "But most of the time..." She leaned over to me. "They look cinnamon," she whispered like it was a secret.

I shrugged. "Whatever you say, teddy bear eyes." I winked.

22

Chapter 22

We pulled up at Lila's an hour before the band was supposed to perform. There was a little crowd but nothing major. Mari said it gets packed around 9 p.m. which is precisely why our curtain call was 9:15. She also mentioned how Lila's social media has blown up with news of the band debuting with a new lead singer.

I hoped I didn't disappoint the band's supporters.

I held the door open for the girls and strolled in behind them.

"How have I never been here before?" Freya said, doing a spin, admiring the place. Lila's doesn't look like your typical bar. It was a mixture of edgy and hippie. There were dark simple, and clean colors but also had random crystals and flower pots and greenery hanging all over the place with a few string lights here and there. If anything, it was the perfect mix of the owners' personalities. Hippie being Mari's mom and edgy being her dad.

"Bars aren't usually my scene, but this place looks nice," Freya said.

"I'm glad you like it," Mr. Santiago said, coming out of the kitchen with a tray full of sparkling clean drinking glasses. He rested them on the counter and walked around the bar to greet us.

"Hi, Mr. Santiago." I waved.

He lifted his head. "It's Adrian." He's been trying to get us on a first-name basis since we met. He hasn't been successful.

Mia shook her head. "It took him years to call my dad by his first name, and up to this day, he switches back and forth from Mr. Harper to Wyatt. So don't even bother trying to stop him." Mia made it sound like it was a lost cause. She's right.

Santiago chuckled, shifting his attention to her. "Hi. You must, Mia." He stuck his hand out for a shake.

She smiled beautifully. "Yes. It's nice to meet you, Mr. Santiago." She shook his hand then placed them on Freya's shoulders. She politely introduced the two.

"Adrian." He corrected them when they began to refer to him as Mr. Santiago.

Mia scrunched up her face. "Yeah, That's weird."

"See?" I gestured to Mia as if to say, "my point exactly."

"How about we compromise? Call me Santiago. Everyone at the office does. And it doesn't make me feel as old. Actually," He scratched his beard. "It makes me feel like I still got somewhat of a cool factor going on." He shoved his hands in the pockets of his ripped black jeans and grinned.

"Dad, accept it! You're aging," Mari said, walking up behind us. Santiago's face grew serious as he considered Mari's words.

"Nope. I refuse. What do you guys think?" he asked the three of us.

We took a minute to take in his appearance. The only time you noticed a hint of aging on this man was when he smiled, and you spotted his laugh lines. Other than that, his olive complexion was unblemished and completely wrinkle-free. No doubt it was the strong Latin genes that made him appear immortal. He had on one of his typical everyday outfits, ripped jeans, combat boots, and loose-fitted sleeveless band t-shirts that looked like he's had it for ages now. It seemed Santiago's office attire was more suited for his age than his casual clothes. But to each their own.

"Honestly, I don't think I could guess your age right if I tried. I feel like you look younger than you are." Mia spoke up for all of us while Freya and I agreed.

He wagged his fingers at us. "I like them!" he announced. "Wings and fries are on me tonight, kids."

Freya whooped with excitement. He winked, walking back to the kitchen but not before he mussed up Mari's hair, causing her to squeal and rush to fix it blindly. She smoothed it down with both her hands until she felt satisfied.

"Do I look okay?" she asked us, her eyes frantically traveled from one to the other and then the next.

"Yes. You're gorgeous!" Freya exclaimed. "And your hair is so pretty." Freya's eyes went wide. "How do you get your curls to look so defined? I've had this mop..." She aggressively pointed to her head. "On top of my head since the day I was born, and no matter how much I nourish and love it, it still dares to frizz on me and or go, poof, when it's humid and rainy."

Light laughter flowed from Mari's lips. "It's not easy, that's for sure. And thank you for the compliment. It took me forever to get ready. After I swore, I was so confident with my outfit, on my way out the door. I took one look in the mirror, and I began to question every style choice I'd ever made in my life." She sighed with a pout. "Eventually, I gave up and just threw this on." She pointed at herself with two fingers.

"Oh no. This outfit is perfect. It complements your figure. This is something I would wear if I had your petite frame." Freya replied with a sigh of her own.

"Psh!" Mari flicked her wrist. "Trust me. Your body is something to behold too."

Freya lightened up again and smiled at her. "Thank you."

I cut in. "Mari, this is Freya." I introduced them. "And this Mia." I wrapped an arm around her shoulders.

Mari stood staring speechlessly at her before she blurted out. "WOW! You're so stunning. I think you might have me questioning if I'm playing for the right team." Mari replied, looking her up and down.

"Um, thank you," Mia said bashfully, bowing her head and tucking a loose strand of hair behind her ear.

"You're welcome. I've been excited to meet you both since Greyson." Mari nodded at me. "Can't stop talking about you two." As if on cue, Freya and Mia glance over at me with matching Cheshire cat grins.

"I don't remember saying much about them," I coolly denied it.

Mia playfully elbowed me, seeing right through the lie.

"EVERYONE! EVERYONE!" Dean shouted, entering the bar with his hands up like he was trying to calm a screaming crowd. A few onlookers were briefly amused while the rest of the people just looked confused. He took off his aviators and stuck them in his shirt pocket. "Please, no pictures and autographs. I know you are all dying to see me but try to contain yourselves. There's enough of me to go around." Dean strolled in with Tobias on the left and Tatum on his right.

Tobias was on his phone, not paying any attention to Dean's obnoxious entrance. Tatum, on the other hand, wanting to separate himself from Dean as smoothly as possible, simply sped up to walk around him, pretending they didn't know each other.

"Hey, hey! Where are you going? We're a unit. We walk together." Dean pretended to scold him. Or was he being serious? I couldn't tell. Maybe it was half and half.

Either way, Tatum dismissed him with a flick of his wrist, not bothering to look back. He joined our group of three, and a smile lit up his face when he saw Mari with us.

"How is it that I haven't seen you all day?" Mari asked him, bringing him into a hug.

"You missed me?" he asked playfully, securing his arm around her back. I knew her response would stir up something in him if she said exactly what he was hoping to hear. It was crazy how the tiniest thing people said and or did could have the most heartwarming effects.

Mari rested her head against his chest and shrugged her shoulders. His question remained up in the air. But her actions spoke volumes.

No one uttered a word, afraid to interrupt their moment. Mari gave him one final tight squeeze then released him, slowly easing out of his embrace. When the two noticed they had an audience, Tatum cleared his throat and shoved his hands into his pockets while dramatically taking a step back. On the other hand, Mari averted her gaze from the group as she rocked back and forth on her feet.

"So," Dean said loudly. He would be the first one to speak at a time like this.

Tobias slipped his phone into his front pocket, entirely focused on everything happening around him. He was also the first to introduce himself to the girls.

"Hi Mia," he instantly recognized her and gave her a friendly smile. "I'm Tobias."

"Nice to meet you," she replied.

His eyes shifted from Mia to Freya. "Hi..." he trailed off.

"Hey," Freya said as they continued staring intently at each other.

Dean cleared his throat, chuckling under his breath.

"I'm Freya. I'm their neighbor." she stuck out her hand but kept her eyes on his face. "And their...Um... f-f-friend," she stammered in a daze.

"Nice to meet you," Tobias said but didn't mention his name. Then again, she probably overheard him, so it was no big deal.

Dean eagerly interjected, swinging his arm over Tobias's shoulder. "This is Tobias. Please excuse his odd behavior. He's usually isn't rendered speechless around pretty girls," he said charmingly.

Tobias glared at him, but he was unbothered.

"Anyways, I'm Dean. Nice to meet you, sweetheart." He winked. Then moved on to Mia. "Hi, Mia." He waved. At this point, everybody should know everyone's name without introductions.

"Hey Dean," Mia replied sweetly.

"Random question," his face grew serious. "Do you have any sisters? Preferably older and single?" he smiled, waggling his eyebrows, but it didn't last long because Tobias flicked his ear. Hard.

"Dude, not cool," Dean grumbled. Tobias just smirked.

Mia and I exchanged looks, and I knew she was silently asking me if they were like this all the time, and I nodded.

"Are you guys like telepathically communicating to each other?" Dean asked, pointing his finger back and forth between the two of us.

"Um," Mia began but was at a loss for words.

Dean continued, "Awe, you guys are so cute. Drinks are on me tonight!" He moved around us to throw both arms around our shoulders. "Wait, you guys aren't old enough to drink yet?"

We shook our heads. Mia isn't even old enough to be in the bar yet, but Lila gave her a pass when I asked her for permission to bring her anyways.

"You aren't old enough to drink either!" Santiago snickered, reappearing behind the bar. "Going around trying to give alcohol to minors and prancing around like you own the place."

"I don't prance," Dean said with annoyance.

"Yeah, you're right. But what do you call this." Santiago imitated Dean's walk to the T.

"That's how you walk when you have...wait for it... swagger." He dusted off one of his shoulders.

"And you wonder why you're still single?" Santiago deadpanned, causing all of us to burst out with laughter.

Dean frowned. "Who said I was looking for a girl?" he lifted a single brow, daring him to provide facts.

"The existence of your tinder profile says it all." He fired back without missing a beat.

"OOHHH!" Tobias and Tatum said.

"Shots fired," Mari added.

Dean rolled his eyes. "You're such a hater. You wish you were my age again so you can go sow your wild oats or whatever it is that you old people used to call." He crossed his arms, looking unamused and uncaring.

"Did you just call me old?" Santiago put down the shot glass that he was drying.

"What? I would never do such a thing, old man," he goaded.

Santiago froze. Then in one quick fluid movement, he slammed his hands on the bar top swung his body over the counter, landing perfectly on his feet like some sort of feline.

Dean became a deer in headlights. "You wanna say that again?" Santiago asked, making slow, menacing strides towards Dean.

"Okay, okay, okay." Dean held his arms out, motioning for him to stop.

"I apolo- SIKE!" Dean made a run for it, and Mari's dad chased him.

This was a pretty normal day with these guys.

CHAPTER 23

We were all sitting at a booth in the back. It was one of the few spaces large enough to hold all of us. We had a few drinks, and by "drinks," I meant Sprite mixed with cranberry juice, but it looked kind of fancy with the cherries and pineapple attached to the cocktail umbrellas.

The place was getting packed, and I could overhear everyone talking about our upcoming performance. The DJ, which was Mari's cousin's boyfriend's second cousin or something super long like that. Anyways his name was Kyle, and he came in every once in a while when he wasn't busy with his internship or online classes. I only met him briefly the other day, but he seemed like a cool dude with excellent music taste, I might add.

When Dua Lipa started to play, Mari grabbed Tatum and said that they were going to dance. Tatum, being Tatum, followed her lead. She dragged him to the middle of the dance floor, and at first, it seemed like he was just going to stand there and let her dance circles around him.

Mari whined her waist, then ran a finger down his chest with a smirk, teasing him, trying to get him to dance along.

A slow grin broke out on Tatum's face, and his hands fell to her hips, pulling her into him, and their hips started to sway to the beat.

"My man's got some moves," Dean said, watching tonight's episode of the Mari and Tatum show right along with us.

"No doubt," I replied.

They danced until the end of that song and then into the next. Tatum twirled Mari under his arm, doing one of those double spins that you'd see those ballroom dancers do, before pulling her back into him.

"Awe! I wish I had someone to dance with me." Freya sighed dreamingly.

Tobias gazed at her but turned away when she felt his eyes on her. Mia and I exchanged knowing glances.

Dean straightened up, slamming one of his hands on the table. "Wait, wait! Trouble at 12 o'clock. Some douchebag is trying to cut in." Dean pointed like an angry spectator.

We all whipped our heads around. Sure enough, a fairly tall red-headed guy waved to Mari, trying to get her attention from behind Tatum. When she finally noticed him, she rushed to greet him with a big hug.

Tatum's face crumbled, watching the interaction.

"She knows him?" Mia asked, tugging on my shirt sleeve.

"I wonder if that's the guy she's been going on dates with him?" I asked the guys.

"She never told us what he looked like," Tobias said, taking a sip of his drink.

"For obvious reasons," Dean scoffed.

Freya snorted. "Yeah, and what would those reasons be?" She crossed her arms. "You got something against redheads?"

Dean let out a hearty laugh. "Don't be ridiculous, babe." He took a single strand of her hair and twirled it around his pointer finger. "I love redheads, especially the feisty ones." He winked.

Freya rolled her eyes, slapping his hand away.

Meanwhile, Tobias' face had "unamused" written all over it.

Back on the dancefloor, there was what can only be assumed as a quick introduction followed by a polite dismissal as Mari decided to dance with the other guy instead.

Tatum stalked off to the edge of the dance floor, leaning against one of the support beams. His eyes traveled over to our booth, and we all quickly diverted our attention from the scene, acting as if we weren't watching the whole thing go down.

"Any more drinks, kids?" Santiago said, walking up to the table, collecting our glasses, and putting them on a serving tray.

"No, thank you. Maybe a little later," Mia spoke for us.

"Alright, I'm guessing you guys want the wings and fries later, too?" he asked, now holding up the full tray with one hand.

We all looked to each other for confirmation. "Yes, please," I spoke for the group.

"Alright then." He looked up from us and out to the dance floor. "Have you guys met Brandon yet?" He nodded in Mari's direction.

We all shook our heads.

"This is our first time seeing the guy," Dean said sourly. The guys had wanted to have a little meet-up with him, but Mari had warned them to steer clear because they were still in the early stages of dating, and she didn't want to scare him off.

I guess she wasn't afraid anymore since she invited him here tonight, and he's clearly met her parents already.

"Hmm." Tobias nodded in agreement.

"He seems like an okay guy. You know he's kind of charming, has great posture and a very manly walk. Unlike some people." Santiago coughed into his hand, saying Dean's name.

We all held back our laughter, except Tobias, who loved seeing Dean get ragged on.

Dean's eyes turned into slits. "Anyways, this isn't about me. It's about your daughter dating a guy that doesn't look like her type."

Santiago lowered the tray. "Does Mari have a type?" he countered.

"Yes!..." he paused. "NO!..." Dean went back and forth. "Point is, he doesn't look good for her."

Santiago regarded his words. "It's whatever makes her happy." He shrugged.

"Yeah, but what's he got on my boy Tatum?" Dean fired back.

"Nothing. Brandon might be taller, and he comes off as overly confident, which isn't a horrible thing but still. He has one of those hairlines that indicates he'll go bald at a young age, and it won't look good."

Needing to look for ourselves, we all peeked over at the guy.

Santiago was right.

He went on. "Tatum's better looking in the face. His thick hair will forever be luxurious, thanks to those blessed Latin roots. He also has a calm demeanor. He's not easily unsettled or dissuaded from his goals. I recognize a bit of me in him. Especially the part that could have been hardened and bitter from the shitty life the universe handed them. But instead chose to be the sun after a storm, chasing away every ounce of darkness where there was once no light."

Santiago sighed. "Then again, I'm biased where Tatum is concerned. He's practically like a son to me. But anyways, Mari and

Tatum don't see each other like that. They're like brother and sister, those two."

Either he was blind, or he refused to see what was in front of his eyes.

"See, even right now, he's standing off to the side, being Mr. Protective. He won't let anyone harm her." He smiled, taking comfort from that thought.

"Right..." Dean had drawled out the word. That was the opposite of how we interrupted it but okay.

The second he walked off, Dean said, "That man is completely clueless." He shook his head. "Welp, nothing I can do about that." He pulled out his phone and checked the time. "We have about 15 minutes until we gotta get set up," he informed us.

"Awesome," Tobias said with a decent amount of enthusiasm. "Hey, Freya!" he called over to her. "Dance with me?" he put with a charming grin, holding out his hand to her.

I saw that one coming. They've been making googly eyes at each other since they met. The only question in my mind had been who would make the first move. I'm finding out that Tobias can be a little shy sometimes, and Freya is no better. So kudos to him for making the first move.

"I'd love to," she said, putting her hand in his.

"And then there were three," Dean said, chugging the last bit of his Sprite.

"Actually," I grabbed Mia's hand, sliding out of the booth with her. "Then there was one." I gave him a two-finger salute.

Dean frowned. "Yeah, whatever. Just leave me here all by my lonesome. I'll entertain myself." He looked a little peeved, but he'd have to deal with it.

"Okay, great!" I said, not feeling the least bit guilty for leaving him hanging to dance with my girl.

Mia and I have danced together before, but we weren't a couple then. So this made it our first official dance. I felt a grin break out on my face.

We were just a few feet away from Tobias and Freya, who looked like they were having fun. Freya couldn't dance to save her life, and Tobias, well, he's not fairing much better than she was. But they're laughing about it, so who cared how they looked to everyone else.

I pulled Mia close to me. I brought both of her hands to rest on my shoulders, then I placed my hands on her hips and started to slow dance.

"Umm... Grey?" Mia said, looking around at everyone. "This is far from a slow dance type of song."

"Is it? I didn't notice." I smirked. I also don't care.

"You're just afraid I'll show you up with my sick dance moves," she jested.

"Ha, haha. Funny." She knew I wasn't the greatest dancer. I haven't had much practice, but I was also not a terrible dancer either.

Mia sighed. "Of course, you wouldn't admit it. I mean, can you imagine? Dancing is one of the things that Greyson McNamara doesn't excel in," she teased.

I see what she's doing.

I chuckled half-heartedly under my breath. If Mia wanted me to dance, I'd dance.

I stepped away from her and did my famous shoulder wave, reaching out a hand to her.

There was enough space for her to do her fancy whimsical dance moves she learned from her years of ballet and contemporary dance. Cute.

I remember when Mia used to put on little dance shows for me every time she learned a new routine, and she wanted an audience to tell her how well she did it. I was biased then like I am now. And sometimes Mia needed a partner, so I may or may not have filled in for a time or two. But absolutely no one needed to know that.

The list of things I would do for this girl was endless.

Some of what we're doing goes to the beat of the song. Minutes rolled by, and I've gone from trying to prove a point to Mia to being turned on by the fact that her dance moves went from artsy to sensual and sexy.

My heart was hammering in my chest, and all I could think was... I lightly pulled Mia by her wrist and tugging her up against me. I cupped her face in my hands, then hungrily, I brought my lips to hers.

Mia moaned upon contact, melting into me, and that was all go-ahead needed to move forward.

I was never one for PDA.

Then again, I've never desperately wanted to be with someone like how I've wanted to be with Mia. So if I wanted to kiss her in the middle of a crowded room, I would. She had no idea how crazy she made me, but I was planning to return the favor.

Mia wrapped her arms around my back, hugging me to her as she fisted my shirt. I deepened the kiss, devouring her mouth, getting a taste of the lingering flavor of cranberries on her tongue.

My body was set ablaze, and everything around us faded away. I couldn't feel anything besides Mia's chest brushed against mine, and I couldn't hear anything but her labored breaths between my attacks on her lips.

When Mia's hands loosened their grips, it was as if someone had just thrown a bucket of water on us. Mia slowly began to retreat.

"Why are you holding back?" I whispered in between breaths, taking little nips at her bottom lip.

As much time as we've been spending together, it was almost like nothing had changed between us. Mia never really initiated anything besides a few quick kisses here and there. We played around sometimes, but she ran off or changed the subject when things started to heat up.

We said we'd be all in, but I know she was still keeping a little distance. And I wanted that space gone.

I meant it when I said I was all in for the summer. Or for forever if she'd let me have that. But maybe I had to step my game up.

If Mia needed more proof, I'd show her how serious I was, and I knew exactly how to do that.

"What do you mean?" Mia answered me but didn't answer me.

I shook my head and placed a light kiss on her forehead. This was safe enough not to freak her out. "Never mind. Don't worry about it." I told her, giving her a soft smile.

Her eyes didn't meet mine, which led me to believe that she's got a lot going on in that head of hers right about now.

The music died down, and we heard someone turn on the mic and double tap on it before speaking. "Hey everyone, welcome to Lila's."

Lila was more persistent than Santiago and wouldn't answer when I called her anything else but her first name. Lila stood in front of the mic, waving to the crowd.

"That's Mari's mom?" Mia asked, and I responded with a quick nod.

If you didn't hear her name and connect the dots, you would probably never guess that Lila and Mari were related. Lila's mom had jet black straight hair and silver eyes with an olive complexion. Almost the exact opposite of Mari minus the height factor. They were both petite women. In the looks department, Mari looked a lot like her Santiago.

"For all those who don't know, I'm one of the owners of this fine establishment." She gave a slight bow, and everyone cheered, and I could tell she felt flattered. "I know you all must be excited about Save the Knights' big comeback." The crowd cheered again, causing her to giggle. "Glad to hear it. Boys! Come and get set up!" she said, talking to us.

"I have to go now. Wish me luck?"

Mia tip-toed and kissed my cheek. "Luck," she whispered in my ear. "Give them a show." She winked.

We separated, and I headed around back to meet up with the guys.

"Okay, the gang's all here!" Dean shouted. "Alright..." he stuck his hand out. "Put them in." He wiggled his fingers, waiting for us to make a circle and do some pre-show ritual. "It's either this or we do a group hug," he suggested like it was worse than the first idea.

"I could use a hug," Tatum said with a half-dead shrug.

"If my girl got stolen by Ron Weasley, I'd want a hug too," Tobias said, throwing his arm around his shoulders.

Not the least bit bothered by this bromance, I joined in too, followed by Dean.

"If anybody asks what we do back here, it's definitely not a group hug," Dean muttered, making us all laugh. "Alright." We split apart. Dean's voice got louder as he added some extra bass. "We got this! This is the moment we've been practicing for! Save the knights, get your head in the game!" he shouted.

We all froze.

"Did he just..." Tatum didn't finish.

"I think he did..." I added in shock.

"Dude, that was so lame," Tobias muttered.

"In my defense, High school musical was really motivational back in the day," Dean told us.

"I think I speak for everyone when I say, agree to disagree," I told him. We shook our heads at him with matching looks of concern about his mental state.

"Fine, fine, fine. Let's just have a good show and all that jazz." Dean flitted his hands in the air.

I grinned. "Now, that I think we can do."

24

CHAPTER 24

Watching Grey up on stage reminded me so much of his dad. From the way, he moved to the music to how beautifully he sang.

His dad was the only reason he dared to pick up an instrument. One, he wanted to know if he had passed down his gift, and two, Grey thought that learning to play the guitar would get him a lot of girls when he got older. He wasn't wrong, but it was more than the guitar that had girls swooning at his feet.

For instance, Grey had the whole bad boy vibes going for him. He rode a freakin' motorcycle, for crying out loud, and when it was raining or something, he drove his dad's old Mustang to school.

Then there's the fact he mostly kept to himself with just a few friends, or it might be better to call those people acquaintances since I was sure he probably wouldn't stay in contact with them after this summer. Not everyone Grey met got to know him well. He usually came off as a mystery.

Not to mention, Grey was one of the most brilliant students in the school. That was how he received a full scholarship. But he doesn't go rubbing it into people's faces or anything.

Grey was also really sweet, caring, funny, and talented.

So it was everything. Everything about Grey was alluring. And I was enamored by it all.

Greyson's eyes have been taking time to travel back and forth between the guys and the crowd jamming out to their performance, but in the middle of that, those breathtaking blue eyes always manage to find mine, and the sexiest smirk emerged on his face.

Dang him. I couldn't contain myself when he did that. So I was grinning back with burning red cheeks.

"You two are making me feel awfully single right about now," Freya said, breaking me out of whatever trance Grey had me under.

We're sitting at the bar with Mari and her date. I swiveled in my chair, angling my body towards her.

I gave her an apologetic smile. "I'm sorry," I said.

"It's cool. You'd think I'd be used to it by now. Everyone I know is in a relationship or actively trying to date while I'm... here." Freya sighed, pulling her shoulders up to her ears then dramatically letting them fall.

I look to the stage and see Tobias looking over at us or, more specifically, Freya. They did share a dance earlier, and then they split up without saying much. I had seen Freya walking back to me with the deepest shade of red, spreading across her cheeks and neck. Her face basically matched her hair, and it was hilarious.

I bit my lip holding back my laughter as I replayed the scene in my head.

"So Tobias is pretty cute," I brought him as Freya kept her back towards the stage, swirling the empty glass of sprite Santiago had given her a few minutes ago.

Freya bit her lip and gave me a nervous glance. "I mean, he's okay. I guess," she mumbled before lifting the glass to her lips and swallowing an ice cube.

"Grey talks very highly of him. Actually, the whole group as a whole. They seem pretty cool. And trust me, Grey's not the kind of guy that gets attached to people, but he likes them. "

"Hmm." Freya said, chomping down the cube.

My eyes went to Tobias at the back of the stage to the far right of Tatum. Each of the guys had their own uniqueness. Not just their personality but their looks too.

Tobias was a little bit taller than Greyson. He had chestnut brown hair and these emerald green eyes. I think he liked to dress in mostly black, but he was always sporting white sneakers. Out of all the guys, he was the most serious, and sometimes he looked like he was brooding but honestly, he was super friendly.

Dean's had a nerdy punk look about him, but it suited him. His confidence, though, was another story. He walked around like Brad Pitt. Maybe the blonde hair and icy blue eyes made him feel that way.

Tatum's looks made him stand out most in the group. He had a smooth tan complexion with dark brown almond-shaped eyes. He was the shortest of the group. If I had to take a guess, I would say he was no taller than 5-foot-9. And his sense of style was a little different. He styled his jet-black hair with a side part. He wore blue jeans, black army boots, and a lime green shirt with black writing scribbled on the front. His personality was calm, relaxed, and occasionally reserved, but not in a bad way. If you were to approach him, he'd be friendly no matter what.

Honestly, when I thought about it. I felt like each of them had a specific Grey personality trait which is probably why they got along so well. Especially Tatum, he was very introverted and independent, and then there was the fact that he had a crush on his best friend, who may or may not be clueless.

Sound familiar?

My attention went back to Mari and Brandon. At first glance, I could tell he liked her. But I felt like something was off between them. Mari seemed a little bit more guarded around him. She laughed at all his jokes, but it came off as a forced laugh.

I just met her, but I've heard how she laughed with guys and Tatum, and it was nothing like that. But why put on an act if she wasn't into him? Does she not want to hurt his feelings? Or maybe she's still warming up to him and trying to feel him out slowly.

Maybe I should stop analyzing all the people around me and their relationships when I need to focus on mine.

When Grey and I were dancing, he said that I was holding back. The words had been a shock to me, but they were true. I was holding back. I felt like Grey might be emotionally putting more into this relationship than I was. But that didn't mean I was any less committed.

For Grey, it was like he flipped a switch, and he instantly went into boyfriend mode.

I, on the other hand, was battling through an adjustment period. I've always had these feelings for Grey, but I was so used to keeping them locked up. So paranoid of slipping up and having him find out.

Now he knew all of it, and I couldn't even handle it. I couldn't handle those forehead kisses, the way he grinned at me when we woke up in each other's arms, how he casually checked me out when he knew I was looking straight at him. The list goes on and on.

But long story short, I was silly. I was overthinking every bit of this. I was going to drive myself crazy.

My attention went back to the guys. They had finished playing an instrumental piece, and Grey was back at the mic along with Dean.

I didn't know Dean could sing. I guess he chooses not to.

I recognized the tune as they began to play it. It's "Take what you want" by Post Malone featuring Ozzy Osbourne and Travis Scott. This wasn't the typical song cover for them, but I knew they could pull it off.

Dean sang for the Ozzy bits to start the song, and I have to say I wasn't the least bit disappointed. The crowd had gone silent, though, most likely as mesmerized as I was by them. Grey took over singing Post's parts, and I was screaming "WOOO!" in the back like a total fangirl. Then when Travis's part came up, my brows shot up when Tatum's voice came through the speakers.

Mari gasped next to me, and all I could think was, "Same girl, same."

But what took the song cover to the next level was the electric guitar solo that Dean didn't just nail it. He killed it.

I noticed Freya in my peripheral glance over her shoulder then away again. She chucked up the glass, going in for another ice cube.

I leaned into her. "So, do you want me to pretend that I don't see you taking secret glances at him?" I said.

Freya's eyes went wide, and she stayed silent.

"So I'll take that as a yes," I teased. I gauged her reaction before saying, "I think he was into you." I shrugged nonchalantly.

Freya started to cough, which led to her just outright choking. I leaped out of my seat and began patting her back until she was in control again.

Her gaze went to the stage, probably to see if Tobias had caught any of that. To her horror, he did.

Tobias kept playing the drums effortlessly without any real focus on the music, but his eyebrows had furrowed, and he had this penetrating gaze aimed right at Freya.

Freya stood abruptly. "Excuse me. I'm going to use the restroom."

I nodded. "Okay."

When the song was over, the audience had gone quiet for a few seconds before erupting in cheers.

All four of their faces had matching smug grins.

And I was so proud of them.

25

CHAPTER 25

Everything I've been planning happens today. I just hoped I could pull it off.

"Hey Mia, can I borrow your truck?" I asked her out of nowhere. It was so random that she had jumped from the sound of my voice, nearly dropping her toothbrush in the sink.

"Sure," she mumbled before rinsing out her mouth. She patted her mouth dry with a towel. "What do you have planned for today?" she asked curiously.

I had already come up with the best excuse, and since the guys are in on it, this lie is perfect. "The guys and I are going to go shopping for some new equipment. I figured it would be best to take the truck since it has all the trunk space."

Mia nodded with no hint of suspicion. "Okay, cool." She turned back to the mirror to twist her hair into a bun.

I stood by the door, watching her going through the motions of her morning routine.

Mia turned to me when she saw that I hadn't moved. Her eyebrows drew together. "Is there something else?"

I shook my head. "Nope. Nope. No, nothing at all." Great. It's not like that sounded fishy or anything. I added a smile for good measure.

"Okay, then." Her eyes shifted from mine then landed on the ground. "So um... Do you mind... you know, leaving?" She toyed with the hem of her oversized t-shirt, swaying her body from side to side.

"I thought we were past that." A stepped inside. "Last week when you had to pee, didn't you come barging in when I was in the shower to use the toilet?"

"That was an emergency! And I told you I didn't peek!" Mia murmured, biting down on her bottom lip.

I smirked. "I wouldn't have minded if you had, sweetheart." I winked. Now her cheeks were beet red. I ran the back of my hand down them, feeling the warmth radiate off of it. "Plus, you've gotten more than a peek at me last summer." I grinned, thinking back to the time we lost our virginities.

Mia tightly shut her eyes. "Whatever," she grumbled, throwing her head back. I knew she probably wished for a subject change—typical Mia.

I chuckled. I leaned forward and kissed her forehead. "I can drop you off at work today if you'd like."

She shook her head. "It's fine. Freya and I are working the same shift, so we've agreed to walk over together. But thanks, though."

My lips tipped up into a smile. "Anything for you."

Mia crossed her arms. "Anything?" she challenged. "Then how about some privacy?" She nodded towards the door, telling me to beat it.

I rolled my eyes. "I walked into that one," I mumbled.

"Totally," she grinned.

As soon as Mia left, it was go time. I rushed to throw on some clothes and then headed out the door to the guys' apartment.

When I pulled at the corner, Tatum was outside with Mari, who liked she was running off somewhere.

I opened the car door. "Morning, guys!" I said to them with a solitary wave.

"Hey, Greyson!" Mari replied first.

"Morning Grey," Tatum said after her.

"What's up?" I asked the two of them, heading in their direction.

"I have a lunch date, and Tatum was just walking me out." She smiled while he frowned.

There's a story there. "Oookay. Well, have fun."

"Why, thank you. I plan to have a lot of fun." She directed the last word at Tatum. Then she winked at us before turning on her heels and walking off.

"What was that about?" I asked him.

He shrugged. "Mari being Mari," he mumbled.

I knew by that response that he didn't want to talk about it. "So, are the guys ready?"

I saw the basement door open down the hall behind him. "YO! Grey is here." Dean waved.

"Hey, man," Tobias said, coming up behind him. "The gang's all here."

"Cool. I think I'll need all the help I can get," I replied.

"We are at your service." Dean saluted.

We unloaded all the new furniture I bought for the balcony and multiple grocery bags three hours later.

"Thank god this stuff is light," Dean said as he and Tobias continued to haul the patio chairs in together.

"Yes, I can imagine weaklings like yourself would have a hard time lifting anything heavier," Tobias replied with a smirk that Dean couldn't see.

Dean scoffed. "Keep saying stuff like that, and you'll have to find a new roommate." It was an empty threat on his part. Everyone knew that from the moment the words left his lips.

"Psh! Like that would be a bad thing," Tobias said smoothly. I didn't know what Dean did this morning to have Tobias poke fun at him all day, but I can't say I wasn't entertained by it.

They walked through the living room and out to the balcony, placing the chairs on opposite sides of the table.

Dean took on a defensive stance, crossing his arms. "If that's how you really feel, I'll go move in with Tatum!"

"No thanks!" Tatum shouted from the kitchen, where he was helping me unpack. "Dean is an absolute slob. He doesn't dry his feet when he gets out of the shower and leaves his wet towels all over the bathroom floor." Tatum shivered with disgust. "Gross. I mean, there are towel racks for a reason." He had a point. Leaving wet towels on the floor was like scattering dirty clothes everywhere in your bedroom. The chaos in all that disorganization would drive me crazy.

I chuckled.

Tobias usually joked about Tatum having OCD, but Tatum had never denied it, and I could see why. His apartment was immaculate, and he was a slight germophobe. He'd only take it easy on you if you're a part of his close circle. Maybe even then, he'd still get on your case about certain things, but not like how he would be completely disgusted by a random stranger's unhygienic habits.

"Looks like you're going to be homeless." A pleased grin appeared on Tobias' face, and he scratched the light stubble on his chin. "Whatever will I do without you?" He sighed as if the thought of having the apartment to himself would make him feel lonely.

Dean stayed silent for a few seconds. "Never mind," he piped up. "It sounds like you'll miss me, so I'll just stay." Dean gave him a pat on the back.

"You guys argue like a married couple," Tatum remarked.

"Disagree." They both responded at once then exchanged looks of annoyance.

Laughter filled the room. "Well, at least that's one of the things they can agree on," I said to Tatum.

I spent the next hour hanging up lanterns and fairy lights and meticulously placing the potted plants I bought around the house and the balcony with some assistance.

The guys and I stepped back to admire our work. "Well, I think our job here is done," Tobias said.

"I don't mean to brag..." Dean began.

Tatum interjected. "Yes, you do."

Dean wouldn't pass up any opportunity to brag. "Okay, maybe just a little bit. But anyway, I think we did good." The four of us took turns grinning at each other. "If this whole music thing doesn't work out..."

"That's why we're in college," Tobias cut in with that reminder.

He stepped out front of us and placed his hands on his hips. "But if that somehow doesn't work out either, we might have a shot at interior design for HGTV," Dean finished.

We all belted out with laughter.

"Nobody ever takes me seriously around here," he muttered. He hung his head, forcing his blonde hair to shade his eyes.

Tatum sighed. "Always the drama queen."

"Moving on from Dean." I saw his head snap up in my peripheral. "I wanted to thank you guys again. I owe you all big time."

Other than Mia, I didn't think I'd ever had friends like these guys. I grew up a loner, only making polite conversation when I had to. I always felt like everyone wanted to be friends with me because my dad was a famous rock star. And after he died, the attention on me died with him. I saw who genuinely wanted to be there for me and who couldn't bother.

It wasn't until middle school or maybe high school when I attempted to branch out and talk to some other people that weren't Mia. Did it work out well? Not really. I was a little too private to let people in. But these guys, it felt different.

"Don't mention it." Tatum held up a fist, and I bumped it. "We're a team. There's nothing we can't do together. So if you need us, we're there." He gave me a swift nod.

"Yeah, what he said." Tobias agreed.

I drove them back to their apartment after that and hurried back home to meet up with Freya. She was also in on this brilliant plan of mine and couldn't have been more excited to help me.

I had been waiting for the elevator when Freya popped into the lobby. "Greyson!" She came barreling through the doors with one hand holding a box of desserts from the café, and the next had a death grip on these balloons.

I rushed over to help her. "You really went all out." I looked at the array of balloons.

This was more than I expected, but I'm not complaining.

"Only the best for our Mia," she replied.

I took the box of pastries out of her hand as we entered the elevator.

"Did you set up everything already?" Freya asked eagerly.

"Yup. The guys helped me out. I think we did a pretty decent job."

She turned to me. "Can I see it?" she said in a rush.

"Of course!"

I opened the door to my apartment and gestured for Freya to step in first. She politely kicked her shoes off then put them on the shoe rack.

I watched her walk into the room then waited for the reaction I was hoping she would have.

Her eyes widened, and she gasped, covering her mouth with her hands. "OHMYGOD! SHE GOING TO LOVE THIS!"

I broke out into a grin. YES!

"Greyson, you guys seriously did a great job. This boyfriend of the year worthy."

I chuckled. "Exactly what I was aiming for. This should earn me more than enough brownie points." I joked. I placed the pastries on the dining table. "Now, I have to get started on dinner. It should be ready by the time she gets home."

"You're cooking too?" Freya sounded surprised.

"Yup. Some of her favorites. By the way, how much do I owe for the pastries and balloons?"

Freya folded her arms across her chest. "They're on the house," she said kindly but took on a firm stance. She wanted me to know that she wasn't going to accept any form of monetary payment.

I figured she would say that, so I came prepared. I picked up the bouquet of orange and yellow Chrysanthemums and held them out to her. "They're a thank you for helping me. And for being a good friend to Mia. And me." Freya looked at me, then flowers, and then repeated the action. "A little birdie told me they're your favorite."

She slowly lifted the bouquet out of my hands and smelled them. "Tobias?" she guessed correctly.

"I'm not at liberty to give away my sources," I repeated the ever so popular line from any secret agent.

She beamed up at me. "It's okay. It was good intel."

"I'm glad."

Freya hugged the flowers to her. "Okay, let me get out of here so you can get to it." She walked to the front and slipped back on her shoes. "I would tell you to tell me how it all works out, but I'm sure I'll hear it from Mia tomorrow." She gave me a knowing smirk.

Grinning, I said. "Hopefully, she'll keep some details between us."

Freya's mouth formed an O. "Oh, scandalous!" She giggled with a little shoulder shimmy.

"Only if I'm lucky. See ya' Freya!" I called out, watching her close the door behind her.

I strolled into the kitchen. I had about two hours to wow my girl.

And I didn't plan on failing.

26

CHAPTER 26

If I didn't know any better, I'd say today was "act weird around Mia" day.

Grey was acting strange, and I've tried to text him throughout the day, saying that I was just checking in. He kept giving me those one-word responses, and it was annoying the crap out of me.

I had to take a deep breath.

Not to mention, Freya was on her phone all day too. She usually left it in the office when she worked, but she kept checking it like a crazy woman today. At one point, she disappeared, and I caught her in the bathroom texting and laughing.

I quietly stepped back out, pretending I hadn't seen anything, and just got back to work.

Two hours before my shift was supposed to be over, I saw Freya packing a box of pastries, but I didn't remember us getting an order in for something like that.

When I asked her who it was for, she said she was doing a favor for a friend and needed to deliver them.

Then thirty minutes before my shift was over, Grey texted me and said that I should let him know when I was on my way home.

That was probably the longest sentence he had sent to me all day. So you could imagine how peeved I was with him.

Regardless, I tried not to be petty and texted him back.

I power-walked home in less than five minutes. Instead of knocking at the door, I pulled out my keys and let myself in.

First thing, my nose was bombarded with the smell of garlic and rosemary chicken, stuffing, yellow rice, and for whatever odd reason, I could smell the scent of vanilla as well.

The second thing, other than the sunset, there were some warm lights towards the living room at the end of the hallway.

I kicked my shoes off and hurried forward.

Grey stepped out into the hall from the kitchen, stopping me in my tracks. He grinned, "I thought I heard you come in." He placed a kiss on my forehead. He lowered his voice, "I have a surprise for you. But you have to close your eyes. Okay?"

I silently dipped my head into a nod and then closed my eyes.

I felt Grey take hold of my hands, gently tugging me along.

"Keep your eyes closed. No peeking." He warned me.

"Okay," I said softly.

I heard a few clicks somewhere off into the distance. And where I had only seen darkness behind my eyelids, I knew there was now light.

What was going on?

I felt Grey's arms wrap around my waist from behind. He kissed my cheek, "Open them," he whispered in my ear.

They fluttered open, and my jaw dropped soon after. My eyes danced around the room, not knowing what to look at first.

The wall behind our couch was covered in a curtain of strings lights. There were plants everywhere, making the room look like a botanical garden, peaceful and serene.

But the real eye-catcher was the balcony.

"You wanna take a closer look?"

I nodded and felt my legs moving before my brain could give them the signal. Grey reached out in front of me and pulled the French doors wide open.

I gasped. Some more string lights were hanging from the railing with some paper lanterns. More potted plants at the end of one side and in the middle were the cutest pieces of outdoor furniture set I'd ever seen.

They were two wicker chairs with grey cushions placed side by side, and across from them was the matching love seat with a decent-sized frosted glass square table, separating the two of them. A bouquet of tulips was resting on the table with two vanilla candles on both sides.

It took me a few seconds to notice, but both corners of the balcony had a lit candle.

This was so dreamy.

"Greyson, what is all of this?" I turned to find him, leaning against the wall with one shoulder.

Grey broke out into a handsome grin. "Our first official date, of course. I wanted to do something special for you." He stepped forward and cradled my face in his hands. I gazed into his magnetic blue eyes. "Just because we agreed to date for the summer doesn't mean I still can't try to win you over. Now that I have you, you're mine. I want to keep you. I want to do things like this for you all the time. I want to show you what you mean to me." He kissed my lips, dragging a sharp gasp from me as soon as he pulled away.

I glanced at the lights and array of candles illuminating every gorgeous and breathtaking feature of his face. "This is too much," I murmured. I was overwhelmed but in the best way.

No one had ever done anything like this for me. That much was obvious. I'd say barely dated, and the one guy I did, not only did he turn out to be a cheating scumbag, he would have never bothered to do something like this. We barely went out on dates like the movies or dinner. Most of the time, we were cooped up at his place ordering take-out and doing the whole Netflix thing but without the chilling bit.

Dropping his hands to my hips, Grey rested his forehead against mine. "You're wrong. It's not enough, but when I'm able to do more. I'm going to give you everything," he said with conviction.

I didn't need to hear anymore. I wrapped my arms around my neck and brought him down to me for a slow, toe-curling, and ultimately mind-blowing kiss.

"Thank you," I murmured breathlessly.

"You're welcome. Now, are you hungry? I made all of your favorites." The corner of his lip tips up into a smirk.

I licked my lips, thinking about the savory dishes that we were about to devour. "Of course!"

We shared out our plates of food, grabbed some drinks then ate out on the balcony. We chatted in-between bites. Everything was as delicious as it smelled, and my tummy was completely happy.

Halfway through the date, I had to apologize to Grey. He couldn't understand why in the beginning, but I was feeling like an idiot. He had been planning this whole date for us while I was getting upset about him being too busy to chat with me.

Naturally, he laughed at me. I swore you could hear it echoing through the semi noisy streets.

"I promise, I didn't mean to. I was busy shopping for everything then hauling it all upstairs." Grey shook his head. "It would have taken me a lot longer if I didn't have the guys helping me. They're lifesavers."

I smiled. "I should thank them. They're beyond awesome." I leaned forward to rest my empty plate on the table.

"I have to agree. But I probably wouldn't say that to their faces. Especially not Dean's."

We belted out with laughter.

"Oh no! The last thing he needs is another ego booster."

"Right." Grey chuckled under his breath. "I knew you would all get along." He took a sip of his cherry coke.

"Of course! I swear they're each like three different versions of your personality," I told him.

Grey lurched forward, covering his mouth with one hand, trying his best not to let the soda go spewing from his lips. I watched his shoulder tremble with the laughter he had forced to keep in. I patiently waited for him to swallow.

"I mean, it's no wonder why you all get along. I'd go as far as to say, those guys are your soulmates but in a friendly way, of course," I added.

Grey scrunched up his face like he wanted to disagree, but he knew he would only be lying to himself.

"I repeat..." I held my hands up, emphasizing for him to chill. "In a friendly way. That's not weird."

"Totally weird."

"Fine. I'll take it back," I mumbled.

Grey smiled with amusement twinkling in his eyes. He loved it when he got his way.

"Anyways, I'm glad you like them." He paused for a second, and I just knew he had something more to say. "I always feel like it's been you and me forever. Whoever I let in my life, I automatically assume they're going to be in yours, so I'm always hesitant about who I let get close to me. To us. I know that I wouldn't let anyone who didn't like you anywhere near you because I'm afraid they would try to hurt you. I guess you can say I'm a little overprotective, but I can't help it."

Grey's forearms landed on the top of his thighs. He hung his head slightly, almost as if he was trying to shield his eyes from my gaze. "Mia, you've been there before all the new people, and you've been there after they've left. It's safe to say you're one of the only constants in my life, and I never want to let anything jeopardize that. If anyone were ever to hurt you, they'd have to deal with me. "

I got up, walking around the table to sit next to him on the love seat. I took his hand in mine and squeezed it.

Grey brought my hands to his lips, pressing a kiss to my knuckles. A trail of goosebumps broke out along my arm.

"We've always been in this together." I rested my head on his shoulder. We fell into this comfortable silence.

A light breeze came and carried the delicious scent of vanilla up to my nose again.

"Hmmm. Is it possible for a candle to make you crave sweets just from the smell?"

Grey laughed. "It's a good thing that I have a box of desserts waiting for you inside."

I lifted my head. "Wait, what?"

"Yeah, I had put in an order in with Freya. She was in on this too." He gave me a smug grin.

I had a light bulb moment. This explained everything.

"OH, so you just recruited everybody."

With a firm nod, Grey said, "It was a secret mission. Needed the whole crew."

I kissed his cheek. "Thank you again. I love everything about this. Not only the fact that you did it for our first date, but I love that this was something you thoughtfully added to our home. We will be able to use this again and again. Like this might be my new fave hangout spot this summer."

"Mine too." Grey smiled.

Before we went in, we blew out the candles, grabbed the plates, trash and then flicked off the lights.

I already couldn't wait for tomorrow night when I could turn them back on and be in awe all over again.

We placed the dishes in the sink, promising to deal with them in the morning, and I rushed over to the dessert box sitting on the dining table. Eyeing the array of sweets, my hands reached for this cheery cheese Danish first, and I took a monstrous bite out of it.

"Ohmygod! It's so good," I exclaimed. My taste buds were delighted.

Greyson walked over to where I was sitting, then he leaned forward like he was going to kiss me, but last minute he diverted his head and took a huge bite of my Danish.

"Hey," I squealed, playfully shoving him away. He chuckled shamelessly. "Bold of you to assume I wanted to share with you." I teased him, taking a few more bites for myself.

Grey grabbed the front of the chair and dragged it. It screeched loudly as he pulled me right up in front of him. He leaned forward, and I leaned as far back as the chair would allow. "You know the Danish isn't the only thing I want a taste of, Mia." He winked, and I could feel my cheeks heating up.

"You're incorrigible," I muttered.

"You like it."

"I never said anything like that," I countered, narrowing my eyes at him.

"Doesn't mean it's not true. You're probably too afraid to admit it." Grey challenged.

Was I going to play this game with him right now?

Grey quirked a brow, waiting for a response. I scarfed down the rest of the Danish. "I...I... I'm going in the shower!" I announced and smoothly slid out of the seat while making a run for the bathroom.

I slammed the door shut behind me and tried to calm my rapidly beating heart. I was such a coward, but he knew that.

I was going to lose no matter what I did or said.

Twenty minutes later, I was grabbing my fluffy robe from the hook behind the bathroom door and sliding it on. I quietly peeked out the door, keeping an eye out for Grey.

With the coast clear, I hurried off to my room, where I froze in my doorway. The surprises just kept on coming. There were balloons everywhere. My favorite kind too, the big clear ones with the confetti inside them. I threw a hand over my heart when I found two glass vases filled with the most enormous bouquets of tulips, lilies, and roses.

I felt Grey's arm drape around my neck like scarf. Instinctively, I leaned into him, covering his hands with mine.

He whispered in my ear, "Do you like it?"

"I love it," I whispered back with awe.

"And today is just the beginning." Grey gave me a light squeeze. "I'm going to take a quick shower. Meet me in my room in 10?"

I nodded speechlessly, causing him to chuckle. He kissed my temple then he was gone, closing the door behind him.

I let out a soft sigh which did nothing to calm my heart.

I was in my PJs long after I heard the shower start, and then I headed over to Grey's room.

Grey's guitar was lying on the bed, and he had a notebook left open with a pencil stuck between the pages and scattered music sheets all around it.

Was he writing music?

I crawled onto the bed, examining the notebook.

Sure enough, there were song lyrics. But there wasn't only one. So this isn't something he just started doing. This book was already partially complete.

I turned to the last page and checked the date up top. There was a song he started to write today.

I read a few lines out loud.

"I think my heart always knew,

Everything in my life revolved around you.

And I've been waiting for the day when you looked at me the same way like..."

The notebook was snatched out of my hands.

"HEY!" I scrambled to my knees, reaching up to steal it back, but Grey held it up and away from me.

Damn him and his very long muscular arms.

"I was reading that!" I shouted, still trying in vain to get that book like my life depended on it.

"Too bad." Grey walked off, placing the book on his dresser.

I slumped back into bed, crossing my arms against my chest. "I didn't know you wrote songs."

"It was a secret," he mumbled.

"Since when did we keep secrets?" I shouldn't be the one to ask this kind of question, but I was anyways.

Grey smirked. "I think we've both kept our fair share of little secrets from each other."

"Like?"

"Like the fact that you were always head over heels for me, your smoking hot and wildly talented best friend." He gave me a smug grin.

I scoffed. "Yeah, right." I rolled my eyes.

I couldn't believe this guy just called himself smoking hot. I snorted.

But then my eyes drifted to his bare chest, and I bit my bottom lip. Couldn't he throw on a shirt? I wanted my eyes to look elsewhere, but instead, they made their way down to his briefs.

Grey was wearing nicely fitted boxer briefs. This was a rare occasion. From the side, his butt looked so toned and... Get your mind out of the gutter Mia! I slammed my eyes shut, cursing myself.

While I knew there was nothing wrong with checking out my boyfriend. I was still slightly embarrassed by the thoughts of him that had invaded my mind.

I opened an eye, expecting him to be enjoying the little show I was making.

With that smirk that might as well be a permanent fixture on his handsome face, Grey gathered the rest of the music sheets along with his guitar.

"Will you play it for me when it's done?" I said, putting my focus back where I wanted it.

I wanted to hear the complete song. I knew it was going to be beautiful.

I noticed the moment his body stiffened at the idea, and he hesitated with his response. "I don't know."

"I'd love to hear," I added some encouragement.

"It's probably not that good." I've never heard Grey so unsure about something.

"It sounded pretty good to me. Especially since I think you wrote it about this amazing girl." I put my face in both palms and fluttered my eyelashes.

I spotted a bit of color creeping up onto Grey's cheeks. He angled his face away from my view. He was totally blushing. Cute.

"Someone might have inspired me," he muttered like it was no big deal.

"I'll have you know that someone is extremely flattered." I smiled, fluttering my lashes.

Grey's gaze met mine as he began to take slow, purposeful strides back to me. He kneeled onto the bed, and his hands gently caressed my face. Did I mention how much I loved when he did this? He cradled my face like I was the most precious thing in his life. Silly, right?

"Mia," Grey said my name with a long exhale. Closing his eyes, he rested his forehead against mine. "I promise to spend my life making sure you always feel like that." He declared.

I pressed my lips to his without warning. It wasn't a long kiss, I didn't let it escalate to all the places I wanted it to, but I did pour my heart into it. And I hoped Grey felt that too.

"Thank you," I said, pulling back slow enough to sense the electricity in the atmosphere between us.

Grey brought his lips back to mine more forcefully, and I moaned upon impact. "You're welcome," he said.

We both broke out into matching grins.

Grey climbed into bed next to me and pulled the covers back. I wiggled under it. Then when he extended his arm, an open invitation to cuddle up to him, I happily took it. He curled his arm around me. Resting his hand on my hip, he swooshed me up against him. I heard him lightly yawn before he said, "Good night," he mumbled sleepily, kissing the top of my head.

"Night, Grey."

He dozed off before I could. Planning and preparing for this day had made him exhausted.

I shifted my head on his shoulder, angling my face so I could see his.

And I mouthed the words I was too chicken to say out loud. Or even while Grey was awake.

I love you.

I gently pressed one final kiss to his lips before I felt eyelids flutter, then eventually close.

27

── ◆ ──

CHAPTER 27

"**A**dmit it! You're going to miss me," Grey said, securing his arms around my waist.

"I will admit no such thing," I told him. My arms were hanging limply at my sides because we'd been standing in the same position for five minutes. This started as a sweet hug goodbye but then turned into this. Me, not bothering to escape Grey and his antics.

"But I'm going to miss you," he muttered sadly.

I was two seconds away from actually falling for that.

"Yeah, well, who wouldn't miss me?" I replied, earning myself a very predictable reaction.

Grey snickered and stepped back away from me. "You can't humor me for a minute?"

I scrunched up my nose at him and stuck out my tongue. "Let's be honest. Whether I was serious or not, the minute you hear that I might potentially miss you, you'll get a big head about it and throw it in my face the entire time you're away." I crossed my arms. "Now hurry up. I don't want you to be late. The guys are probably waiting for you." I handed him my truck keys.

Two days ago, Grey and the guys got a call from an old friend of Lila's. They asked if they could play at their rehearsal dinner and wedding reception. Their band had quit last minute, and they thought the guys would be a great replacement.

The guys didn't have anything else planned for those days, and the location was within a reasonable driving distance, only five hours away. Also, they made them an offer they couldn't refuse. It's easily one of the biggest paydays for the band.

Supposedly, the happy couple was loaded, and I wasn't surprised. Santiago and Lila were pretty well off too. By the way, Santiago, Lila, and Mari will also be there while one of the managers holds the fort back at the bar. They asked me if I wanted to tag along, but I declined.

This would be the first guys' trip that Grey had been on. I was not counting all those times he and my dad hung out and went fishing by the lake. So I think it would be good for him and the guys to bond. I mean, they're practically four peas in a pod at this point but still. I wanted him to enjoy this and experience the whole band thing.

"Fine. Gimme a kiss for the road, and I'll leave." Grey lowered his head, and I stood on my tippy toes to meet him halfway.

Once our lips touched, I melted into him, savoring every second of it.

I parted my lips giving him access and our tongues collided. He tasted like Cinnabon and espresso. I wrapped my arms around his shoulders.

Grey grabbed my hips, pulling me to him and effectively eliminating the tiny space between us. Good.

I didn't know how I managed to ignore the fire between us for as long as I did.

Everything about this kiss, the way Grey's tongue hungrily chased after mine one minute, then how he expertly took nips at my bottom lip the next, I was in an absolute state of bliss.

He released a deep sexy groan, and my thoughts went to the dirtiest place.

I broke away first, but it took me a minute to gain some composure before I slowly blinked my eyes open.

I watched a slow, smug grin take over Grey's features.

"Yeah, you're totally going to miss me." He winked.

See! That right there was what I was talking about.

"Whatever." I rolled my eyes. I said the first thing that came to mind, desperately needing a subject change. "Anyways, I want updates. Call me when you get there and check in to your hotel. And please drive safe. We have one car since someone wanted to be impractical and ride a motorcycle around," I teased.

"That's a lot of instructions from someone who says they're not going to miss me."

I gave in and finally muttered the words he wanted to hear.

Grey cupped one of his ears. "I'm sorry. What was that?" he asked obnoxiously.

I repeated it louder. "I guess I'll miss you just a teeny bit." With my pointer finger and thumb, I measured a centimeter to express how little I would miss him.

Of course, I was going to miss him way more than that.

He chuckled. "You know what, I'll take it." He swept me off my feet, and I planted another kiss on his lips. "Are you sure you're okay with this? I mean, it's too late for me to back out now, but if you were lying, I'd at least like to know the truth."

I interlocked my hands at the back of his neck. "Let's say for the sake of argument that I was lying. What would you do?"

"Unpack my bags and stay home with you, of course," Grey said with a straight face, and I knew he meant it.

I shook my head.

"Is that how you feel?" he rushed on. "You want me to stay?" His eyebrows scrunched together, and a slight frown tugged on his lips.

"No. I'll miss you like crazy, but I want you to go out and do this. You've loved spending time with the guys. Out of all your hobbies, I've never seen you dedicate so much time to something like how you have been with playing music."

While working, Grey was with the band practicing most of the time. He tried to come home before me, or he picked me up from work so we could spend the rest of the day together. But even at home, Grey had his guitar nearby. When he suddenly got inspiration, he grabbed his notebook and started strumming a few chords.

I've been begging Grey to play me that song he wrote, but he continued to insist that it wasn't finished yet.

I didn't believe him, but okay.

"You're wonderful, you know that?" he said in awe.

I laughed nervously because that was an unexpected compliment. And let's be honest, my heart still got swoony when Grey said these things.

"I mean it, Mia." He stared deeply into my eyes. "I know this summer is supposed to be about us, and I don't want to lose focus of that. I want to spend as much time as we can together together."

I palmed his cheek. "Don't worry about it. We have all the time in the world. I want you to do this, and I need you to know that I'll be cheering you on the entire way."

I earned myself another kiss, and I was downright giddy about it.

"Okay. That makes me feel a lot better." He placed me on my feet. "I can ditch you now and go have the time of my life," he joked.

"Yeah yeah, whatever," I grumbled.

Grey's phone started to ring, and he dived into his pocket for it.

"Hey, Dean... Yeah, man... I'm on my way... No problem...Cool... Bye." He pocketed his phone. "Dean says to tell you you're an angel, and the guys can't thank you enough for letting us borrow the truck."

I waved it off. "It's cool. Anything for my favorite band." I winked.

Grey grabbed his guitar case and duffle bag. "Okay, I'm leaving right now," he said, walking backward.

I nodded slowly.

"I'll be gone for like three days. Away. From my girlfriend." He pouted, and I was sure my face matched his in every way.

I ran to hug him. He dropped everything and wrapped me in his arms.

"Why are you making this so hard?" I whispered.

"Because it feels like I'm leaving my whole heart behind," he replied instantly.

"I'll be one phone call away. Most importantly, I'll be right here waiting for you when you get back." I pulled away from him to show him my very reassuring smile.

Grey smoothed back my hair with one hand and then kissed on the top of my head.

"Alright. I'm leaving for real now."

"Okay," I said.

"So, um, Mia, you know you have to let me go, right?"

I pouted, but he couldn't see it. "Hold on, let me get my fill."

He chuckled.

"Okay, okay." I reluctantly released him. "Hurry up and go," I ordered. I shooed him in the direction of the front door. "And hurry and come back," I mumbled the last line, jutting out my bottom lip.

"Will do. I'll see you soon."

I waved, watching him pick up his bags and finally head out the door.

28

CHAPTER 28

Ella was at the café today and had to admit I missed seeing her face these past few days.

"Hey, beautiful," I said as she walked in.

A grin broke out on her face. "Hi, Mia!" She waved excitedly before walking over to the empty counter.

"How's the knee, kiddo?" I asked. She scraped it up a couple of days ago when she crashed into Grey on her skateboard.

She looked down at her exposed knee, which was still sporting a bandage, and shrugged. "It's not too bad. Healing pretty well for the most part."

I nodded. "That's good. What did your parents say about it?" I noticed she didn't come in here with her skateboard today.

Ella paused and diverted her eyes from mine. "Um, Nothing." She tucked a strand of hair behind her ear. "My mom was kind of worried, and my dad doesn't like to see me get hurt. So I'm sure he was thinking about either placing me in a plastic bubble for the rest of my life or just locking in me the house period altogether." She sighed. "Glad, he came to his senses though because I would have rioted."

I laughed. "You don't strike me as the rebellious type," I told her.

She smiled. "I'm not. Up until the other day, I barely left the house. I still feel out of my element here. I miss South Korea, but the US is growing on me. And I've met some great people here too."

"I'm glad. You already know I haven't left the continent, but I can imagine the culture shock you must feel sometimes." I had visited Montreal with my dad a few years ago, and just being in a city that mainly spoke a different language was my version of culture shock.

"Yeah. I'm sure I'll get used to it eventually," Ella said optimistically.

"What about your sister?" I asked randomly.

Something flashed across her eyes before she quickly masked it. "Hmm?"

"Is she transitioning okay?" I asked randomly. I knew Ella didn't talk about her sister much, and it sucked that she doesn't have her to lean on when they're on this new journey together.

Ella swayed her shoulders. "I think so."

"Oh, okay."

It was silent for a few beats, and I took the blame for that.

"So um, I wanted to stop by and ask you something." Ella bit the corner of her bottom lip anxiously.

I leaned forward, resting my forearms on the counter. "Sure, what's up?"

"So my birthday is tomorrow..."

I smiled but didn't interrupt her.

"And I know you have the day off. So I was wondering if you wanted to hang out at the arcade tomorrow with me?" Her features pinched together as if she was bracing herself to hear me reject her.

"I would love to."

Her eyes widened, and she clapped her hand together. "Really? Like seriously? You don't mind?" She rushed to say. She almost looked like she was in a state of disbelief.

I didn't know why when it was no secret that I loved spending time with her.

I shook my head. "Of course not. I love arcades. But what about your family? Are they going to be there or..."

She cut me off. "My mom is flying in from overseas tomorrow afternoon. My dad is working most of the day, but he took the night off for me. He said it's alright if I want to go out and hang out with friends until we have dinner in the evening. He's cooking all my favorite Korean dishes, and he's also setting up one of those huge blow-up projectors in the backyard so we can watch Transformers." She made her hands into fists and shook them. "I'm so excited!"

"I can tell." I laughed. "Alright then. You, me, arcade tomorrow." I held up my hand for her to high five, effectively cementing our plans.

Ella slapped it enthusiastically.

"Here! Give me your number." She handed me her cellphone from her back pocket.

I put my number in then called myself so that I could get hers too.

"Thanks, Mia," she said sweetly.

"No problem." I winked. "So were you planning to leave after giving me that invite, or did you want to do something sweet?" I whispered the last few words conspiratorially.

Ella cupped her mouth with one hand and said, "I always want something sweet," she whispered back like it was a secret between just the two of us and then she winked.

"Don't worry. I got you." I gave her a thumbs up and went into the kitchen to grab the freshest batch of cherry cheese Danishes.

Later in the evening, Freya came over for a girl's night. We ordered pizza and watched The Matrix.

I was glad we had the same taste in movies because I wasn't about to watch the typical chick flick, like Mean girls. I cringed.

"Is it sad that I can't remember the last time I had a girl's night?" Freya asked me out of the blue while she continued to struggle with wrapping her hair in a messy bun.

I laughed and scooted closer to her on the couch to help her. "Nope. What's sad was that I've never had a girls' night. I was always hanging out with Greyson. When I got invited to a few sleepovers, I worried about Grey being alone that night, and I usually made my dad cancel for me last minute with some bs excuse."

"Wow," she muttered.

"Exactly." I wrapped her bun perfectly before bringing her scrunchie around it. "There," I said, sitting back to admire my work. Freya's hair was the prettiest shade of auburn, but it was long and sort of curly hair when she didn't apply products. I couldn't figure how she managed it, but I did know she preferred to wear it out most of the time rather than attempting to style it into something like a bun or ponytail.

Except for when she was at the bakery, of course.

"Thank you." She smiled up at me. "So you've been in love with Greyson since you guys were kids," Freya said.

I thought it sounded like a question, but I think it was a statement.

"Psh! No." That sounded like I was in denial, and it wasn't intentional. What Freya was saying could be true. Who knows exactly when I fell for Grey? All I knew was that one day I looked at him and everything he'd ever done, everything he'd said just came rushing to the forefront of my mind, and suddenly, it wasn't one thing I liked about Grey... it was everything. It was an overwhelming thought at first. It seemed to keep building up to the point where I wasn't sure what to do anymore.

I knew I was afraid of screwing up our friendship for something that felt one-sided. Then again, even when it didn't feel one-sided anymore, I was simply scared. I suppressed my feelings for a while in hopes that Grey wouldn't ever find out. Then I kind of screwed up last summer. Okay, maybe screwed up isn't the best phrase, considering I didn't regret what happened between us. I just regretted how I handled it.

Freya laughed, and it ripped me out of my train of thought. "You two fell in love with each other a while back. I don't think you guys realized until now."

I waved off her comment. "Yeah yeah." I tried not to blush.

I quickly changed the subject. "So you and Tobias..." I gave her the opportunity to finish that sentence for me.

"Just friends," Freya said straight-faced.

"That's how it always starts." I bumped her shoulder.

She giggled nervously like didn't know what else to do. "I don't think he's into me like that. And he doesn't date, so there's that."

I think I remembered Grey mentioning that to me once. "I wonder why?"

Freya shrugged. "It's a mystery to me too. He doesn't talk about it, and I don't push it."

I frowned.

She continued. "Other than that, he's pretty awesome. He's kind of sweet and funny in a sarcastic way." She gazed off for a few seconds and started to laugh about something in her head. "He's a good listener. He remembers everything I tell him. I could give him an "All about Freya" quiz, and I think he would get a 100," she said with absolute certainty.

I picked up the second to last slice of pizza. "He's one of the good ones."

Freya took her time answering. "Yeah."

Before I could reply, our phones vibrated at the same time. We both reached for them on the coffee table.

"It's Grey."

"It's Tobias." We both said at once.

"They made it safely after taking more than a few pit stops," I added.

"Tobias says he blames Dean."

"I'm not surprised by that."

"Me either. I don't know how they put up with him," Freya said.

"I think they're immune to his antics," I supplied.

"I think you're right."

We busted out into laughter.

"I can honestly say those guys are one of a kind," Freya told me.

"Definitely." Without a doubt.

"Just like us."

I dramatically flipped my hair over my shoulder. "Of course," I put on my preppy girl voice.

"Thanks for hanging out with me tonight," she said randomly. "This has been really fun."

I grinned. "Anytime."

29

CHAPTER 29

"You're here!" Ella said, rushing to hug me as soon as I walked through the doors.

I laughed. "Hey, birthday girl," I told her, giving her a big squeeze.

When she pulled away, I admired her outfit. Ella was wearing light blue skinny jeans with slits at the knees, a loose-fitting sleeveless white blouse that fell to the waist, and it had two tied bows at the side. Then she was sporting all-white converses, and topping it off, she had her jet black hair in a high ponytail, but it was curled with a few locks falling down her back.

"You look beautiful," I told her with a soft smile.

"Thank you. I decided to put in a little more effort than usual, considering it's my day and all," Ella said with a bit of sass.

"Of course, I don't blame you." She giggled. "I have a gift for you, but I left it at my place when I was rushing to get over here." I looked at her apologetically.

Her eyes widened, and she shook rapidly shook her head. "You didn't have to get me anything!" she blurted.

I flitted my wrist. "I wanted to." I brought her into a side hug.

"Thank you," Ella said, peering up at me.

"Don't mention it. So what are we going to do first?" I asked, finally taking in the place.

Most of the arcades I've been to had a retro theme to them. This one had nicely polished dark wood floors and dark blue walls adorned with framed autographed movie posters. Televisions were plastered almost everywhere. Some grey couches were in the middle with a few coffee tables. Then there was a super sleek wood counter that took up this whole corner, and it looked like they had prizes, snacks, and beverages back there too.

Ella shrugged in response to my question. "Anything, really." She looked around with me. "When I visited Japan, I think I tried playing one of everything until I found something I liked. OH! I forgot. They also have a bowling alley. It only has three lanes, but it's still pretty cool."

I quirked. "You like to bowl?"

She nodded enthusiastically. "Don't mean to brag or anything, but I'm kind of a pro." She grinned, dusting off her shoulder.

"Hmm. What do you know?" I got eye level with her, "So am I."

Ella clapped her hands together. "Okay, game plan. We make our way through the classic arcade games," she pointed to where the Pac-man and Tron machines are. "Then we travel to the pinball machine area." She gestured to the middle-ish area. "Followed by the air hockey, skee ball, and basketball." I nodded, my eyes following hers. "Lastly, bowling." She pointed to the furthest corner.

How big was this place?

I saw a food and drinks sign right next to it, and I think I spotted some dining tables and a kitchen in the far back. "Do you want to grab some lunch in between too?"

"YES! They have the best hot dogs and chicken nuggets."

I laughed. "Okay, let's grab some tokens and get started then."

Ella responded by grabbing my hand and pulling me behind her.

After about two hours later, we had a bucket filled with tickets, a half-eaten pack of those rainbow Twizzlers, and some Oreos. Plus multiple video clips and photos on our phones, and now grumbling tummies.

We made our way to the bowling alleys, and I ordered some food to be sent over.

"I'm going to the restroom before we get started. Can you put our names into the computer?" Ella asked, walking backward.

I gave her a thumbs up. "Yup."

As Ella ran off, her phone began to ring, I turned to call out to her and let her know, but she was already out of sight. I scooted over on the love seat and looked at it.

It was her mom. I could let it ring, but if she was calling to check in, it might make her nervous if Ella didn't pick up even though she could call back in five minutes.

I answered the phone for her. "Hi, Mrs...." Crap, I just realized she didn't tell me her last name. "Hi Ella's mom," I said instead. "This is Mia. Ella just ran to the ladies' room, and she accidentally left her phone behind," I told her.

I waited for a response, but it was silent on the other side. I had to double-check to make sure I had answered it.

"Mia?" I heard a voice say from the other end. A voice I knew all too well.

"M-m-mom?" I sputtered.

"What are you doing with Ella's phone?" she said in a rush. "Are you with her? Wait, how are you two together?"

"Mom?" I said again. It was like my brain couldn't fully grasp the facts.

"Yes, honey, it's me. Is everything okay? Why do you sound like that?" she asked, panicked.

"Ella is..." I thought it through in my head. All the conversations we've ever had and how weird she used to get when I asked about her family.

I came to meet someone. She had told me at the café.

My mom and dad split up when I was younger, but they got back together a few years ago.

I have a big sister, but we're not super close.

"MOM!" I shouted into the phone as the realization hit me hard, forcing me to jump to my feet.

"MIA?" She responded in the same tone. "You're making me anxious talk to me."

"I didn't know," I told her vaguely.

"You didn't know what?"

"Ella's my sister, and I didn't know," I said softly.

"How could..."

I cut her off, palming the top of my head. "She never told me." And if I hadn't answered the phone. I wouldn't have known.

"Mia, you're not making any sense."

"MIA!" I heard Ella call out my name.

"We'll call you back," I told Mom.

"Okay, sure thing," Mom said all too calmly.

"Mia, I was thinking..." Ella began to speak, but she noticed me with her phone in my hand. "Th-that's m-my phone," she stammered. Her brows caved in, and she looked from me to her phone, then repeated the action.

"Did someone call?" she asked cautiously. I could see the rapid movement of her chest rising and falling.

I nodded silently.

"W-who was it?"

I stared at her. How come I couldn't see it before? The striking resemblance to our mom. Especially the eyes. The same brown hues as my own. But Ella's were more beautiful.

Ella stared at me. "Who was on the phone?" her voice was hoarse.

I gave her a small smile. "It was our mom," I told her.

Ella's eyes began to water, and her bottom lip trembled before all the words tumbled from her lips. "I'm sorry. I didn't mean to keep it a secret. It's just that I was dying to meet you, to know what you were like, and to see if I could get you to like me too. I met you, and I thought you were so nice and sweet." Tears are flowing down her cheeks, but she does nothing to stop them. "I thought if you knew who I was, it would make things weird, and or you'd hate me. And I didn't want to lose you." She shook her head, forcing her ponytail to swing from side to side. She said between sobs, "I'm so sorry, Mia." She covered her face and cried into her hands.

I immediately pulled them away and wiped all her tears. For a few seconds, I was speechless, but I found the words. "You're my sister Ella. I could never hate you."

She hiccupped.

I cupped her cheeks, "I love you," I told her, giving her another reason to start crying again. Except for this time, I cried with her, bringing her into the biggest hug ever.

"I love you too," Ella whispered.

My heart was grateful to hear it. I kissed her cheek.

"Okay." I pulled away, resting my hand on her shoulders. "My little sister, I can't believe I've had you here with me the whole time." I shook my head in disbelief. "That's why you wanted to celebrate with me?"

Ella gave me a firm nod. "It's my first birthday with my sister."

"In that case, I think we have all the more reason to go all out. I have a lot of catching up to do."

Ella blinked up at me a few times. "You mean it?"

"Of course. I'm not missing a single moment of your life, starting now." I pointed to the ground to affirm my statement. Ella flung her arms around me. It caught me off guard and nearly had me stumbling back. I laughed regardless.

Smoothing down her hair, I said, "How about we wrap up this game?" I checked the clock on the wall. "Then we can go over to my place and talk. You have a lot of explaining to do."

Ella lifted her head and cheesed at me. "ME?" she asked innocently.

"Hmm," I confirmed.

"Fine, fine. You're right. But it's a long story," she told me.

"I'm sure it is."

Back at my place, Ella explored the apartment, going from room to room, looking amazed by it all. Even the tiniest little touches of décor, she took the time to admire.

It was cute.

"I love this place!" she exclaimed in the middle of the living room while doing a little twirl.

My family hasn't visited yet. I was a reasonable distance away from home, and it's only been about two and half-ish weeks since I've seen my dad, but we talk all of the time. He promised to take the time to visit soon. So did Grey's mom.

Having Ella in my apartment, though, I don't think I could put into words how exactly it made me feel. I loved that she was here, and I was going to try my best to incorporate her more into my life. I felt comforted that Ella liked my place and seemed so happy to be here.

I nodded. "Yeah, Greyson and I have similar tastes when it comes to décor. So it was easy to decorate the place."

Ella smiled then her eyes caught the balcony. "OHMYGOSH, A BALCONY!" she said, running over to unlock the double doors. "This is so pretty!" she shouted over her shoulder.

I went over to switch on all the lights, including the ones in the living room. It wasn't dark enough to appreciate the beauty of them, but oh well.

"WOW, WOW, WOW!" Ella ran her fingers along the hanging string lights.

I laughed out loud. Stepping outside, I told her, "Okay, all of this is practically new." I gestured to the furniture and potted plants. Grey surprised me with a charming dinner date the other night, and we ate out here for the first time."

Ella placed a hand over her heart. "AWE, that's so sweet of him."

I felt myself beginning to blush as a flashback of that night played through my mind.

"Mia?"

"Hmmm," I replied absentmindedly.

"You're blushing," She sang teasingly, pointing to my cheeks.

I covered my cheeks with my hands and playfully glared at her.

"My sister is in love." She made little kissy faces at me.

I rolled my eyes. She was living up to that little sister stereotype right about now.

"Nothing to be embarrassed about." Ella looked down at one of the chairs. "Can we sit out here?"

"Of course." I sat across from her.

Ella looked up and down the street. "This is a great view. It almost makes me wish I had my sketchpad to draw it." She pouted a little.

"You can come back and bring your sketchpad anytime you want."

Her face lit up like a firework. "OKAY!"

"So now that we're settled spill the beans. Give me the whole story."

Ella's eyes flitted around, focusing on everything but me. "What did mom say when you answered the phone?"

She was stalling. "She was just as surprised to hear my voice as I was to hear hers. She wanted to know how we were together," I said.

"But she didn't sound mad or anything, right?" Ella asked carefully.

"No, she wasn't mad. Just confused."

"Okay, okay, that's not bad. I guess." She nodded to herself.

"Yup..."

"So," Ella began. I had believed she was about to explain how she found me but instead, she asked, "When's Grey coming back?"

"Ella," I said firmly.

"Hmm." Her face looked entirely too innocent for a girl who was skating around an important subject.

"You don't want to tell me?"

"Does it matter at this point? I mean, we're together now." She shrugged.

I let out a soft sigh. "I'd still like to know."

Ella thought about it. "Fine," she grumbled. "I did something bad," Guilt was written all over her face.

Ella told me that she had overheard her parents talking about me late one night. Unlike me, she always knew she had a sister, but she never knew where I was. When she found out that I had just moved into town with Greyson, she went snooping around mom's office. She searched through her phone, reading her texts until she read the ones sent to my dad. They talked about where I worked, how I was doing if mom should reach out to me, etc.

After that, Ella concocted this plan to visit me at the café, but she saw me and chickened out when she got there. So she took the table furthest away from the counter and tried her best to stay quiet, keeping herself busy with homework.

When I had gone over, it took her by surprise. She wanted to talk to me, and she didn't care what we talked about or how we hung out just as long as she was around me. She thought it would have been best for us to know each other before she told me the truth. She was afraid if she told me too soon, I wouldn't want anything to do with her because she heard mom say that I wasn't sure if I wanted her back in my life.

I had interrupted Ella and told her whatever was going on between mom and me, doesn't affect how I felt about her. Had she told me the truth sooner, I would have been spending more time with her like this from the very beginning.

"Do you think Mom will get mad once she finds out?" Ella bit her bottom lip as her eyebrows pinched together with worry.

I shrugged. "I'm not sure. I think she will be happy that we're together and getting along. So I hope not."

Ella's shoulders relaxed.

"Listen," I leaned forward, resting my elbows on top of my thighs. "I can understand why you did what you did, but you should have been honest at some point to the both of us. If mom gets on your case about anything, it will be that."

"I know, I know." She hung her head. "I'm sorry."

I walked over to where she was sitting, and I wrapped my arms around her shoulders, giving them a big squeeze. "Don't worry about it." I kissed her temple. "It's going to be fine."

My phone interrupted our sisterly moment.

"It's mom," I announced to Ella before handing the phone over to her to answer.

Ella looks at me disapprovingly and shakes her head. "Hey, mom ... Yes, she's right here..." She looked over at me, and I lifted a brow. "I don't think that would be a good idea... Yup... I know... I will... Okay... I'll ask her now." She met my gaze. "Mom asked if you can drop me home, please."

I nodded.

"She said 'yes. Okay, we'll leave now. Bye." She hung up and handed me back the phone. "I thought big sisters were supposed to be the mature ones," she snickered.

"I'm new at this." I elbowed her. "Come on, let's get you home." I stood and held out my hand to her. "WAIT! Crap!" I slapped my forehead. "I don't have a car."

"What do you mean?"

"I lent it to Grey and the guys."

Ella slowly nodded with understanding. "You're terrible at this sister thing," she joked.

I pouted. "Learning curve. Cut me some slack." I had a light bulb moment. "Wait here!" I ran inside, through the front door, and across the hall.

I double tapped on the door and waited. Robbie opened it up, and Freya stood behind him. "Hey, guys. I need a massive favor." I gave them a huge grin with the prayer hands in front of my chest.

Thirty-five minutes later, we pulled up at Ella's house.

"Wow, you managed to make it right on time despite driving ten under the speed limit," Ella said sarcastically. I narrowed my eyes at her in the rare view.

I thought when I knocked on Freya's door and asked to borrow her car. I would have hopefully gotten the keys to her Kia SUV, not the keys to Robbie's BMW. I swore I tried my best to reject his offer, but he insisted. Freya had looked at me like I was crazy for even thinking of turning him down, so I took it.

The next thing I knew, I was driving turtle slow all the entire way over here. It would eat me up inside if I let something happen to his car. The last time I remember being this nervous about driving was the day of my driver's test.

"HA HAHA. My little sister is a comedian." I clapped my hands.

Ella stuck her tongue out at me before unbuckling her seatbelt. She grabbed the gift bag by her foot along with the giant Pikachu teddy sitting next to her. When we cashed in all our tickets, we decided that we wanted a giant teddy bear. We instantly chose Pikachu when the lady at the counter brought it to our attention.

Ella reached for the door handle to step out.

I saw Mom open the front door at the same time. She waved at me, and I gave her a half-smile.

"You know, you can come in and join us if you would like. Mom wanted me to let you know," Ella said, glancing back at our mother.

"It's okay. Maybe some other time." I promised. I still needed more time to think through the whole Mom thing.

"It's okay. I figured you'd say that." While Ella had expected to hear me say that, I could still see that she was disappointed about it. "Even if you don't want to come by today, you can totally stop by anytime you want. Alright?" she added.

I gave her a firm nod. "Got it. I'll see you later, okay? Enjoy the rest of the birthday."

"Okay," Ella gave me a huge smile. "Thanks, love you!" she blew me a kiss.

My heart just about melted. "Love you too!" I waved.

I caught Mom smiling, watching the whole display.

I knew things had to change if I wanted to keep this relationship with Ella. I knew it would be best to have that talk finally. But I couldn't help but wonder if I was emotionally prepared for it all.

This talk would involve potentially forgiving my mom for leaving me the way she did and choosing not to come back until years later.

I felt like we would have to open all the old wounds that I liked to ignore and finally give them a chance to heal.

And that seemed so scary to consider, but I'd do it if I had to.

I'd do it for Ella, and ultimately, I needed to do it for me too.

30

CHAPTER 30

Before I could get out of the truck, my mom flung the front door open and sprinted across the front yard.

She didn't care that her fuzzy socks were going to get dirty or that her wet hair was still wrapped up in a towel, taking the shape of an ice cream cone. I met her halfway, and she slammed into me, wrapping her arms around me.

"Hey, Mom," I said, hugging her back.

I heard sniffles.

"Mom," I complained. "Stop acting like I'm coming back from war."

"This is the longest we've been apart. Leave me alone and let me have my moment."

"Awe, you missed me?"

She answered with a snicker as if to say don't call her out on it.

A very distinctive chuckle came from behind me, and I mentally rolled my eyes. I bet any money that was from Dean.

"Not surprised he's a momma's boy," Dean mumbled.

I knew it."Mom," I whispered. "You're embarrassing me," I joked.

I didn't care, but Mom would never let me go if I didn't break this up.

"Alright, alright." Mom pulled away and looked up at me with a beautiful grin.

She cupped my cheek with one hand before pinching them.

"OW!" I grumbled.

"You're eating well." Then she stepped back to examine me. "You're taking care of yourself." She nodded with approval.

"Don't sound so surprised," I mumbled.

"I'm not. I was just stating facts."

"Yeah, right. Anyways, Mom, I want you to meet the guys." All three of them take that as their cue to step forward.

Mom held the towel up with one hand as she used the other to wave at the guys. "Hi, I'm Stephanie, or you could call me Mrs. McNamara. Nice to meet you guys."

I feigned shock, leaving my mouth in the form of an O. "Wow, you didn't assault them with hugs? Are you sure you're my mother?" My mom had always been a hugger. It's in her nature.

Mom gave me the sweetest of smiles before evilly pinching my biceps, causing me to flinch. I rubbed my arm, knowing it was slowly going to turn red. This was my mother. No alien abductions took place here.

The guys all chuckled then introduced themselves.

"Are you boys' hungry? I cooked a feast because if all of you eat like Greyson, then we wouldn't have enough otherwise."

"You know I'm technically still a growing boy, at least until the age of 21 or something," I told her.

"Yeah, scientists have backed up that fact," Dean nodded.

"You would agree to any excuse that lets you eat more food," Tobias muttered under this breath, causing Dean to scowl at him.

"You're one to talk," Dean fired back with the quickness.

Tobias shrugged.

"As you can already guess by now, I'm the only normal one here." Tatum smiled politely at my mom.

Tobias and Dean grunted in disagreement, and Tatum looked offended.

Mom, on the other hand, was highly entertained.

"I can see why you like them," Mom said to me, but she wasn't quiet about it.

"Come on, let's get inside before more of the neighbors get to witness me in this state." She gestured to her hair and outfit.

I wrapped my arm around her shoulders, and we walked inside.

"You have a lovely home," Tatum said, admiring the place.

"Thank you," Mom said as we followed her into the kitchen.

"WHOA WHOA WHOA!" Dean made a scene in the hallway. He paused in front of one of dad's RIAA-certified gold plaques on the wall. "This is a piece of rock music history." He said in awe. "Quick, take my picture!" He shoved his phone at Tobias, who reluctantly obliged.

"You guys were huge fans of Roman's?" Mom asked in both shock and approval. She instantly likes almost anyone who is a fan of dad's music.

Tobias snapped a couple of pictures with Dean making various poses.

"If Grey is up for it, maybe he can show you his old room, which was his studio, office, and man cave rolled into one. Gosh, Roman used to love to spend hours upon hours in there," Mom told them as we continued to walk into the kitchen.

I chuckled, sliding into the breakfast nook. This is where the two of us, mostly have our dinners, but it's large enough to hold about eight people. "One time, mom got annoyed with dad after he said he'd come to dinner in five minutes. She barged into the room, grabbed him by the ear, and she dragged him down the hall."

Mom laughed at the memory. "In my defense, his five minutes were long up."

The room filled with laughter as all the guys slid into the breakfast nook. Mom sat at the end next to me.

She pointed out all the dishes in the middle of the table, and then she let us dig in.

"This is so good, Mrs. M," Tobias spoke first, layering another helping of mashed potatoes onto his plate.

"Mhmm," Dean mumbled with one cheek full of food and nodded vigorously.

"Delicious," Tatum said, moaning into his bites.

I shook my head, but I couldn't help but smile at all their reactions.

"I'm glad you like them," Mom said happily. Watching people enjoy her cooking warms her heart. "Eat your bellies full, please. I won't need all these leftovers."

The guys gave her a thumbs up, passing the dishes back and forth.

In-between bites, we all took turns telling mom about our wedding gig. She was so excited that we had booked something like that, and she said that this could be the start of something even bigger. Dean, being Dean, agreed and said that the band has star potential.

We wrapped up dinner with some Oreo brownies and almond milk.

I felt my phone vibrate in my pocket, and I fished it out.

Mia's name lit up the screen, I quickly replied.

"It's Mia, isn't it?" Mom asked, poking my cheek and making me aware of the fact that I was grinning like a fool.

The guys all chuckled under their breaths, and I pinned them with a look. Then they each pretended to be extra into the desert in front of them.

I schooled my face and cleared my throat. "Yeah, she was just checking in." I shrugged nonchalantly, slipping the phone back into my pocket.

"Hmm," Mom said, eyeing me suspiciously. "I won't pry. Not today anyway." She gave me a smile that promised she would bug me about this later, but for now, I was grateful that she wasn't going to push it. She probably decided to have mercy on me because the guys are here. "Anyways," she braced her hands on the table and stood. "I'm going to try to do something with all of this." She motioned to her hair that's still perfectly wrapped in a towel and exited the kitchen.

"Your mom is cool," Tatum said first, taking his final bite and sipping on his milk.

"I agree," Tobias nodded.

"Yeah, she's pretty awesome." Dean chimed in. "She reminds me a little of my mom. Except for my mom always dresses like a senior citizen and wouldn't be caught dead with a towel on her head. Her cooking skills, though, they're amazing."

"Of course it is. She's a chief," Tobias pointed out.

Dean waved off his comment, silently communicating that wasn't the point.

Tatum stood and gathered all our plates. "I'll put them in the dishwasher."

"Thanks," I told him.

"So, what's the plan for the rest of the day?" Dean asked, stretching his arms out.

I messaged the back of my neck with one hand. "So um... I kind of wanted to visit my dad. Then we can do whatever you guys want afterward. There's a lot of stuff in town that won't close until late."

"Can we go with you?" Tatum asked, taking me off guard.

My eyebrows pinched together. "I..." I didn't know how to feel about this.

"I think the three of us would like to pay our respects as well," Tobias said before I could finish. "It would be an honor. But it's not okay with you. We understand."

I took turns meeting all of their gazes, and I could sense that they genuinely wanted to be there with me.

I nodded. "Yeah, sure." Their faces lit up.

Dean double patted my back. "We're here for you, bro. That and you're kind of stuck with us, but you already knew that." He gave me a lopsided grin.

I chuckled. I'm oddly okay with that.

A few minutes, I told mom we'd be right back as we were heading out. I opened the front door and nearly walked into a man who had a bouquet in one hand while the other was a fist raised in the air.

"Can I help you?" I asked him. Who was this guy? He must have the wrong house.

He lowered his hand and straightened up. I had a few inches on him, so he had to tilt his head up to meet my gaze. "Hello there." He opted for a small wave. I saw his eyes glance over my shoulder, probably looking at the guys crowding behind me.

He cleared his throat before speaking again. "I'm Gabriel. I'm here to see Stephanie."

I quirked a brow and took a step back. So this is the guy my mom's been dating. I took a good look at him. He looked as if he could be her age or maybe younger. I think she might have mentioned that. He wasn't dressed like her type. I mean, I always thought my mom was into the bad boy-looking types, but this guy was dressed like an elementary school history teacher.

Anyways, I'd like to think he's smart enough to figure out that he's talking to her son. But in case he still had no clue. "Is my mother expecting you?" I asked him, crossing my arms against my chest defensively.

His eyes widened for a second, realizing that I wasn't going to make this easy for him. "I um... well... no. She hasn't been answering my phone calls since yesterday. We had a minor misunderstanding." His face grew guilty.

Dean stepped up next to me. "Excuse me, sir, define misunderstanding." I nodded, wanting to know what he meant by that too.

Panic swept across his face. "It's complicated, adult stuff." He scratched his beard.

Tobias was next. "Give us the PG version then. If we hear something we don't like, we're slamming the door shut," he said, deadly serious.

Gabriel grew pale. "I-I-I..." he shook his head. "It's not..."

"BOYS!" Mom shouted from behind us.

We all turned into innocent angels. We answered with a mixture of "Yes, mom, yes, ma'am, and yes, Mrs. M." Tatum even threw in a polite smile. Out of all of us, he was usually the one least likely to get into trouble.

Mom glared at us from the bottom of the stair. Her hair was now half dry and half wet, making half her head look like she had gotten electrocuted.

"Lay off the man," she gestured with a stretched arm.

"Come on, we were just messing with him," I said. "He showed up with flowers looking like he committed a crime."

Mom rolled his eyes. "That's because he did," she grumbled.

"What!" I turned my attention back to him and scowled.

She ran forward and grabbed his arm, pulling him inside. They breezed right past us and went upstairs to her room. I heard a door slam.

Was I supposed to be okay with this? I realized I couldn't very well interfere in every aspect of my mom's life but still. I sighed.

"Anyways," I said, trying to pretend I wasn't peeved; my mom just let that guy in after admitting he had done something wrong. I was making a mental note to talk about it with her later. The last thing I wanted was some guy thinking he could take advantage of my mother. Then again, Mom can handle herself pretty well. It would be hard for anything to slip by her. I rubbed my temple, thinking of what the situation might be between those two, then I changed my mind before it wandered too far. "Let's go for real this time."

I motioned for the guys to head out behind me.

"Wait, can we take the mustang!" Dean blurted out, pointing to the car in the driveway.

"It might be a tight squeeze." We're not exactly little guys.

"That's fine. Tatum and Tobias can cuddle together in the back." He threw them a looking over his shoulder before yelling, "Shotgun!" And sprinting down the driveway.

Thirty minutes later, we were pulling up at my dad's resting place. Dean carried the flowers since the passengers were obligated to hold these things.

The guys stayed a step behind me, letting me lead the way. I made it to dad's tombstone and kneeled in front of it. "Hey, Dad," I whispered. "I was in town and thought I would stop by." I gave him a quick life update and then added. "I brought some friends today that would have loved to meet you."

Dean walked over first and kneeled next. "Hello, sir, I'm Dean." He placed the flowers in the vase. "Huge fan and an even bigger admirer." Then Tatum and Tobias followed, taking a knee as well. They introduced themselves then they each started to talk about what they loved about his work.

"I'm sure you already knew this, but you left your son with some serious talent, and he was obviously wasting it, but now he has come to his senses." I elbowed Dean, and he grunted, holding his rib cage.

"He's right," Tobias said. "We're nowhere close to being the star he was, and who knows if we'll ever get there but what matters is we're all in this together."

"If any group can make it, why can't it be us?" Tatum joined.

"My talent can take us far." We shot an annoyed look over at Dean. "I mean, it's good to have you guys as backups, though," he added.

Tobias shoved him, forcing him to lose balance, and we all laughed at his expense when his butt he the grass.

"Fine, we're all talented in our way." He jokingly rolled his eyes.

Tatum shook his head, but he had a smile on his face.

"So Grey, I know in the beginning we said we'll give you until the end of summer to decide if you wanna stay in the band, but I think you unconsciously made a decision already." He rested a hand on my shoulder, grinning.

I looked around at all their faces and smiled.

I wasn't looking for new friends, and I indeed wasn't looking to join a band. But I've slowly made myself into a member of this brotherhood that I never knew I needed.

I stuck my hand out in front of me. "Save the knights," I said.

One by one, they each joined in, repeating the same thing.

"You guys are stuck with me," I told them, cementing my place in their world and them in mine.

CHAPTER 31

Grey's been glued to my hip since he's been back.

I wasn't complaining, only stating an observation. Grey said he missed me, and the feeling was mutual.

I was trying not to be a clingy or obsessive girlfriend while he was away. But when he didn't get random updates from me throughout the day, it bothered him. So he asked me to text him whenever I felt like it, even if it was about something silly, like I saw a cloud shaped like a banana, which I did.

Grey told me the guys were offered to do a few more events, and he joked about it being a mini American tour. When he had asked me how I felt about it, I told him I was happy the band was getting higher-paying gigs, and I thought they should do as many as possible.

His eyebrows had pinched together, and he looked at me with a concerned expression before saying, "I know this summer is supposed to be about us, and I didn't want you to feel like we haven't spent enough time together or something."

I reassured Grey that that wouldn't be the case. I wanted him to go off and be awesome, and I'd be waiting right here when he returned.

That brought a big smile to his face, and he looked so relieved.

While he went into the shower, I went into the kitchen to whip something up for dinner.

I had my head stuck in the fridge reaching for one of the water bottles in the back when I heard my phone vibrate with a text.

It was probably Ella. We've been texting on and off all day, getting to know each other even more.

Ella: Is Mom there? She just stormed out of the house and said she would be right back.

Me: You don't think...

I didn't get to finish the text before I heard a pounding at my door and I ran to grab it.

Mom was standing there in joggers and a white tee with her hair in a messy bun. She breezed right past me and walked straight into the living room.

I panicked. "Mom!" I intended for that to come more calmly, but it came out harshly. Grey was in the shower, and I still hadn't told him about her yet or Mia. I hadn't decided what I was going to do.

"Okay, I can't take it anymore. I have been trying to give you space these past few weeks. But since I saw you with Ella, I haven't been able to think of anything besides having my two girls together and with me." Mom looked upset and defeated.

"Listen, Mom. It isn't a good time. It's late, and Grey is..."

I saw the moment he must have stepped out of the out bathroom and into the hallway. Mom's eyes had looked over my shoulder.

"Hello, Greyson. It's been a while." She smiled politely at him.

Oh no. Oh no. I didn't bother turning around to see Grey's facial expression. I could just imagine him being confused and or slightly angry.

I didn't know what I expected him to say, but this wasn't it. "Hi, Mrs... er..." He didn't know what to call her since she and my dad had split up. Heck, not even I knew her new last name.

"You can just call me Lydia, dear." Mom waved off his confusion.

"Uh, sure. How are you?" I heard his footsteps come up behind me. He was being nice, acting as if he knew about her all along, and it was no surprise seeing her here.

Now, I was really in a panic. Grey was taking this too well.

"Pretty good. Just trying to talk some sense into my stubborn daughter." Mom smiled at me.

I laughed nervously.

"Is there any way you could help me?" she asked him sweetly. "She's bound to listen to you more than me. I've been trying to convince her weeks to come to visit me, talk to me, maybe even go on a few trips this summer with her sister and me."

My heart was pounding in my chest, and my throat was clenching up.

Grey nodded like this wasn't the first time he was getting this information. "I think that would be great. Maybe Mia needs to warm up to the idea. I know it's been weeks, as you said. But you know Mia's not someone to make any rash decisions. She liked to think things over thoroughly."

"Maybe too thoroughly if you asked me," Mom snickered.

I tried my best not to glare at her.

"Anyways, I'm sorry to barge in at this hour. I was at home, and I felt like I was going to explode, driving myself crazy with all of this." She took a deep breath, looking between the two of us. "I'll show myself out now," she said, walking past us. "Grey, can I count on you?" she said over her shoulder with one hand on the doorknob.

"Leave it all to me." I heard him say while I glared daggers at the back of his head.

Mom looked back at me, waving and saying goodnight.

I waited for the door to close before I tightly shut my eyes.

"So, when were you going to tell?" Grey snarled.

Crap. I was in trouble.

32

CHAPTER 32

Mia averted her eyes. "Grey, I wanted to tell you. I was going to as soon as I decided what I wanted to do. I just..." She closed her eyes and took a breath.

I crossed my arms against my chest. We never kept secrets like this from each other.

"You mean you were going to tell me after you decided to go off and travel with your mom." I laughed bitterly. "It's just like you to run off when things get serious."

Mia's eyes flew to mine, and she rapidly shook her head.

"It's not like that," she argued.

"Then what's it like?" I paused, waiting for her to answer. When she didn't, I continued. "I know you. You push me away whenever we get serious, or I get close. While you don't verbally give me an excuse, you do find a way to completely ignore the fact that something happened between us and return to being good ole besties with me." I shook my head.

Mia toyed with the loose hem of her shirt. "I was afraid," she mumbled.

"And you think I'm not?" I fired back.

"You didn't let me finish!" she shouted. "As much as I swear I know you, I was always afraid I wouldn't be enough for you. I was afraid to take it too far because what if you suddenly decided that being in a relationship with me wasn't what you wanted anymore." She swallowed, then cleared her throat. "I was afraid I'd be like every other girl you've been with, like every hobby or obsession that temporarily kept your interest before you moved on from them."

I opened my mouth, but nothing came out. I wasn't expecting Mia to say something like that.

"You know the best part about this summer deal?" Her eyes glanced up at mine, but then they settled on the logo in the middle of my t-shirt. "I felt like even if you changed your mind about us, at least I could say I got to spend the summer with the guy I've always wanted to be with. Knowing that you were mine for just a brief moment in time would make my life. "

"Mia," her name came out gravelly as it passed my lips.

"Why do you always seem to be chasing the next big thing, and what happens when I'm no longer a part of that dream?" Mia asked, her brown eyes turbulent.

"You always will be. That's why I wanted the chance to prove it. Did you ever think that maybe this isn't just about me and my so-called forever-changing hobbies? That maybe you have a bit of a problem too with that fact you're afraid to let people in fully?"

Mia scoffed like my judgment was off.

"And it all started when your mom left," I said.

When her jaw dropped, she rushed to say, "Don't bring her into this!"

"It's the truth. You grew up loving her just as much as you love your dad, but the minute she left, you were unbearably hurt. You swore you would never forgive her. Now she's barging in and asking for some kind of relationship with her daughter. But you're so hurt from the past that you can't even consider it."

Two massive steps forward, and Mia was up in my face. As angry as I was with her, something in me wanted to hold her close and makeup. "And what about you? You gonna pretend this didn't all start after your father died?"

"That's different!" I growled.

"Different how? You're practically walking in his footsteps."

I sighed, pinching the bridge of my nose.

"You can't be him, Greyson," Mia added.

"Why not! Why can't I tour with my band and live life to the fullest? He had everything to lose, and he still went out of his way to be a hero and lost his life."

It had been the last day of his American world tour. Dad was heading out to his tour bus when he heard some screams. He went over, running, and saw that one of the fans he had just met backstage was getting assaulted. Dad being Dad, swooped in like a hero to save her. But he didn't know that the guy had a gun. He shot him when they started to fight. The guy ran off, leaving Dad with a deadly wound to the chest.

When they rushed him to the hospital, there wasn't much time left for him.

Mom and I had gotten there a little too late.

I remember the last conversation with Dad, and I will forever be grateful that it was a good one. But I could never get over it because it was the very last one. Never mind that he told me he was proud of me for doing well in school and that he was happy. I always tried to make mom smile when she seemed sad about him being away.

Never mind that we both said, "I love you" and "I'll see you soon." It hurts to replay the conversation in my head, knowing I could still hear his voice so clearly in my mind, and that's what I'd have for the rest of my life. I should be happy that my memories of him haven't faded, yet it's still bittersweet.

"I'm still alive. I can try anything I want, be anything I want. I have nothing to lose." That might sound like I was willing to take any risks with or without consequences, which would be true. Living on the edge became something to fill that space Dad left behind. And a part of me wanted to surpass him in a way that would make him happy.

I had to try everything. I had to be everything. I knew this would become a problem, but not to the extent that it would affect my future with Mia.

"You have your mom. You have your friends. You have me."

I shook my head. "I'm not sure I even have you."

And with those words, I did one of the most irrational things I could think of.

"I need some air," I told Mia before walking out the front door.

33

CHAPTER 33

Grey slammed the door on his way out.

I thought I'd give him a few minutes to cool off. But when an hour passed by, it occurred to me that he might not bother coming back home tonight.

I brought my knees up to my chest and curled into a ball on the couch. I let the tears come from the frustration of this whole situation.

I knew this could've been prevented. But the other stuff, we said to each other, I felt like that was something we'd both been bottling up for some time.

I didn't think either of us was wrong, but I knew it would take some time to let those words sink in.

Meanwhile, I needed to vent.

I marched down to Freya's apartment in my fuzzy socks and Hello Kitty pajamas and lightly knocked on the door.

She opened it, took a good look at my state, and pulled me inside.

"OHMYGOSH! What happened, Mia?" She asked with concern, dragging me over to the couch.

I hung my head, focusing on my chipped fingernails. "Grey and I got into a fight, and he stormed out," I sniffled.

"I didn't know you guys fought. You guys may bicker at times, but you two are so close. I can't imagine the two of you having such a huge blowout."

We've never argued this before.

"It's kind of my fault." I went on to explain the whole story.

Freya listened, only nodding her head between my pauses and inserting a few comments here and there. "I can see where you're coming from. I can see where you're both coming from, and I think you two just need a little space to think and cool off."

"You think he'll come back?" I asked her.

"Of course, honey! There's no way he can stay away from you. That boy loves you!" she exclaimed.

My jaw dropped. "What?" My eyes widened with shock.

Freya smiled sweetly and reached for my hand. "You mean to tell me that you have no idea Greyson loves you?" She quirked a brow. "Anybody, literally anybody with eyes, could see that. He's absolutely crazy about you, and that's not going to change." She gave my hand a comforting squeeze. "So, don't worry about it. Couples fight all the time. Completely normal." She flitted her hand in the air.

"Okay." I nodded slowly, feeling slightly relieved.

"Trust me," she added.

I smiled weakly. "Alright."

Freya jumped to the next issue. "Now about the Mom situation,"

I grumbled, rolling my eyes.

"Nope. None of that. Go straight to your mother's and stop stalling. Tell her how you feel."

I sucked in my bottom lip.

"Do you want me to go with you for moral support?" Freya wrapped one arm around my shoulder, hugging me to her.

I shook my head, then rested it on her shoulder.

"No, I need to do this on my own, but I appreciate the offer. Thank you," I told her.

"No problem. I'm always here if you need me." She brought me into a hug, and I leaned into her embrace, soaking in all the warmth and support I needed.

A few seconds later, I gathered all the motivation I could muster and stood up.

"I'm going to do it!" I told Freya. "And I should do it now before all the motivation goes out the window."

Freya cackled. "In that case." She jumped to her feet and shooed me. "Go, go, go!" She walked me to the front door and gave me another hug. "Let me know how everything goes, okay."

"You got it." I winked.

Freya watched me walk down the hall to my apartment, and we both waved at each other before going inside.

I ran to my room to change into some sweats and a hoodie. Next, I grabbed my phone, wallet, and keys as I rushed out the door once more.

Time to talk to my mother.

Thirty minutes later, I glanced at the clock on the radio. It said 10:30 pm. I knew that wasn't super late to some people, but I thought it was late enough to be an inconsiderate time to storm into someone's house.

Then again, that someone was my mother, so shouldn't I get like a pass or something. At least this once?

I brought my forehead down on the steering wheel, weighing my option. If I tried to come back again tomorrow, I might not have the nerve. And how could I possibly sleep with all of this on my mind? Plus, I was already here.

And Mom did say I could stop by anytime.

I started tapping my head against the steering wheel, annoyed with myself. My thought process was getting me nowhere.

I blindly fished out my phone from my pocket when I felt it vibrate.

Ella: Are you outside? Is that you in the truck?

I saw one of the lights on the second-floor flick on, setting the window a glow.

My cover was blown. I should get out and face the music.

Opening the car door, I hopped out, waving to Ella, who had her head sticking out of the window with a massive grin.

I heard something like a squeal before she ran back inside.

Before I could make it up the three little steps in front of the door, Ella swung it open excitedly, banging it against the wall inside.

"MIA!!!" she screamed, loud enough to wake any of the sleeping neighbors.

"Hey, sis." I pulled her into a giant bear hug, kissing the top of her head.

She pulled away slightly. "What are you doing here?" she asked, craning her head up to look at me.

"I wanted to talk to Mom. Is she still awake?" I asked, smoothing down her hair.

She nodded.

"Mia?" Mom stepped into the doorway, and I saw a man standing behind her. He was a tall, slender man with black wavy hair and mossy green eyes. His face looked warm and friendly.

Ella spun around. "Dad, this is Mia, my big sister." She politely introduced us.

He nodded with his lips curving into a smile. He stepped around Mom, holding his hand out. "Hi, I'm Matthias, but you can call me Matt. It's nice to meet you." We shook hands.

"Likewise," I told him. I looked from him to my mother, who was still frozen where she stood. She was probably unsure of what to say or do. Maybe she was waiting to follow my lead. "I'm sorry to stop by so late. I..." I started.

Matt cut me off. "Nonsense, you're family. You can stop by any-time you like. Now, please come in." He waved me in, and Ella tugged me inside after her.

I heard the door close behind me as I stood frozen in the middle of the foyer.

"Wow," I mumbled under my breath, but I didn't think anyone heard me.

This house was even more beautiful on the inside. It was a mod-ern architectural masterpiece.

As soon as you walked in, there was an L-shaped charcoal grey, and white staircase with stainless railings and glass to the left—the color of the stairs and the wood floors were the same throughout the house. The chandelier and light fixtures are steel and with a unique geometric design that I have never seen before. There's photography everywhere with a few art pieces. Most of them were black and white, but a few were in color.

I took my shoes off at the door, and Ella, so kindly, put them in the coat closet before leading me into what could be described as the formal living room. This area was just as impressive as the front of the house. There wasn't much furniture, only two white love seats facing each other with a marble table in the middle.

"Is everything alright? What brings you over tonight?" Matt asked, pulling my attention away from the furniture.

"I was hoping to talk to Mom." I sat down.

Mom's steps faltered like she couldn't believe it. She was acting as if she wasn't just at my house, begging me to open up to her. She took a seat across from Ella and me.

Matt looked over at Mom with a smile on his face. "Okay. Can I get you something to drink?" he asked.

Ella jumped up and said, "I know what she likes." She headed into what was probably the direction of the kitchen.

Matt chuckled. "Alright, then. I'll leave everything to her," he said, walking in the same direction.

I heard Ella mumble something in Korean, and her father replied.

"Would you believe me if I told you that her first language was Korean?" Mom said, drawing my attention to her.

I shook my head. "What? Really?" I never knew that.

She nodded with a smile. "She was living in Seoul with her grandparents. It was all she knew in the beginning. While her father's family speaks English and Japanese, Korean is their first language, so it was natural for them to speak it around Ella. I was the only person who spoke to her in English most of the time. She's such a smart girl. She soaked up the language like a sponge. Which was great because my Korean sucks." Mom laughed lightly. "It's a bit better now. I think. Matt and Ella tell me that it is, but I think they're lying to me," she whispered the last bit.

It was my turn to laugh.

Mom stared at me with a tilt of her head. "I missed that sound," she said out of nowhere, effectively killing my laughter. I could see her eyes doing that thing where they glazed over all my features.

"Mom," I said. "I meant what I said earlier. I want to talk, and I want to explore the possibility of us rebuilding our relationship."

Mom nodded as she processed my words.

"I would like to hear your story, and then maybe you can listen to mine," I suggested.

"Of course." Mom got up, walking over to me. She reached for my hand, and I was almost hesitant to have her hold it. I thought it would be awkward, but I felt oddly comforted by this. Maybe it was because I was choosing to be open with her. I was choosing to let her in with the hopes of something good coming from this.

I looked down at our hands.

I remembered when Mom's hands used to cover my own entirely. Now they're practically the same size. "Before I tell you everything, I need you to know that I never stopped loving you. Even when you said you hated me and didn't want me to come back."

My head whipped up, and my eyes met her gloomy gaze. "Dad told you that," I asked in disbelief.

"No." she smiled sadly. "I was on the phone, hoping to talk to you, and I overheard you say that to your father. After that, I decided to give you some space."

I tore my eyes away from hers, slipping my hands out of her grip.

I saw the hurt flash through her eyes in my peripheral. She probably thought I was pushing her away again when she's finally gotten so close.

"You know when you say things like you're giving someone space, they expect you to come back, but you didn't." I felt my heart clench painfully at the memory.

"I'm so sorry, Mia."

I shut my eyes. I was trying my very best to accept the apology without staying bitter about the past.

So I took a deep breath. "It's fine," I mumbled. It all felt far from fine, but I didn't want to stop our progress. "Tell me what happened."

Mom took a few seconds to put herself together calmly. It was evident that she was wrecked with every kind of emotion.

She began to tell me that she and Dad had briefly separated when I was four years old. She was unhappy, and she thought about being with another man. She had met Matt through a mutual friend at the museum. They worked closely together on a few projects that involved South Korean international Art students. But she swore nothing happened because she remained faithful to Dad.

When she had told Dad everything, he told her it was okay and that he just wanted her to be happy. Then she left to see where that other relationship could go. I remember at that age, Mom went on a lot of "business trips." Obviously, those weren't business trips.

That was her flying to and from South Korea to visit Matt.

Long story short, she quit her job, moved to South Korea, and had Ella. But when things started to fall apart with Matt, she left Ella with her Dad and returned with us. She went to therapy with Dad to work out their problems. Dad knew about Ella from the beginning, and they made a deal to tell me about her when I was old enough to understand.

Mom visited Ella as often as she could, but everything changed when she got the news that she was sick.

Matt reached out to her and asked her if she wanted to be there for Ella throughout her surgeries. The doctors weren't sure if they would help with her condition or draw out the inevitable.

Mom broke down one night and told dad everything. Dad being Dad, he put his feelings aside and encouraged her to go to South Korea and be with Ella.

Mom mentioned that Dad had been dying to tell me the truth, but he didn't feel like it was his secret to share, and Mom had begged him to keep quiet.

"So, you see, I've made some stupid decisions, and I know I can't use all these excuses. The minute I felt like I failed you as a mother, I was terrified to go back. I wanted to beg for your forgiveness; I wanted to hold you in my arms so you'd know that you were still very much loved. But then months turned into years, and like a coward, I couldn't face you. Your dad gave me updates. It took him a while to forgive me, especially after I showed up on the doorstep asking to see you."

"He told me that he chased you away. He was still healing. We both were," I told Mom.

"When he finally cooled off. He said that he knew you'd eventually forgive me, but I couldn't forgive myself." She swiped a tear from under her eye. "I let you down, and I didn't want to own up to that." Mom shook her head.

She continued, "Once your dad told me that you were happy again and smiling, I thought that you'd be fine without me. He was doing such a good job raising you while I was across the world. He never complained. He never thought any less of me, even after finding out about Ella or when I told him I felt like I was developing feelings for Matt again. Gosh, he deserved better than me. You both did. And I can't say I'm sorry enough." She buried her face in her hands and started sobbing.

A part of me was fuming mad at her past decisions, while the other was just tired of holding a grudge.

Nothing would change how she practically abandoned me back then, but she was here now, and I didn't think I could walk away from this.

Not when Ella was involved and not when I knew Mom desperately wanted to fix everything.

I sighed. Taking one arm, I wrapped it around Mom's shoulders. "I forgive you," I said in a whisper. I never thought I would utter those three words to her, and what shocked me the most was that I knew in my heart that I meant them.

Mom removed her hands from her face. Her cheeks were burning red, and her eyes were glistening. She opened her mouth, but no words came out.

"This doesn't mean everything will be perfect between us. It just means that I'm willing to put in the effort."

"Mia," she croaked, and suddenly, I was wrapped up in her arms. She kissed my cheek. "I'm never going to forget this, and I swear I will never let you down again."

And I believed her.

We spent minutes just holding onto the other for dear life before she pulled away and asked if I would tell her more about my life. She wanted to know anything that Dad might have missed.

I cracked a smile and started from the beginning.

I yawned as I felt my eyes slowly closing.

"Why don't you spend the night? I don't want you to drive home so late," Mom told me.

"I'm not sleeping," I mumbled.

"Silly girl, you can barely keep your eyes open." I felt Mom's fingers run through my hair.

"You should let Grey knows so he doesn't worry."

"He doesn't like me very much right now." I think I gave her the cliff notes version of what happened between us. I didn't know if it made sense because I felt like I was muttering gibberish in my sleepy haze.

"Oh, no, honey. It's my fault."

I shook my head against the couch cushion. "Don't worry," yawn. "About it." yawn.

"We'll talk about this more in the morning. I need to set up the guest room for you."

I felt myself nod.

"Or she can sleep with me?" I heard Ella say from somewhere off in the distance.

"That's fine, too," I mumbled.

I heard a pitter-patter of footsteps, and then a finger poked my cheek. I slapped it away.

"Are you gonna get up or what?" I heard Ella say.

I grumbled in response.

"She's always been a cranky sleeper," Mom muttered, causing them both to giggle.

"Not true." I pointed in the direction of where I heard her voice.

"Yeah yeah. Come on, Aurora." Ella pulled on my hoodie sleeve.

"Fine, fine." I sat up, opening one eyeball before slowly getting to my feet.

I stuffed my hands in my pockets. "Lead the way, El," I told her with a nod of my head.

She skipped by me, way too chipper for whatever time of night it was.

I dragged my feet behind her and Mom and walked carefully behind them.

I wanted to take in more of the house, but I would have to do that in the morning. My brain couldn't register anything more at the moment.

When we finally made it to Ella's room, I sighed. That walk was longer than I would have liked.

Mom stood in the doorway, "Good night. See you two in the morning!" She blew us a kiss and closed the door behind her.

Ella dived onto the bed excitedly. "Do you want some PJs to change into? I have some oversized T-shirts and stuff that will fit you."

I shook my head, giving her a small smile. "Nope. I sort of came prepared." I slipped off my hoodie and my joggers, revealing my PJs underneath.

Ella busted out with laughter while I neatly folded my clothes and placed them on the edge of her dresser.

"Hello, kitty, though?" she asked with her eyes flickering to my shirt.

"Says the girl in Transformers PJs." She glanced down at herself, then back at me. "Touché." She playfully rolled her eyes, and I cracked a smile.

I pulled the sheet back and climbed under the covers, getting myself snuggly and cozy.

"MIA!" Ella whisper-yelled.

"Hmm?"

"This is our first sleepover!" I peeked over at her and saw her mouth form an "O."

I grinned. "Yeah, I guess it is."

"AWESOME!" she whisper-yelled again while fist-pumping the air.

I officially have the cutest little sister on the planet.

It was silent for a few minutes, and my eyes fluttered shut.

"Mia?" I heard Ella say again.

"Ella?"

"Are you and Greyson gonna break up?" she asked me softly. I opened my eyes and saw that she was lying on her side, facing me.

I reached to caress her cheek, smoothing my thumbs across her freckles. "I don't know. He seems pretty mad at me earlier. Truth be told, we were only supposed to date until the end of summer."

"What!" Her cinnamon eyes expanded.

"Yeah, it's a long story. I'll tell you about it in the morning, Okay."

I pulled my hand away, tucking it underneath the pillow.

Ella nodded before adding one final thing. "I don't think you see it. But you guys are like soul mates. So that means, no matter what problems you two have, you're supposed to be able to work them out," she spoke with such confidence in us.

"You're amazing. You know that?" I told her.

She grinned, and those dimples that I adored made an appearance. "I've been told that a time or two."

"Because it's true." I yawned. "I love you, Ella," I told her, shutting my eyes.

"I love you too."

34

CHAPTER 34

I knew I'd be able to work through my thoughts after talking it over with someone. And who better to listen to my problems than Tatum. Nothing against the other guys. I just felt like he would be able to relate more than Dean and Tobias.

I knocked on the door and waited for him to answer.

He opened the door, looking at me with one eye open.

"Grey, what's up?" He said, covering a yawn with the back of his hand.

He didn't wait for me to answer before waving me in.

"I'm sorry, didn't mean to wake you," I told him with an apologetic smile.

"It's fine. You alright? You never pop up like this?" He asked with concern.

"Is it cool if I crash here for the night?" I answered his question with one of my own.

"Sure." He nodded, crossing his arms against his chest. "Just as long as you tell me why you're here instead of at your place with Mia."

I walked over to his couch and plopped myself onto it.

With a sigh, I raked my fingers through my hair. "We got into an argument, and I stormed off," I muttered. Every time I replayed the moment in my head, I became uneasy.

"Okay," I watched Tatum grab two water bottles from the fridge, a bag of kettle chips, and pretzel MMs from the cabinet. Then he pulled out two Styrofoam bowls. "I'm going to need more details. You're probably here because you want to talk, right?"

I nodded.

He walked over, handed me one bottle then placed the snacks on the coffee table in front of us.

"Alright, so I'm all ears." He opened the bag of chips, pouring some into one bowl before sprinkling MMs on it and passing it to me.

I chuckled. "Thanks." I'd be lying if I said this wasn't comforting food, which was kind of what I needed.

I tossed a chip into my mouth. "I found out Mia kept a massive secret from me, and I went off on her about it. We've never argued like that. Not since the eighth grade when she heard some dumb rumors about this girl named Kacey something and me." Someone had told Mia that she saw Kacey and me kissing under the bleachers during gym class, and they swore we were going out. Mia got mad because I had told her days before that I didn't like Kacey and thought I had lied. What didn't help my case was whenever Kacey saw me, she decided to stick to me like gum on the bottom of a shoe. That girl was a thorn in my side. She couldn't take a hint.

It wasn't until I saw her step up to Mia, talking a bunch of non-sense about being jealous and secretly in love with me, that I straight up told her she would never have a chance. As I've always said, whoever messed with Mia messed with me. Her fights were my fights.

I explained the whole argument with Tatum, telling him who said what and asking him what he thought this meant for our relationship. I also added the part about us making a deal to date for the summer.

His jaw went slack upon receiving that info, but he regained his composure. Out of everything, I told him that was the one thing that caught him off guard.

"What were you planning on doing at the end of summer?"

I shrugged. "I was hoping I would have changed Mia's mind by then and convinced her that we could make it. I never wanted to have Mia as some summer fling. She means more to me than that. I was just afraid to tell her that I wanted her for longer. I was worried it would freak her out. So I concocted this plan and figured I would take baby steps in that direction." I slumped back into the couch before grabbing a handful of MMs. "Now, I see no matter how she feels about me, she probably would have broken it off anyways because she was afraid. Afraid that one day, it would be all over, and she would have lost her boyfriend and her best friend. She wouldn't know how to recover from that."

Tatum nodded, listening intently. I couldn't believe this man wanted to go to law school when he was clearly missing his calling as a psychologist. "Do you believe that would have happened?"

I shook my head. "Heck no. She's it for me. But if she doesn't want to see it that way. What can I do?" I shrugged with defeat.

"So you're giving up?" he asked in disbelief.

"I might be taking a step back. Maybe this is what we both need." I mumbled, as much as it pained me to say that. I only wanted what Mia felt was best for us.

Tatum punched my bicep. "Nope. Wrong answer."

I lurched forward, nearly dropping my bowl, and grabbed my bicep. "DUDE! Not cool!"

Tatum looked at me with a straight face. "Don't be an idiot!" he shouted. "Or I'll hit you again. Maybe you need a slap upside your head to knock some sense into you."

My eyes widened. Tatum was never this aggressive. I looked at him speechlessly.

"Mia doesn't want this to end. She wants this as much as you do. If you stop showing her that, whose say she's going to come to the conclusion you want all by herself. You need to fight for her." Tatum urged me.

"I know that, but it would be good if she wanted to fight for me, too," I admitted. "We do almost everything together. We're a team. It has always been 50/50. So was it terrible that I wanted the same amount of effort that I put into this relationship? Was it hard to believe that the guy needed to feel wanted too?"

Tatum went silent. "I get that. Man, I do." He huffed out a breath. "Okay, the next course of action." He clapped his hands together. "It's been a long night. How about you sleep on it?" he suggested.

I nodded with a yawn. "Sounds like a plan."

"Cool," he smiled before getting up and heading to his closet. "Catch." He tossed me a blanket then grabbed a pillow, which he slipped into a cotton pillowcase. "Make yourself at home." He gave me the thumbs-up.

"Thanks." I got comfy, laying back and stretching out my legs. I was grateful his couch was large enough to accommodate me.

Tatum's studio apartment wasn't overly spacious, but it was good enough for him. It had a modern flair with a large brick accent wall and massive windows that looked like they went from floor to ceiling. The kitchen was a decent size, it's functional, and it opens up to the little dining area he has with a basic round wood table and four matching chairs.

Since the space isn't necessarily divided by anything, Tatum's found a way to make it appear that way with how he's lined up his furniture, etc.

A place like this close to the campus wasn't super cheap, but he got the Santiago family discount.

I could see what Santiago said when he talked about Tatum. That guy had a rough life, but you could never tell by how he carried himself and or how he treated the people around him.

"Lights out?" Tatum shouted from across the room.

I shoved a thumb my thumb in the air, hoping he would see it. When I heard him chuckling, I saw the lights go off.

I slipped my phone out of my pocket and watched the screen come alive. I decided to text Mia and let her know that I wouldn't be coming home tonight. I didn't want her to worry.

"Texting Mia?"

"Yup." I wanted to write more than that simple text, but I voted against it.

"So predictable," I heard Tatum mumble as he laughed quietly.

"I don't wanna hear it." I waited to see if Mia would respond, but she didn't.

I tried not to be disappointed.

I placed the phone on the coffee table and rolled over into a prime sleeping position.

"Night, Grey," Tatum called out.

"Night," I said.

I prayed Mia and me could work all of this out tomorrow. I didn't care what happened long as I got to keep her in my life.

The smell of bacon hit my nose in the morning. Hearing the sound of breakfast cooking and smelling it was my favorite way to wake up.

Then I thought about Mia kissing me awake by pressing kisses all over my face and down my neck.

I groaned. Never mind. I take it back.

Waking up to those brown eyes would forever be my favorite way to wake up.

I sat up on the couch and spotted Dean, Tobias, and Tatum all in the kitchen.

"Awe, look, sleeping beauty is finally awake," Dean said, making everyone turn in my direction.

"Morning," I said with a half-assed wave.

"Hey, Grey," Tobias said. "Tatum is being super hush-hush about whatever happened last night, so care to explain?"

I scratched my chin. "Mia and I got into a fight," I mumbled.

"What?" Dean exclaimed. "What did you do?" He instantly accused me.

My lips turned down into a frown. "It's complicated. But the blame should be split 50/50."

Dean looked confused.

I saw my phone light up with a notification in my peripheral.

I grabbed it.

There were messages from Mia.

I was eager to read through them.

"Tatum can give you the cliff notes version," I told them. "I'm going to freshen up," I said as my legs began to move faster than my brain could register to the bathroom. I shut the door behind me and opened the messages.

Mia: Hey, Grey. I hope you're still not mad at me because I'm really sorry. You were right, and I should have told you from day one instead of making all these excuses. I do that a lot. Make excuses when something is hard for me to talk about, and I shouldn't.

I should stop pretending that my feelings will go away if I ignore them, and I should stop being afraid of them.

Mia: Just like I want to stop acting as if I could live with this relationship ending here or at the end of the summer. I don't want that. I want to take that leap with you because I do trust you. And if you still want to give us a chance after last night, I'm going to prove it.

Mia: I want to say a lot more than this but in person. So when you're ready to talk, let me know. Until then, I'll be spending the day at my mom's. We talked through everything last night, and we're choosing to move forward. Anyways, please text me back.

Mia: I'm sorry again.

I felt myself grinning.

She wants to stay with me. Like in it for the long haul, remain with me.

I reread the messages.

I couldn't believe it.

I wondered what could have changed her mind. Maybe that talk with her mom worked some kind of magic.

I shook my head in disbelief.

In a rush, I flung the door open. "You guys..." I began just as a knock on the door interrupted me.

"It's probably Mari," Dean said when all four of our eyes looked to the door.

Tobias went to open it. "Um... Can I help you, munchkin?" he asked, looking down at someone.

I craned my head to look around him and spotted her. "Hey, Freckles," I said, walking towards her. I opened my arms to hug her. But instead, she took a swing at me.

That was two punches in less than 24 hours. I rubbed my arm then looked into those maple syrup eyes. They were fiery, filled with the determination of a girl on a mission.

"What are you doing here, Freckles?" I asked her, trying not to be offended that she came at me maliciously when I welcomed her so warmly. I probably deserved that, though.

Ella leaned her skateboard against the wall and then unfastened her helmet.

"Is someone going to explain who this little girl is?"

Ella glanced over at Dean, and I saw him stagger back. "Is it me...?" He started to point furiously at her. "Or does she look a lot like Mia?"

Ella grinned, flattered to hear of the resemblance she had to her big sister.

I could see it more clearly now. If you took away the dark hair, she'd be a dead ringer for her sister, minus the freckles and dimples. Mia doesn't have those but still. The resemblance was sort of unmistakable unless you're me, of course.

I mentally rolled my eyes at myself.

When I had seen them standing side by side the other day, I swore I got a strange feeling.

The fact that Dean spotted it when I never could blow my mind but okay.

"This is Ella, her little sister," I told him, then did some quick introductions.

"It's nice to meet all of you." She waved. "I'm sorry to barge in, but I wanted to talk to Grey." She met my gaze.

"About?" I asked, bemused.

"Getting my sister back, duh." She slipped her helmet off and smoothed down her hair. "If you wannabe my future brother-in-law, you need to step your game up. Today's your chance," she added.

"OOoo! I like her. She can hang with us!" Dean announced.

Ella giggled then started to blush when Dean winked at her.

I elbowed him, signaling him to knock it off.

"Anyways," I said, bringing Ella's attention back to me.

"I have a plan!" she blurted out. "I mean, well, it's part of a plan. Maybe you can help fill in the rest."

Tatum offered her some food, and she took a seat at the dining table with us.

Ella went over this idea that she had gotten this morning. Then she pulled out a sketch of the set-up from her back pocket.

"WOW!" Dean said, his eyes growing wide. He slid the picture over to him. "You are so talented!" he praised her, and she ducked her head, her hair shielding her face. She was blushing again. At this rate, the poor girl would be crushing on this fool.

I cleared my throat, and Dean getting the hint, toned it down a bit.

"Okay, I know exactly what we can do from there," I said.

I told her my plan, and a slow grin took over her face as her dimple came out, then braces made their appearance.

Ella squealed with joy. "Yay! She's going to love that!" She sang the words.

I chuckled. "I hope so. How much time do we have?"

She checked her watch. "Not much, and I have to head back. I don't want Mia to get suspicious even though I told Mom to cover for me."

I lifted a brow. "She's in on this too?"

"Not officially. But she felt bad and wanted to help. You know she's always liked you, right? I mean, there's no one else she would have been okay with Mia dating." Ella said, sliding her chair back to stand.

"I didn't know that," I told her with a smug grin.

"Well, you do now." She smiled. "So Operation sunset serenade is a go!" She held her fist up for me to pound it.

"I can tell your going to be a cool bro-in-law." Ella winked, then waved goodbye to the guys. "See y'all soon," She told them.

"Text me when you get home," I told her. She had given me her number for updates, etc.

"You got it." Ella slid on her helmet and grabbed her skateboard. "Later!"

I waved, watching her jog down the hall, heading for the elevator.

I shut the door and turned to the guys.

"You know you're like really racking up on the list of favors you're going to owe us in the future," Dean said with a smug grin while the other two shook their heads.

I rolled my eyes. "And if in the future either of you needs assistance like this, I will gladly help out. Deal?"

"Sure thing," Dean spoke for the majority.

"Cool. Now, let's get to work."

The guys all grinned. No doubt about it, this was the team to best team to be on.

35

<hr>

CHAPTER 35

When I opened my eyes, I found an empty space beside me.

"Ella?" I mumbled in my sleepy haze, but I heard nothing.

I sat up, rubbed the crust out of my eyes, and headed for Ella's bathroom. It was so cool that she had a bathroom attached. I didn't take a good look around her room yet, but I already considered it to be bedroom goals.

Back at home, Dad and I had a modest house. Even with Dad's money from starting his practice, he's never thought about moving to a bigger place.

Not that it was necessary. It's been just the two of us with occasional visitors. It had four bedrooms, two and a half bathrooms, and a two-car garage with a huge backyard. We remodeled about two or three years ago and had some pretty cool upgrades in the bathrooms and kitchen. That place was our only home; we wouldn't trade it for anything.

I freshened up in the bathroom, using Ella's face wash and her Listerine. I'll ask her or Mom for a toothbrush in a minute. I wanted to make sure I at least said good morning with fresh breath.

I looked at my hello kitty PJs and debated whether I should slip back into my joggers and hoodie. I shrugged, voting against it.

When I heard a knock, I peeped out of the bathroom door.

"Good morning, sunshine." Mom was grinning from ear to ear.

"Hey, Mom." I smiled back.

"Are you all done?" she asked with a raised brow.

I nodded. "Hmm."

"So Mia, don't freak out, but I want to show you something."

I stepped out, nodding slowly. "Sure." I drew out all of the sylla-bles.

"Okay, follow me," Mom said excitedly.

We walked down the hallway.

"How many bedrooms does this house have?" I asked.

"Only six. And then we have five bathrooms," she said over her shoulder. "Speaking of bedrooms." She opened one of the doors. "This one is yours."

My jaw went slack.

I felt Mom take hold of my wrist and pull me in. My eyes bounced off the walls, which were painted the softest shade of blue, and the room was furnished with a queen-sized bed and two nightstands with a dresser. The bed wasn't made or anything. The mattress and the pillows still had plastic on them.

I felt Mom's hand grab my shoulders and twist my body to the right.

"OHMYGOSH!" I said, seeing that there's an attached bathroom.

"I remember when you were a kid watching HGTV with me, you used to make such a huge deal about having a bedroom with your own bathroom." She giggled. "I used to think it was funny because you were an only child, so technically, you had a bathroom to your-self." She did have a point, but it was not the same.

"That was different. I wanted to get up and walk six feet to the bathroom, not down the hall." I squealed, running into the bathroom and turning the lights on. "I can't believe this," I mumbled. On the counter, there was toothpaste and a new mechanical toothbrush.

Mom laughed. "I know you live close by, but if you ever want to sleep over for the holidays or the weekend. Or you wanna hang out with Ella or me, and you can stay here anytime."

I ran to hug her, making sure I gave her a good squeeze. "Thank you," I told her.

"Anytime," she whispered.

"Also, Greyson can stay over too. As long as you guys are responsible and adhere to all the important house rules." She pointed the finger at me as her eyebrows drew together. It gave her the illusion of being a stern mom. But she was always the softie. More so than dad. Then again, when you have kids who don't rebel, there's no need to have this constant stern parent mentality. I eased away from her. "So, no funny stuff with Grey under my roof."

Hearing Grey's name made me pout and feel like crap all over again. I crossed my arms against my chest, hugging myself.

"You want to talk about it?" Mom asked. "If it's not, it's fine." She waved it off.

I sat on the mattress and patted the spot next to me. "We have a lot of these talks to catch up on anyway."

Mom took a seat, and I told her something I didn't mention last night. "Grey had said some things about me being afraid to put my whole heart into any relationship because I didn't want to get hurt like how it hurt when you left me. And he was right."

Mom tore her eyes away from mine and folded her lips into a thin line.

I didn't want to upset her, but I needed her to understand.

"For the longest time, keeping people at a distance was my thing. I made friends, but they never got as close to me as Grey. He's been with me through it all. I never felt I needed or wanted anyone else to know my whole life story. But I've been slowly changing my mind about a few things. I've watched Grey change and grow, and he's been rubbing off on me. I've made a few new friends, and I can't imagine keeping them at arm's length. They've all been so wonderful and helpful, you know?"

Mom nodded with a small smile.

"Anyways, I also not only do I feel like a crappy bestie, but I also feel like a crappy girlfriend."

I told her about the deal we had made.

Mom's eyes went as wide as saucers. She opened her mouth to speak, but I was afraid she'd shout or scold me, so I said something first.

"Wait! I know that probably sounds crazy. But it's the best deal we've made. Grey wanted me to see how perfect we fit together and as terrified as I was to see it, I do now. And I want him to know that he's not the only one who will be giving one hundred percent anymore. I will too."

Mom sighed. "I see that I really wasn't prepared for these kinds of grown-up talks." She softly laughed, shaking her head.

"It's not the kind of simple relationship talk that you were expecting." I giggled.

"Exactly." She agreed with a nod. "Mia, I think everyone around the two of you knows how you feel about each other. They've had faith in you forever, including your father, so believe me when I say I don't think loving Greyson will ever hurt you. And loving him back is nothing to be afraid of because he will cherish it. Just as I suspect you will when you finally tell him how you feel." She pinned me with a knowing look.

"Why are moms always so intuitive?" I grumbled, pretending to be annoyed with her.

She shrugged. "It's a gift." She bumped my shoulder.

"Thank you."

"Don't mention it."

"No, I have to. Not just for the relationship advice but everything." I angled my body towards her."Thank you for not giving up on our relationship when I gave you all the reasons to." Mom's eyes began to water."Thank you for listening to me and understanding. Thank you for making room for me in your home. I can't tell you how much it means to me." The last few words came out muffled.

My voice became hoarse, and my vision grew blurry. This room was proof of her commitment to fixing our relationship and how much she cares about keeping me a part of her life."OH, honey." Mom brought me into a hug."No thanks are necessary. I love you."

"I love you too."

I freshened up again, but this time in my own bathroom.

I kept replaying the conversation I had with mom in my head, and I decided to text Grey. I told him that I didn't want this relationship to be just a summer thing, and I wanted to prove it. There's a lot more I wanted to say, but I told him I would prefer to say it in person. Then I told him how I'd spend the day and my mother's with Ella. Hopefully, he texted me back so we could talk. I didn't want this fight to go on longer than needed.

Afterward, I skipped downstairs for breakfast.

When I walked into the kitchen, I asked about Ella."She went for her morning skateboard ride," Matt told me."She should be back soon. Depending on how far she went," He flipped a pancake with the spatula."She can go for miles on that thing," he chuckled, shaking his head.

Then he turned to me as I took a seat on one of the barstools."So, how's everything, Mia," Matt asked with a bright smile. It was a vague question, but it was easy to pick up on what he was really asking me.

I frowned, and his face grew concerned."Honestly," I began with a sigh. I paused for dramatic effect and watched him nervously comb his hands through his hair. It's great!" I blurt out with laughter.

Matt looked confused at first, but then he caught on soon enough. "You were messing with me." he feigned disappointment, but I saw him crack a smile.

"Sorry, I had to," I told him.

"Glad to see you two getting along." Mom came in and kissed Matt on the cheek.

"Ella isn't back yet?" she asked him.

"Nope. I thought she would have skipped the morning ride to spend all her time with Mia," Matt replied.

Mom shrugged. "She does, but you know how she likes her little morning rituals."

He nodded. "You're right."

I joined Mom at the breakfast table, and we had some coffee.

"I'm back!" Ella, I heard a shout from the front a few minutes later.

"How was your ride?" Mom said with a wink as they exchanged looks.

"Great. Just what I needed," Ella said with a smirk.

"You two are being weird," I commented.

Their heads whipped around to me.

"You think?" Mom replied nonchalantly as if she couldn't possibly understand why I would have said that.

Ella, on the other hand, just shrugged. "I don't know what you mean."

Matt looked as confused as I did, but he let it slide.

We gathered at the table for breakfast and had a light chat.

Matt had to wrap up some work but promised he'd free up his schedule for the afternoon.

Mom and Ella wanted a girl's day filled with movies and an at-home spa day.

Naturally, I couldn't say no.

36

— • —

CHAPTER 36

Before the official start of our girl's day, I had to run back home to shower and grab a few things.

Grey hadn't responded to my messages, so I crossed my fingers that he would be home.

You couldn't imagine how bummed I was when I found out that he wasn't.

Was he that mad? I thought to myself, and my heart filled with dread and worry.

What if he wouldn't forgive me for this? What was going to happen with our relationship?

My head was spinning from thinking of all the worst-case scenarios.

When I reached Mom's house, she took one good look at my face and instantly knew something was wrong.

She mentioned that I liked to jut my bottom lip out a lot when I was upset. I also tended to murmur and avoid contact. Supposedly, that was something I've been doing since I was a kid.

Mom and Ella offered to listen if I needed to vent, but I told them not to worry about it. Right now, I needed to relax and clear my head before I drove myself crazy.

By mid-afternoon, I had rainbow-colored nails, thanks to Ella. My wavy strawberry locks had been washed, blown out, and then curled to perfection for a more dramatic effect. I forgot how awesome mom was with styling hair.

Unfortunately, she didn't pass down any of that talent. Hence, my hairstyles usually consisted of basic styles.

During all of that, we had watched Captain America parts one and two. I made fun of mom when she became all googley eyed as Steve took off his shirt. Not going to lie, I was gawking at him too, and when I tried to cover Ella's eyes as a joke, she wasn't having it. She hit me with one of the cushions. It was safe to say Steve Rogers was eye candy for women everywhere.

Every hour or so, I couldn't help but check my phone to see if Grey replied. I tried to be understanding, but it hurt like hell.

Mom and Ella cheered me up a lot, though. I was grateful to have this time with them.

"Dad, are you all done now?" Ella asked when her father walked into the room.

He nodded with a smile.

"I was thinking, we should have a BBQ, and then we can take this movie night outside to the inflatable projector." Mom suggested, looking back and forth from Ella to me.

I gasped. "I totally forgot you have one of those!"

"Yeah, it's so cool," Ella said with a huge grin.

"Yup. I'm totally on board with this plan. I'll get the stuff ready," Matt said, walking towards the kitchen.

"We'll need to set up outside." Ella eagerly launched to her feet. "Mia, you should see the string lights and tiki torches at night. They're so pretty."

"I bet." I winked. "What do you guys need me to do?" I asked mom.

"Depends... Are you still good at baking?" She smirked

I answered her with a smile.

"I like chocolate, peanut butter chips cookies!" Ella informed me.

"I'll see what I can do," I promised.

Ella opened her mouth to say something, but then her phone went off. She grinned, looking down at it. "This one of my friends back in Seoul, she just got back from a modeling gig in Japan, and I told her to call me when she got back home." Ella bit her bottom lip like she was having a hard deciding if she should answer right now or not.

I didn't want her not to talk to her friend because of me. "It's fine. Talk to your friend. We got everything covered."

She beamed. "Okay, I won't belong," she told us before skipping off.

An hour later, I had a massive amount of cookies drying on three different trays. We made Ella's favorite, and I'm sure she's going to devour them.

Mom made a huge fruit platter. She even took the time to cut them into cute little shapes. Think of the Edible arrangement's style.

Matt had all the chicken legs and burgers seasoned to perfection for ready for the grill. He also whipped together some shish kabobs and promised me that they would be one of the best things I've ever eaten.

Outside, I helped Ella set up the table and the umbrellas as mom took some time to water her rose bushes.

Ella's phone rang again, and she rushed inside to answer it.

I went over to Matt by the grill. "Um... Matt?" He glanced at me from over his shoulder. "Do you always make this much food?" I eyed the grill curiously. There was enough food to feed a small village. There's no way we could eat all of that.

He traded a look with my mom and shrugged. "We like to have leftovers."

I nodded. Okay, sure.

Ella came rushing outside with a flash drive in her hand.

She didn't say anything, but when she looked at mom, mom hurried over.

"What's going on?" I asked, noticing that they definitely weren't acting normal.

Whatever was going on, everyone was in on it but me.

I pouted, hating to be out of the loop.

"Mom, get the lights. I know they won't be as vibrant at this hour, but still." Mom flicked on all the twinkling yard lights.

Ella plugged the flash drive into the projector then turned to me with a bright smile. "You know I love you, right?" she said.

Regardless of all my questions, I nodded, waiting to see how this would play out.

"Okay, this was my idea, but some other people did put in their two cents, so I can't take all the credit," she added.

"I'm still as confused as I was three seconds." Ella went in for a hug, then mom came in, wrapping her arms around the both of us.

"Alright, I've been waiting to do this all day." Ella clicked play on the remote, and a video came up.

I sat at a park bench looking out at the pond when Greyson came and scared me. I yelped, thrusting my arms out and bringing a knee to my chest. Then his laughter echoed through the park. It was deep, hearty, and, honestly, one of my favorite sounds.

"Mia, you're such a sacredly sometimes," Grey said.

"You could have been anybody. Even a serial killer or kidnapper."

He scoffed. "As if I would ever let anyone hurt you."

And I remember how he rolled his eyes after saying that, causing me to shove him playfully. Grey broke out into laughter again before taking a seat next to me.

He turned the camera around and told me he was doing a video.

I mumbled something like, "Of course, you would want to record scaring me."

As he held it up, he asked me to smile and wave. Then he threw his arm around my shoulders and kissed my temple.

"Mia, you know you're like one of my favorite people in the world, right?"

"Yes. Just like you're one of mine too."

I watched as a slow handsome grin emerged.

Gosh. That smile would give any woman heart palpitations.

The corner of my lips tipped up, thinking back to how my heart swelled. Grey always thought of himself as my protector. This was only the ninth grade, but I think that's when I noticed that I might be feeling more than friendship towards Greyson.

Then the projector started to show a series of pictures, starting from our childhood. I heard a guitar being played, but it didn't sound like it came from the slideshow. Thinking my ear must be deceiving me, I glanced behind me and saw Greyson strumming his guitar.

My jaw hit the ground, and my heart started beating wildly in my chest.

Grey was wearing a white three-quarter button-up dress shirt with these fitted pair of black jeans and his favorite black boots. He's been wearing his hair spiked up in the middle with the sides slightly trimmed. But today, his dark locks were hanging down just slightly above his eyebrows.

"Greyson," I murmured when his eyes met mine, and they transformed into glittering topaz gems.

He just smiled and started singing as he took slow strides towards me.

I didn't recognize the song at first, but it hit me the more I paid attention to the words.

He was singing the song from his notebook. The one he said was unfinished but had told me he would sing for me when it was complete.

My hands flew to my heart. I felt the beats vibrating under the palm of my hand.

Greyson walked until he was in front of me. The song's lyrics kept flowing from his lips, and I let them wash over me, feeling the emotions behind his every word. His eyes stayed laser-focused on me, but I also saw so much love in them.

I grinned hard enough to make my cheeks hurt.

The slideshow was still playing behind him, and I glanced over at it now and then, but I didn't want to miss more than a few seconds of the actual show.

I watched Grey strum the last few chords before his fingers fell from the strings and his guitar hanged loosely from his body.

I heard cheering from behind us, but I didn't dare turn around.

Grey slid the guitar behind his back, then eliminated the remaining space between us.

"Mia," he uttered my name, slipping his arms around my back and placing a tender kiss on my forehead. "Did you mean everything you said in the texts?"

I nodded. "Of course." I craned my head up to look into his eyes. "I meant every word. I'm sorry about not telling you the truth.

Most importantly, I'm sorry for holding back when it came to us. You were right. I was afraid and tiny part of me still kind of is. But I don't want that to stop me. I trust you." I brought my hands up to caress his cheeks. "I love you, Greyson."

His eyes widened, and his lips parted as he took in a sharp breath.

I stood on the tips of my toes and gave him a quick peck on the lips. "So trust me when I say, I believe in us too, and I want to make this work. No matter. I'm in it for the long haul."

Grey's eyes frantically searched mine as if he were trying to decipher if this was real.

"Mia," he spoke my name like a prayer, rested his forehead against mine, and closed his eyes. "I love you so much."

I grinned before bringing his lips to mine. It was gentle, like the last one. I wanted to pour my heart into this one.

We heard whooping and handclaps.

Crap crap crap. I forgot we had an audience, and two of the said audience members were my mom and her husband.

I reluctantly broke away from him.

Grey's face was the epitome of joy, and I couldn't be happier about that.

I felt a deep blush coming up my neck, traveling up to my cheeks at the thought of us having to turn around and face everyone who had just witnessed our little moment.

Oh gosh.

Greyson chuckled, picking up on my obvious distress.

I heard hurried footsteps before two slender arms wrapped the both of us.

"I'm so happy for you guys." Ella squealed.

Then I had a lightbulb moment thinking back to what she had said a few minutes ago. "Hold on a sec! This was your idea?" I looked down at my little sister.

She nodded with her famous grin. "Just the picture slideshow. Grey came up with the rest."

I shook my head in disbelief. My eyes flickered between the two of them.

"Thank you," Grey said, leaning over to kiss the top of Ella's head.

"Anytime, bro." she winked.

Ella's released us and faced me. "How much did you love it? We called this operation sunset serenade. Personally, I think it was a huge success." She dusted off her shoulders. "If I do say so myself."

"It was perfect," I told them. And I love that they worked together on this.

"Yay!" She started jumping up and down, clapping her hands.

Too flipping adorable.

"So now that you love birds have confessed your love, you should know that the food is getting cold!" We all turned around to the voice.

Dean stood with his hands, cupping his mouth and a massive grin on his face.

As a matter of fact, they all appeared to be grinning—Minus Freya, who was wiping a tear from her eye while Tobias patted her back.

"Dinner time!" Mom shouted, waving one of the metal tongs in the air.

"Oh, thank god!" Dean responded. Everyone broke out into a symphony of laughter.

Look at my little family, I thought. A few people are missing, but most of the gang is all here.

Ella took one hand; Greyson took the other, and together we walked side by side.

Life couldn't get any more perfect than this.

37

CHAPTER 37

I couldn't feel my face.

I spent hours laughing with everyone and taking so many pictures. I swear my cheeks were sore.

Mom got to meet all my friends, and she instantly loved them. Matt seemed to quickly bond with the guys too.

Ella fit right in, which wasn't surprising considering she and the guys already spent some time together when they were secretly planning this whole thing. Then Freya couldn't stop gushing over Ella and mentioned multiple times that she was a mini-me.

I was hoping Ella wouldn't get annoyed by that, getting compared to me all of the time, but the way her face lit up when Freya said it, I knew that she loved it.

A part of me was tempted to disagree, though, because Ella being compared to me didn't do her enough justice. Ella was 100x times more impressive than I could ever be, and I loved her for it. I haven't known her long, but everything I've learned has made me proud to be her big sister. So this goes without saying, but I couldn't stop gushing over her either.

After dinner, we had the desserts I made while we watched a movie. We had taken a vote between watching the live-action Lion

King or Aladdin. Aladdin won by mudslide because we all agreed we couldn't watch Mufasa die. I didn't care how old I got, I would forever fast forward through that part of the Lion king.

Dean started this sing-along throughout the movie, and we all joined in, surprised most of us knew all of the words minus mom and Matt. They just laughed at our impromptu Disney concert.

It was about 10:30ish when we all decided to call it a night. We didn't want the neighbors filing any noise complaints.

The guys and Freya helped clean up, and then they left first since they had carpooled.

I asked Mom and Matt if Ella could come over for dinner tomorrow night, and they agreed. They decided to make tomorrow a date night for themselves. So then Ella asked if she could spend the night instead. I looked to Greyson, and he scooped her up in his arms and said, "Of course you spend the night, freckles." He spun her around, and she started giggling.

Mom and I had a little heart to heart and told them that dad had his suspicions about Greyson and me for a while now, but he was waiting for us to confirm. This meant that Grey and I finally needed to have that talk with our parents and tell them the news.

No doubt, his mother will probably start planning our wedding the minute we tell her.

Anyways, we all said our goodbyes and headed home. When Grey saw me yawning, he offered to drive, and I gladly gave him the keys.

Back at home, I kicked my shoes off at the door and slid them onto the shoe closet. Grey flicked on the lights, and I stretched my arms above my head, walking down the hall. "It feels so good to be home," I said.

Grey treaded behind me quietly. His eyes were glued to the ground as he appeared lost in his thoughts.

"I'm going in the shower," I told him.

He nodded, then his eyes met mine. "Can I come with you?" He whispered.

I shrugged, pretending that my heart hadn't decided to act like we were running a marathon. "Sure." I smiled, hoping it didn't give away any of the nervousness I was feeling.

I headed towards the bathroom, not sneaking a peek behind because I'm sure I would chicken out. When we made it to the bathroom, I heard Grey close the door, and I went to turn the shower on, giving it a few seconds to warm up.

For a minute, I stood facing there, facing the shower with my back turned to Grey.

"Mia..." I heard him mutter.

"Hmm..."

"Turn around, please."

I did as I was told.

Grey moved forward until he was a foot away from me, and then he began to unbutton his shirt.

I watched his fingers go through the motion before he slipped the shirt right off his shoulders, letting it drop to the floor. His glorious abs were on display.

Grey smirked, then his eyes flickered to my halter top.

I reached for the hem and lifted it over my head.

His eyes widened when he discovered that I wasn't wearing a bra underneath. There was a built-in bra that gave the girls some support, so I didn't bother with a real one.

A slow smile crept up on his lips.

I waited for his next move. His socks came off next, and I crossed my arms, pouting.

That was the least exciting article of clothing to come off.

"Patience, babe." He winked, stuffing his socks into one another and placing them on the counter.

I see the mirror begin to fog up from the steam.

Grey zipped down his pants, chucking them onside, and then finally, he slipped off his boxers.

I gasped, biting down on my bottom lip hard enough to leave a bruise.

"I'll go first." He stepped around me, and I heard the shower door open and shut.

I took a deep breath, finished undressing, neatly folded my clothes, and put them off to the side.

Stepped into the shower, Greyson had his back to me, and my eyes followed the droplets of water that slithered down the curve of his back.

Wow.

He slicked back his soaking wet hair then spun around to face me. His eyes traveled up and down my body before a handsome smug grin appeared.

I felt my legs moved forward, and I didn't know what I was doing.

My hand slid up his chest to the back of this neck while the other snaked around him to pull him up against me.

Grey lowered his head and devoured my lips.

Goosebumps, sparks, heart palpitations, I felt everything all at once. Grey hoisted me up, and I wrapped my legs around his waist.

"I've had fantasies about us in the shower," Grey confessed, kissing alongside my neck and collarbone.

A soft sound escaped my lips.

"I want you, Mia," his husky voice sent shivers down my spine.

"Here?" I asked stupidly.

Grey grinned. "Here, in my bed, wherever you want."

Instead of answering him, I rubbed my hips against his and bit the corner of my lips.

"I guess that's my answer." He brought his mouth to mine, and we got lost in each other.

Later we moved that party into his room, and if I thought doing it in the shower was fun, but it was nothing compared to what happened in that bedroom.

We made love, and my body has never felt more content in all its life.

Grey cuddled into me, wrapping his arms around my back and pulling me closer to him. I giggled a bit, but it wasn't loud enough to wake him.

I brushed a lock of hair from his face. The more I looked at this man, the more I was grateful to the universe for bringing him into my life when it did.

We've been leaning on each other from day one, and neither of us had the faintest idea that all those years of friendship would have to lead us here. Together.

It used to be a fantasy, having my best friend as my boyfriend, my lover. I used to think I was crazy and delusional, that I could never be so lucky as to have Greyson as both.

And that's what made all of this so special.

Grey was everything a girl could ask for wrapped up into one. And I loved him.

I pressed a soft kiss onto his lips, hoping not to wake him.

He remained blissfully unaware of it, making me smile.
What was I so worried about? I never had anything to lose.
Not when it came to Greyson.

38

EPILOGUE

After the night of the BBQ, summer went by in a blur.

Greyson and the guys got booked for events all over. Now, they were blowing up over social media with over 40k followers on Instagram in less than two months.

They were still performing at Lila's, even though Santiago always joked about no longer being able to afford them. But with Santiago as their landlord and friend, the guys wouldn't dream of not playing at the bar.

Dean said when they were a broken band, and they weren't sure where to go, Lila and Santiago always invited them to play there. They encouraged them to move forward and not give up.

The guys weren't sure how long they wanted to ride this music wave, but they all agreed that they wouldn't continue any of it if they weren't altogether.

If that wasn't the most adorable and loyal bromance, I didn't know what was.

Mom, Ella, and I, finally went on those trips. The first stop was South Korea. No surprise there. We spent a week in Seoul, and Ella was beyond excited to see her family and old friends and show me her old stomping grounds. Ella showed me where she likes to eat, play computer games, go shopping, and enjoy the sunset. I loved every minute of it.

We came back home for about a week and a half until we were off again, but this time to Tokyo, Japan.

That trip was a bit shorter than the last. We only spent four days, but somehow mom and Ella managed to squeeze everything they wanted me to experience in those days alone.

Along the way, I tried to pick up bits and pieces of the languages. Thankfully, I didn't start as terribly as mom did. Ella and Matt said that I was a natural and took a lot of pride in that.

The week before classes, we made our final trip. We revisited Japan, but this time we stayed in Osaka. It was pretty epic.

So yeah, Grey and I traveled a lot, and we missed each other like crazy. But out little reunions, well, they felt like the greatest thing ever.

Almost every other weekend, Grey and I tried to go home to see our parents. Ella had tagged along a few times too. She and Dad automatically become close. He gave her one of the spare rooms to make her own, so she didn't have to stay in the guest room whenever she visited. He said she's family, and he called her his second daughter.

I remember a few weeks ago when Grey and I sat down and told our parents the news, how happy they were. They high-fived each other, and then dad pulled out his wallet to hand Stephanie a hundred-dollar bill. Supposedly, she and my dad had made a bet about how long it would take for us to get together.

Dad had said next year because he knew I liked to be stubborn.

But Stephanie had said before Thanksgiving because she knew Greyson would have cracked and told me about his feelings after spending so much time with me.

It was pretty hilarious.

I hung out with Ella, Freya, Mari, and the boys when I wasn't traveling.

We've become a close-knit group, thick as thieves.

"Ella! If you don't hurry up, you'll be late." I shouted from the kitchen. It's the first day of school for both of us, and she's being obsessive about her hair not being perfect enough.

"Freckles! You look perfect. You don't need to change anything," Grey called out.

"You haven't even seen me yet!" Ella yelled back.

He chuckled under his breath. "I don't have to."

We waited for her to answer back, but we were met with silence.

Grey and I maneuvered around each other in the kitchen. Separately, we tried to assemble a different part of our breakfast feast.

Grey flipped the pancakes, and I scrambled the eggs, sprinkling cheddar cheese on them.

"Okay, okay." Ella stepped into the kitchen. Her long dark hair was half up, half down, and she was wearing light denim shorts that fell to her knees with a baby blue t-shirt that had these tiny white stars all over it.

"AWE!" I said because I thought she looked adorable.

Ella scrunched up her face at me. "AWE?" she repeated, "I don't wanna look 'awe,'" she frowned.

I turned off the stove and started sharing portions of the scrambled eggs onto three plates.

"Then how do you wanna look?" I asked her.

"Like...Like..." She threw her arms up with frustration. "I don't know. I give up."

"Relax, freckles. You look great," Grey told her with a warm smile.

She looked back and forth between the two of us. "You guys do know you're totally biased."

We both nodded.

"Bias and proud," Grey said, and I agreed with him before we all broke out into laughter.

Grey and I finished sharing the food for each of us and then sat down to enjoy it.

Ella told us about the classes she would have this year. She mentioned something about her guidance counselor, saying that she should pick up at least two years of a language to look good on her college applications. As much as Ella loved to learn languages, she hated that the school had limited options. She would prefer to learn Mandarin, but she said she would give French a try instead.

For our first semester, Grey and I had two gen-eds together, but that was it. From there, we had our introductory classes for our majors.

After breakfast, we threw the dishes and pans into the dishwasher then headed out the door.

Mom and Matt called us on our way to Ella's school to wish all three of us an excellent first day.

We pulled up at Ella's school 20 minutes later. She unbuckled her seatbelt then I watched her slide her leather backpack onto her shoulder before she moved forward and kissed my cheek. "Have fun at college." She grinned.

I grinned widely. Were all little sisters this sweet? Gosh, I swore I had one of the best.

"You too, Grey." She winked, lightly punching his shoulder, then proceeded to hop down from the truck and slamming the door shut.

We watched her walk up the steps, and then she waved goodbye one last time before heading.

"They grow up so fast," Grey said, pretending to sniffle and wipe away a nonexistent tear.

I erupted into giggles. "Yeah, they do."

Another 15 minutes later and we pulled up in one of the university's many parking lot spaces.

I took a deep breath before getting out after Grey. We handed him my bag from the backseat while he only grabbed a notebook and a pen that he pens, which he stuck in his back pocket.

Grey was wearing one of my favorite outfits. Okay, I liked a lot of his clothes, but honestly, this was in my top three. He wore a pair of dark blue jeans, a white three-quarter Henley, that hugged all his defined muscles, and then he wore his black boots.

Also, we seemed to be matching today. Grey had picked out my clothes this morning, and I was grateful I didn't have to bust my brain trying to put an outfit together. So I was wearing jeans that were pretty close to the color of his. Then I had on a flowy white top with combat boots-my style. Grey knew me well.

I watched him do a 360, admiring the place. I couldn't help but be excited about the next step in our journey: all the new experiences and the new memories.

I was glad I had Grey to share these things with.

I looked up to meet those blue eyes that I love more than anything. I reached for Grey's hand, and he interlocked our fingers, smiling down at the gesture. "We got nothing to lose, right?" I repeated his favorite phrase.

Greyson grinned, giving me one of those forehead kisses that I adored. "No," he said, tucking a strand of hair behind my ear. "Only a whole lot to gain."